THE EXTRA

Cover Design by Melissa Williams Design

Director's Chair and Film Lights copyright 2019 Quarta; artinspiring, AdobeStock

Movie Reel and Film Strip copyright 2019 Brainstorm331; aTomislav Forgo, Shutterstock

Janci's author photo by Michelle D. Argyle
Megan's author photo by Heather Cavill

Published by Garden Ninja Books

ExtraSeriesBooks.com

First Edition: May 2019

0 9 8 7 6 5 4 3 2 1

THE EXTRA

THE EXTRA SERIES *Book 1*

MEGAN WALKER & JANCI PATTERSON

For Ken Grey and Marilyn Koffman,
who always believed

ONE

Going out to lunch in Beverly Hills probably isn't the best way to handle the loss of my thrift-store boutique job, but I've convinced myself the leftovers of my college fund will last a year or so yet. Now that I've stopped actually going to college, that is.

Besides, this lunch isn't about me or my "shocking lack of enthusiasm for vintage Prada." Apparently when the door to one career slams in your face, another one opens.

The door opened for my roommate instead.

"Seriously, Anna. I'm so excited for you. This is crazy." I take another sip of the fruity Beaujolais Anna-Marie ordered for the occasion. It's not my favorite, but it's her day and thus her wine choice.

"I know, right? I can't even believe it. I was so giddy between takes, I'm pretty sure I actually giggled. *Giggled.* The director probably thinks I'm a total airhead. Or insane." She shakes her head in mock remorse, her long, chestnut-brown hair dancing around her shoulders.

"You're a soap opera actress now. He probably thinks you fit right in."

Anna-Marie laughs. She may have been the Ranchlands Beauty of Everett, Wyoming, every year in high school, but she also captained the debate team to a national championship and kills at Scrabble even when she's drunk. She's got more going on upstairs than most of the small town girls that swarm LA every summer looking to make it big.

The waiter brings our entrees, setting them down without taking his eyes off Anna-Marie. A bit of marsala sauce slops over the side of my plate onto the white linen, but he doesn't notice.

"Can I bring you anything else?" With his soft Latino accent and mysterious dark eyes, he could be a younger, slightly-less-handsome version of Enrique Iglesias. I imagine that this waiter, too, is waiting for his big acting break, going to auditions between shifts. I wonder if I'm the only one in the restaurant not desperate to become a star.

"No, thank you," Anna-Marie says, flashing her patented megawatt smile, soon to brighten the TVs of stay-at-home moms and retirees across America. "Gabby? How about you? More wine?"

The waiter visibly starts, only now seeming to notice my presence. I've been hanging around with Anna-Marie for over a year now; I'm used to the reaction.

"No, I'm good."

The waiter nods and shoots Anna-Marie one last saucy look. Her lips twist coyly in return.

"Delicious," she murmurs when the waiter leaves earshot.

"And I thought you were here for the risotto."

She shrugs, then her blue eyes widen. "Did I tell you who my first scene was with?"

"Bridget Messler?" I've never been much of a soap opera fan and have only caught the occasional episode of *Passion Medical* when I came back from class early and Anna-Marie had it on. But even I know about Bridget Messler, legendary matriarch of the show and twelve-time Daytime Emmy nominee (though never yet winner).

Anna-Marie droops a bit. "No, not yet. But guess again! It's pretty obvious. I mean, my character just got back from

6

boarding school in Switzerland. She's going to want to see the mother who abandoned her. And that mother is in . . ." She pauses expectantly.

"Um . . ." I fish around my brain for what she's looking for, but come up empty.

"A coma!" She flourishes a forkful of mushroom risotto. "At Passion Medical!"

"I still think that's a terrible name for a hospital. What doctor would want to list that on their resume?"

She ignores me. "And her attending physician is none other than Trevor Everlake."

"The guy who used to be in the mafia?"

She sighs in clear disgust. It sounds like an eerie echo of my former boss after I said that the latest line of celebrity-inspired purses looked like they were attacked by a blind five-year-old with a bedazzler.

"Eww. No. That's my character's uncle. Trevor Everlake is the gorgeous young genius who has risen from obscurity to be the head doctor at Passion Medical after only two years of practice."

"Two years? Sounds like Passion Medical has never heard of malpractice suits."

"He's the one with the incredible eyes, and the . . ." She gestures at her face vaguely, and I instantly know who she means. In a sea of blandly attractive pseudo-celebrities, he stands out as being the swoon-worthiest face on daytime TV.

"Hot Doctor!" I exclaim, loudly enough that the couple next to us—two well-dressed men in matching hipster glasses—frown pointedly in my direction.

Anna-Marie grins. "Yep, Hot Doctor. His real name is Ryan Lansing."

I wrinkle my nose and take a bite of my chicken marsala. It's fabulous, but I can't help thinking of the price listed next to it on the menu. I really should have gone with the side salad, celebratory lunch or not. "That sounds almost as soap-operaish a name as Trevor Everlake. I'll just keep calling him Hot Doctor."

"Your call. But now that I'm working with all these famous people, you're going to have to learn their names eventually. And their dramatic backstories."

"Well, I'll certainly have more time to watch TV now."

Anna-Marie pauses with her fork midway to her mouth. "What do you mean? Oh god, Gabby, did you get fired?"

The speed at which she jumps to that conclusion doesn't give me great hopes for a future in on-trend retail.

"It's okay," I say. "Now I don't have to wear any more perfume designed by the latest reality star of the month. My clothes all reek of desperation."

She shakes her head with a rueful smile. "The way you talk about that stuff, you'd think you were the import from hillbilly land, and not the one of us who probably learned how to pronounce Louboutin in preschool."

It's not just the way I talk that would make anyone think that, but I try not to compare my stocky build and thoroughly average features to Anna-Marie's seemingly made-for-LA willowy body and perfect facial symmetry. That way lies madness.

"Well, it just means I've had long enough among all this crap to realize how little any of it—" My attempt at deep philosophy is interrupted by the return of Anna-Marie's fawning waiter, who refills her water glass even though she's barely touched it.

As she laughs at a witty remark he makes about the risotto, I consider my comment. The truth is, I've learned in the last several years just how fleeting all the money and designer labels and any prestige associated with it can be. But that doesn't mean I don't miss it. Just a little.

I drum my fingers on the cheap Target purse on my lap, feeling through the faux leather to the Chanel wallet within, a gift from my mother when I went off to college. I've gotten rid of so much of my former life, but not everything.

After the waiter leaves, I manage to turn the conversation back to Anna-Marie's new acting gig—not difficult, given her level of excitement. Which I totally get. This is a huge breakthrough for her, considering her biggest previous star credit had been as "girl in white dress running through field of wheat" in a tampon commercial. And I really don't need to go into details on my most recent life failure. This isn't the first job I've lost, and we both know it won't be the last.

"You know," Anna-Marie says, pausing after a very detailed description of her scene with Hot Doctor. "My new job might open up certain . . . opportunities for you."

I raise an eyebrow, a little afraid. I'm not sure exactly what opportunities her knowing Hot Doctor might provide for me, but knowing Anna-Marie, it could be anything.

She smiles. "What do you think about becoming an extra? For *Passion Medical*."

"An extra what?" A brief moment of confusion imagining myself fetching coffee for some production assistant is replaced by the dawning realization of what she really means.

"An extra," she says again. "You know, the people in the background of a scene. Ordering coffee or walking through the park, that sort of thing."

"The people smiling like idiots while they mouth the words 'strawberry watermelon strawberry watermelon' to each other, you mean." She looks a little surprised and I shrug. "I grew up in LA, remember. I do know some things about the acting business."

"Then you should know they get paid pretty well for doing that. And you need a job, don't you?"

She takes my silence for the consideration it unfortunately is and pushes ahead. "The best part is, *Passion Medical* tends to use the same extras over and over. They want the sense of it being a real town, so somebody used in a hospital scene might show up in the coffee shop in an episode the following week. Which means it might even become a regular gig. Well, as regular as it can be."

"If they use lots of the same people, why would they hire me?"

Her smile widens. "Because they just fired a couple of them

today. Two of the 'nurses' at the hospital"—she puts the word "nurses" in air quotes—"disrupted a scene by getting into a fight when they found out Ryan Lansing slept with both of them this morning. There was hair pulling and everything."

"He's into hair pulling? Hot Doctor sounds kinky."

She laughs. "In the *fight*. But yeah, he probably is. I guess you'll just have to find out for yourself when you take the job."

"A paycheck and the chance to bang a soap opera star, all in the same day? Sounds like my parents' dreams for me are finally coming true."

"I'm serious," she says. "About the job, anyway. I don't suggest you do Ryan Lansing, but you wouldn't be the first. Or the fifty-first."

"I don't know, Anna. I don't really have any acting skills."

"Well, then you know what that means." She smiles as the waiter brings us our check, and hands him her credit card, shaking her head at me as I bring out mine. "I've got this," she says.

Despite a brief flush of pride, I gratefully allow it. "Thanks" I say, as the waiter leaves again. "So what does my lack of acting skills mean?" But I already suspect what she's going to say.

"You can finally come with me to my acting class on Tuesday."

I groan. She's been trying for weeks to get me to go to this acting class with her. And for weeks, I've been coming up with excuses to spend Tuesday nights in my sweatpants watching Netflix instead.

"It would be good experience," she says. "Get you used to being in front of people. My instructor has offered free trial classes to people before. And there's lots of cute guys there . . . " She trails off with a waggle of perfectly groomed eyebrows.

I almost make a joke about how I've been dying to meet a narcissistic starving actor, but rein it in just in time. Anna-Marie gets my sarcastic nature in a way few others do, but that might be crossing the line.

"I'll think about it," I say.

"Which part?"

"Both."

"Okay. That's all I ask," she says. But I can tell she's formulating more reasons why I should try my hand at being an extra on her soap opera, none of which will be more convincing than the paycheck argument she began with. My bank account isn't exactly empty, but if it ever becomes so, I'd end up having to leave my apartment and the life—meandering and uncertain though it may be—that I've built for myself and move back into my parents' house.

The thought is terrifying.

As she signs the bill and we get up to leave, Anna-Marie flashes one last broad smile at the waiter, who appears ready to desert the table he's currently taking orders from to come talk to her one last time. He frowns, then turns back to his customers. I'm not overly worried for him. Anna-Marie may be beautiful, but beautiful girls to flirt with aren't exactly rare here. This is LA, after all.

We leave the dark restaurant and pass into the bright early spring sun, both of us blinking and squinting and pulling our sunglasses from our purses. A light breeze, the faintest remnant of a winter that never really touches this sun-drenched city, tickles my arms. The valet brings around my silver Hyundai. He looks slightly insulted as he hands me the keys, as if being forced to drive such a pedestrian car has sullied him.

We climb into my car and jack up the volume on the hit single of this debut band, Alec and Jenna, so loud the valet jumps. We laugh the better part of the way home.

Faking a good mood isn't so hard. Maybe I should be an actress, after all.

I drop Anna-Marie off at our apartment in WeHo, telling her I have errands to run. Then I pull my car into a metered spot only two blocks down the road from our apartment. I do indeed have some errands I can run, but today's latest firing seems to require a celebration of its own.

The rundown Chinese/American restaurant squished between

a dry-cleaner and a liquor store fits my mood much better than any swanky Beverly Hills restaurant.

Fong's All-American is dimly lit inside, but with far less prestigious atmospheric effect than the restaurant we just had lunch at. I don't particularly care about the atmosphere, the flickering lights above the bar, or the chef who always pokes his head out from the kitchen when the door chimes just to scowl at me. The food here is the best in all of LA, but I'm not here for the Sweet and Sour Pork and Beans or their oddly delicious Cheeseburger Lo Mein.

I slide into a cracked-leather booth, and refuse a menu from the pretty, petite Chinese waitress who seems to live here for all the many times she's served me. She always has a wide smile and her hair pulled into strange configurations with plastic neon hair clips.

"I'm going for the big guns, Su-Lin," I say.

Her smile drops. "Oh no! Boyfriend problems?"

"Not this time. Got fired."

"Awww, that sucks," she says, then yells back to the kitchen, "One Breakup Tub. Extra cookie dough."

I wish she wouldn't yell my order like that every time, but the few other patrons here at four in the afternoon barely stir.

"You'll get a better job next time," Su-Lin says. She brightens suddenly. "Maybe you can work here!"

The chef's hearing must be extraordinary, because he pokes his head out of the kitchen at that and scowls at me a second time.

"I don't think so," I say. "Where will I go for my Breakup Tub when I get fired from here?"

She smiles sadly and pats my head like a fond aunt, though she looks like she's several years younger than I am.

When she leaves, I allow myself the thoughts I felt too guilty to acknowledge in my best friend's presence. Anna-Marie is getting her big break, another perfect feather in the ever-fashionable hat of her life. She's moving forward, toward something she loves and is really good at, and I, as usual, am stuck in some kind of early-adult pothole of pathetic jobs I don't care about and college plans I can't muster the interest to see through.

She's moving on, and it won't be long before she's left me behind. Like my family.

My nanny LaRue used to say to me, "You have a smile so bright, Gabby, you make everyone around you shine." It was meant as a compliment, I'm sure, and at six years old, I took it as such, beaming gap-toothed grins wide enough to illuminate the world.

She said other things, too, about the teenage girls who zoomed past our house every morning on the way to school in a shiny silver convertible ("Daddy's money is the only difference between them and the streetwalkers") and about men ("Fellas who fish off of too many docks are only gonna catch crabs,") but none of that seemed to apply to me. LaRue was let go a year or so later, after Mom found her smoking pot out by the pool while my little brother Felix and I were inside watching *Dora the Explorer*.

I remember the day she was fired. Pressed against the sliding glass door, I had heard the screaming. My mother, bright and Easter-egg pretty in her pastel cardigan and slim white pants, shrilly denouncing the apple-cheeked Southern woman who cooked fat-back bacon for me on the sly and played Johnny Cash for Felix and me to dance to.

LaRue gave back as good as she got, trading her usual sweet drawl for a yowl about how she'd found the pot in Mom's own drawer and how dare she judge—a tirade punctuated with words I only realized years later were probably the real reason Mom fired her rather than laughing the whole thing off and joining her for a poolside toke. My mother wasn't a woman used to being challenged.

My fingers and face made smudges on the glass as I watched, little clouds obscuring the fight. I pressed my lips to the glass and blew, puffing my cheeks out wide, hoping to blow some of my bright smile onto the door. Hoping to make them happy and shiny and forget their argument.

Instead, Mom sent me to my room. She came in a while later with an apologetic smile and began a long, one-sided discussion of why LaRue was needed with another family, one whose children weren't as well-behaved and special as we were. She brought a dish of old Halloween candy to help persuade me. Mom tightened her lips at every bite of simple carbohydrates that crossed mine, but even she wasn't above the occasional well-placed bribe.

LaRue might have been wrong to steal her employer's weed and smoke it while tending children, but at that moment, it seemed the woman had been right about one thing. When I smiled at my mom, she shone brightly back.

Everyone around me continued to shine and shine, though, and they did so just fine even without the help of my smile. My older sister Dana, in elementary school during LaRue's unfortunate exit, took first place in virtually every academic competition she entered, eventually earning her PhD in chemical engineering. And then, after being featured prominently in several trade journals and winning more awards than I thought a single field of study could realistically have, she went on to prove that women really can have it all by marrying a handsome fellow engineer and having an adorable baby boy.

My little brother Felix picked up the cello in fifth grade and never looked back. He didn't even bother applying to any other school but Juilliard, and didn't need to—he got an enthusiastic acceptance back from them almost instantly. Mom swears it was due to all those classical music DVDs for babies she put on when we were little, and maybe that was the case, but every so often I used to hear him break into Johnny Cash's "Ring of Fire."

My parents were only slightly more thrilled by the successes of their progeny than by their own heights of achievement. Mom was a realtor during a time when California beachside mansions lasted on the market for less time than your average celebrity marriage, and Dad climbed the accounting ladder until he was the lead accountant for a major film-production company.

With all this shining going on, I don't think they even noticed how their middle child, little smiley me, faded blandly into the background. Constant. Plain. Middling grades and even lesser drive. Thoroughly average in every way.

A few minutes into my morose thoughts, Su-Lin brings out the Breakup Tub, a glorious mess of chocolate ice cream and thumb-sized chunks of cookie dough, covered in caramel sauce and whipped cream, and quite possibly dusted with crack for all that I crave this on a near-daily basis. I force a smile at Su-Lin, even though I've long since learned the truth—LaRue was wrong about the power of my smile. I might make everyone around me shine, but only in comparison to how little I myself do.

It was a relief, once I finally realized I didn't have to brighten everyone around me with all that infernal smiling. They would be bright enough on their own. I could just go about my mediocre life, walking in as needed on the sets of their grand dramas.

I have always been an extra in someone else's show.

And that's when I know Anna-Marie is right; it's time to start getting paid for doing it.

"To bigger and better things," I toast to myself softly as I take the first bite.

TWO

In the end, Anna-Marie convinces me to try her acting class as a kind of preparation, even though I haven't told her yet of my decision to take her up on being an extra on *Passion Medical*. I dutifully arrive at the local community college a few minutes early, hoping I can sneak into some hidden corner in the back of the class where no one will notice me, but where I can still technically fulfill my promise to her. From behind a large potted fern, perhaps. That always works in movies.

The chances of a community college classroom having a large potted fern are low, but I'm nothing if not optimistic about all the wrong things.

I walk past the bland hallways filled with over-papered bulletin boards and nondescript classroom doors, looking for room 114. A metal rack holding a stack of community education catalogs captures my attention, and I pick one up, eyeing the grinning woman on the cover dubiously. She's sitting at a pottery wheel, her clay-smeared hands resting on a perfectly shaped vase, her laughing expression indicating that she's having way more fun with pottery than anyone has had since the movie *Ghost* was filmed.

Still, a sticker on the cover announces "Try a class for free! Details inside," and I find myself flipping through the pages to see what other classes the catalog offers (having already ruled pottery out after a disastrous event in the seventh grade involving a pottery wheel and the long hair Jenny Denton had been growing out for Locks of Love).

"Gabby? Gabby Mays?"

I startle and cut my finger on the page advertising, ironically, a First Aid class.

I immediately recognize the guy standing next to me, and my throat dries up. Will Bowen, still with those perfectly mussed blond curls and those green eyes and still tall (*of course he's still tall. What, did I think he was going to shrink over the last two years?*) and still . . .

Still the guy who once fired me from a job I actually kind of enjoyed.

"Will," I say, forcing a smile and likely doing a ghastly job of it. I can feel heat creeping up my neck, the same reaction he used to elicit from me two years ago. "Hey."

His brows draw together as he looks down at my hand. "Sorry, I didn't mean to startle you. Is your finger—?"

"No, no problem, it's fine. Just a paper cut." I stick my throbbing finger in my mouth and suck on it instinctively to stop the blood flow, grimacing at the sharp tang on my tongue. Then I realize how creepy I must look and remove it.

Please don't let me have blood on my teeth, I pray to the same god who will probably not answer my plea for a large potted class fern either.

"How have you been?" he asks. "It's been a couple years, right?"

"I think so, yeah." Feigned casualness is not my strong suit, but I go for it. "Doing good, you know, usual stuff. How about you?"

"Well, I'm not at the bookstore anymore, so that's something."

I want to ask him if he got fired by the person he had a massive crush on over one stupid microwave fire in the break room or if that sort of thing just happens to me, but I bite back my snark and just nod noncommittally.

"Are you here for the screenwriting class?" He gestures to the

17

booklet in my hand.

Screenwriting. I bark out a laugh. "Oh god, no. I want to actually get paid someday."

He cocks an eyebrow, and I remember how he used to spend his lunch breaks huddled over his laptop, typing away. Working on his novel.

I cringe. "You're here for that class, and I'm a big ass."

He grins, and he still has the stupid adorable dimple on his left cheek that I used to daydream about. "I'm actually teaching it."

"So I'm an even bigger ass." But I'm smiling for real now. I had only known him for two months before the firing, and it's not like we'd had loads of soul-baring conversations. But even small talk had always felt more comfortable with him than it should have, like he genuinely cared how my day was going and what my feelings on the latest *Saturday Night Live* skits were.

And there had been that *one* conversation about top hats and monocles and my tragic sketching ability.

"More like practical," he says. "And maybe a little blunt. I always liked that about you."

I feel a thrill at him saying that he likes me, even if he's talking purely about my tactlessness, but a pit forms in my stomach. He liked that about me, but not enough to not fire me after one tiny mishap. I mean, I put out the fire before it spread past the break room countertop. All we lost was the stale box of donuts that had been sitting out for three days, and, well, the crappy microwave that caused the whole thing. Good riddance to both.

"So what *are* you here for, then?" he asks.

"Um . . ." I scuff the front of my sneaker on the linoleum floor. "Acting class, actually."

The look on his face makes me laugh, despite the heat undoubtedly turning my face a lovely shade of Solo-cup red. "You're wanting to revise that whole 'practical' thing you thought about me," I say.

"Acting, huh?" He shakes his head, his green eyes glinting.

"I'm going to have to revise a *lot* of the things I thought I knew about you."

"I'm just trying it out. For a friend. Not that there's anything wrong with acting," I add hurriedly, in case he also moonlights as some off-off-off Broadway leading man.

"So the drawing thing didn't work out?" His lips twitch.

I blink in surprise. *He* remembers that conversation too? It wasn't like it had been anything special, not really. Well, to me, maybe, but considering it was a major step up from the previous longest conversation I'd had with him—in which he'd confessed to his deep and abiding hatred for ranch dressing—it had always stuck out in my mind as a meaningful exchange. And a lost opportunity, maybe.

I gather my wits as best as possible under that gaze. "Shocking, right? Given how talented I was."

He grins, and I know he really does remember.

"Acting, drawing, writing," he says. "They're all good, unless you want to get paid someday."

"Well, maybe a paycheck is overrated."

His smile drops the smallest amount, his expression ever so briefly hesitant, and I wonder if he's going to bring up the fact that he once took away my paycheck. If so, I wonder if I would shrug it off and tell him that he was just one in a long string of managers who've done so. That he was just the one I regretted the most.

Never. Blunt or not, I don't want Will Bowen to think of me as pathetic. Or least any *more* pathetic.

"Maybe so," he says, and I let out a breath I'd been holding, not sure whether to be disappointed or relieved he didn't bring it up. "But I'd better get to class and earn mine. I've grown accustomed to electricity and running water."

"Snob."

The dimple is back, and my stomach does a little flip.

"Good seeing you again, Gabby," he says, and heads further down the hall, disappearing into one of the classrooms at the end.

I chew the inside of my cheek and look down at the community education catalog, at the overly cheerful pottery student on the cover. Have I *ever* had something—a job or hobby, some kind of passion—that brought me catalog-cover-level joy? Something that, like Will, I would do even knowing it was hard to make a living at?

Certainly not drawing—I'd proven that well enough back at the bookstore. On one particularly slow day, I'd picked up a "Drawing for Kids" book I was supposed to reshelve and decided to try it out.

The book claimed to be able to teach kids of all ages to draw various animals, each in under five minutes. I did draw something in under five minutes, but it didn't much resemble the toucan it was supposed to be. I was tilting the paper at an angle, trying to figure out if the beak was supposed to be that large in relation to the body, when I heard a muffled step on the carpet behind me. I turned just in time to see Will, my impossibly cute manager, standing right behind me.

"Huh," Will said, looking over my shoulder at the picture I'd drawn. "Nice . . . chicken eating a banana?"

I'd hoped the flush of warmth in my face—both from embarrassment and how very, very close Will's body was to mine—wasn't radiating heat off the back of my neck right onto him.

"It's a toucan." I tried to say this with some dignity, but really, he was absolutely right. It looked like some malformed chicken. Eating an overlarge banana.

I expected him to smile vacantly and nod, the kind of pandering expression I was used to seeing on my mom whenever I'd mention learning a musical instrument or figuring out how to sew a revolutionary-war era dress (I'd been really into the revolutionary war for about two months in middle school after falling in love with Heath Ledger in *The Patriot*.)

My mom hadn't exactly been wrong to lack enthusiasm for my attempts at gaining a talent, either. Whether suffering the less-than-dulcet tones of beginning clarinet or nearly sewing my finger into the folds of a misshapen bell skirt, my trying to pick up a new skill always led to some sort of pain.

Will, however, just looked thoughtful. "Well, yeah," he said, after a moment in which I realized that he smelled like books and Swedish Fish. "I mean, if you'd finished it, that would be obvious."

I frowned, eyeing the picture, while trying to decide if books and Swedish Fish is actually a sexy smell combination, or if it just seemed that way on Will. "It *is* finished."

"No it's not. It's missing the top hat and monocle."

I looked at him skeptically. "Top hat and monocle? This is supposed to be a toucan, not Mr. Peanut."

"Trust me, this is basic art advice."

I added the top hat and monocle, or at least my best artistic approximation. Now it looked like a really haughty chicken eating a banana.

Will grinned, and there was that dimple, the first time I'd seen it up so close or directed at me. "You see? Clearly a toucan now. I'm actually really disappointed this book didn't tell you how to properly finish the picture. We shouldn't be selling this book here. We could ruin an entire generation of budding artists."

Then he'd grabbed the book from the table and tossed it into the trash next to the register, reached over and squeezed my hand, and then headed back into the break room to finish up his lunch break of Swedish Fish and words on an old laptop. And I knew then that I'd gone from thinking my manager was cute to imagining us on our honeymoon in the rainforest, where we'd outfit toucans in top hats and monocles.

About two weeks later, I'd blown up the microwave, and he'd fired me.

Too bad, toucans. No looking like old-timey British gentry for you.

"Gabby!" Anna-Marie approaches me from down the hallway, and though she's wearing her post-work clothes of a

21

fashionable tunic shirt over skinny jeans and boots, I can smell the hair spray wardrobe douses her with even from this distance.

"So sorry I'm late," she says as she reaches me. "Ryan offered to drive me here on his way home, and even though he has a Boxster, he drives like he's afraid of taking it over sixty and . . . What's up? You have a weird expression. And why is your finger bleeding?"

I ignore the finger question. "I'm fine, just excited to start my acting career."

She swats at my shoulder. "Shut up. You're going to love it."

A little deluded part of me hopes she's right.

THREE

Anna-Marie's acting class is actually down at the end of a different hall, and I can hear the chatter from the students inside. So much for my early arrival plan.

The chalkboard inside is still full of notes about the Italian Renaissance from the day's actual college class. The air smells of coffee from a small machine brewing atop one of the desks in the back. There's something surprisingly utilitarian about the whole set-up—the Styrofoam cups stacked neatly by the cheap coffee machine, the desks pushed back against the wall. No large potted fern for me to hide behind.

The fellow acting students break into spontaneous applause when Anna-Marie and I enter the room. They've heard about her big break, apparently. Their faces are pasted with broad smiles, but despite taking classes in this sort of thing, many of them fail miserably at hiding their jealousy. I wonder if I should warn her against drinking the coffee.

Their interest in her first week of work on *Passion Medical* is genuine, however. They pepper her with questions of all kinds, from what it's like working with Bridget Messler to what kind of food catering provides. She basks in the attention, telling the same stories I've heard nonstop for the last couple days, until a slow clapping from the front of the room interrupts her description of the director's "passion for artistic detail."

We all turn, and the class quiets. A tall, lanky man with a preternaturally smooth face despite his advanced age stands at the doorway. Peter Dryden, star of the late 90's hit cop drama *Cuffs*. Despite the obvious Botox (or perhaps because of it), he hasn't aged well. The past twenty years since the show's cancellation haven't been good for him. After all, he's stuck teaching Tuesday night acting classes in a back room of a community college. I kind of feel for the guy.

He claps a few more times in slow emphasis. "A star is born," he intones in a deep, overly theatrical manner that I at first assume is some kind of joke. But when I look around to see if anyone is about to laugh, I discover it is not. "Congratulations to Miss Halsey. May this break lead to the Hollywood Walk of Fame."

The cheering begins again, until a glare from the man brings it to a stuttering halt. "The 'big break' you all long for, however, will not keep you in this business if you have not learned the art, if you do not make love to the art, breathe the art, take it into your very soul."

The class is nodding, rapt, while I try to figure out how exactly one makes love to the art. Maybe I missed a very special episode of *Cuffs*.

"You must surrender to it, stalk it, take—" he stops, turning his icy blue glare to me. "Who are you?"

I am about to say that I'm just a student who showed up really, really late to my Italian Renaissance class and duck out, but Anna-Marie senses my impending flight and grips my arm tightly. "This is my roommate Gabriella, Mr. Dryden. She's been interested in acting for some time, and I told her you allow one free class. To . . . see if she's a good fit."

Despite that small flicker of hope from earlier, I can already tell I am not a good fit and so apparently can Mr. Dryden. He sniffs loudly. Then, as if I don't exist anymore, he resumes his speech about the art. I only barely pay attention, wishing they had some donuts to go along with the coffee. Of course, this being a class for wannabe stars, I would be far more likely to find a tray full of celery and organic quinoa.

While Mr. Dryden rambles on with a shocking number of sexual metaphors for what one should do to the art, my thoughts make their way back to Will, who is here in a classroom very similar to this one, possibly teaching his students about how to make love to writing.

I fail to hold in a giggle at the thought, though I'm pretty sure Will could never be that pretentious, and I wince as Anna-Marie pinches me on the arm. Peter Dryden clears his throat, and for one panicked moment, I think he's directing it at me specifically. But no, his eyes sweep the room. "We need one more volunteer for this first exercise."

Anna-Marie starts to pinch me again, but I bat her hand away. I don't need to be pinched into action. I'm perfectly capable of actively screwing this up all on my own.

Come on, Gabby, I coax myself, *you're here now. There's no harm in trying. At least you won't start anything on fire.*

I suck in a breath and raise my hand. Peter motions me and four others—including Anna-Marie, who'd apparently volunteered when I'd been daydreaming about Will—to stand by the chalkboard. His expression is already weary, even though the class has just started.

The scene we are supposed to improv starts in a bank. I've done all my banking online for years, and so I'm immediately uncertain what to do as the customer I'm assigned to be. Do I just stand in line and look at my phone? Pretend to fill out a deposit statement?

Fortunately, my confusion about whether I should just approach Anna-Marie, who is the bank teller in this scenario, is interrupted. One of the other "customers"—a short red-haired man with more freckles than pores—pretends to pull a gun from his waistband and waves it around wildly, shouting, "Everybody down! This is a robbery!"

Well, that makes my decision easy. I drop to the ground and

crawl under the nearest desk, putting my hands over my head. I assume the others are doing the same, but I am staring at the floor like a good little hostage.

"No, no," barks Peter, and when I glance up, I see this time it *is* directed at me, his forehead creasing as much in frustration as the Botox-stretched skin will allow. "You need to *add* something to the scene, not suck the very life from it!"

My cheeks flush, and Anna-Marie looks to be already regretting forcing me into this. Isn't acting about portraying things realistically? So why on earth, if I *were* caught in a bank robbery by a gun-toting fanatical actor hopeful, wouldn't I just do what he says and slide my phone over to him and sit silently? Every movie I've ever seen has informed me that trying to be a hero in this kind of situation ends badly for anyone who isn't Liam Neeson. Hell, Peter should know this sort of thing from five seasons of *Cuffs*.

The other three actors are still standing too, each looking like they're holding guns as well. Was I the only real customer in this bank? Or was I supposed to be a robber, too?

Anna-Marie saves the scene—or at least turns the attention away from me—by cleverly turning her banker character into some unholy mix of an ex-CIA operative and Jessica Rabbit, distracting the robbers with a sexy saunter and a few slick kickboxing moves from her Tae-Bo DVDs.

Just as she prepares to battle the final robber, he turns the scene into a musical, and Anna-Marie plays gamely along, crooning back at him and copying his dance steps in nearly perfect precision. The other robbers climb back to their feet and do the same, and suddenly I'm huddled under a desk with my hands over my head while the rest of the troupe appears to be auditioning for *High School Musical 5: Community College Edition*.

"Is this still a robbery?" I ask, wondering if this is some kind of test. "Should I be pretending to call 911?"

The musical stutters off at my words, and everyone stares at me. Anna-Marie shakes her head, but I can see she's trying to hide a smile.

"Cut," Peter Dryden says.

I last through two more torturous exercises in what appears closer to utter insanity than anything resembling acting, then slip out to my car to wait out the rest of the class. I unwisely haven't brought anything to read and my phone battery is practically dead, so I thumb through the community education catalog I cut myself on earlier.

Finances. Musical instruments. Photography. Stress reduction. Foreign language. Much like when I flipped through my college course book every semester for three years, nothing really speaks to me. I wonder, not for the first time, if I am fully without a talent or passion for anything other than locating amazing desserts at dive restaurants. I wonder where I should start applying for my next short-term job.

The class ends a half hour later, and Anna-Marie comes out with her acting friends, laughing and giving several of them hugs. She wasn't wrong about the cute guys, though I think most of them were far more into each other. She climbs into the car.

"Sorry," she says, as I pull out of the parking lot. "He's usually not that bad."

"No big. It's not every day I get to be called an 'atrocious waste of time' by a second-rate TV cop."

She winces, and I feel bad. I know she was just trying to give me some practice before I have to pretend to be held up by hot doctors having nervous breakdowns in hospital cafeterias in front of actual rolling cameras.

"Honestly, Anna, I'm fine," I say, tossing the booklet into the backseat. "I'm just better informed now of what songs to sing should I be caught in a bank robbery."

She chuckles, and we sit in silence for a moment. I debate telling her about Will, but there's nothing to tell, really. A cute guy who fired me two years ago actually remembers who I am and didn't actively avoid saying hi to me. *And* he has a single, perfect dimple when he smiles.

Maybe it's worth at least a mention.

My phone buzzes from the cup holder, and Anna-Marie picks it up. "It's a text from your brother."

Thoughts of Will flutter away and I sigh. "What does he have to say?"

"Mom says you're avoiding her again. You should call her."

"Et tu, Brute?" I murmur as I switch lanes. Felix usually takes my side of things, or at the very least, stays as far from our family's usual drama as he can. He moved to the other side of the country, and I'm not convinced his music scholarship was the only reason why.

In my peripheral vision, I see Anna-Marie chew her lip pensively and I worry I'm in trouble. "Don't tell me you want me to call my mom, too."

She shakes her head. "You know, Gabby, you weren't really that bad tonight."

Before I can respond, I slam my brakes and honk at a red Ferrari that blows a red light and nearly t-bones us. We both jerk forward and back again to the seats. My heart feels like it's jumped up to my eyebrows, while my stomach has settled somewhere near my ankles. A brief flash of a middle finger from the Ferrari driver's window, and the car is off weaving at a breakneck speed down a side street. I wonder which celebrity I'll see featured in a mug shot on TMZ in the morning.

We start driving again, my breathing stabilizing. Anna-Marie hardly seems fazed by our near brush with death. She only really freaks out at this kind of thing when *she's* the one driving. For all the things Anna-Marie is good at, driving is not one of them. She's been especially terrified of driving in LA ever since the first month she arrived and was hit by one of those Tours of the Stars Homes buses while making a u-turn.

We have a good system worked out: she pays gas and way more than her fair share of rent, and I drive her to work or wherever else she needs, as long as I'm available. I consider this both a financial win and a public service to the good people of Los Angeles.

"I wasn't that bad?" I say. "You were *in* the class, right?"

"Okay, so improv isn't your thing. But you played the scenes themselves in a realistic way. When you placed your coffee order with the barista who had Tourette's Syndrome, you were really convincing."

"I think Mr. Dryden called it 'masterful.' Oh wait, he followed that with 'lack of creativity.' "

Anna-Marie nods. "Okay, yeah, maybe for the improv exercise. But for actually ordering a cup of coffee—that's what extras *do*. You'd be great at that. I know it."

I hope she's right. We drive past Fong's All-American and I wish I could settle in for another round of the Breakup Tub. But I live in the land of salads and juice cleanses, and while I don't necessarily buy into all that, I'm health conscious enough to save my total nutritional meltdowns for special occasions.

If my foray into acting is any indication, I'm sure I'll be celebrating one of those again soon.

I let out a sigh as we're walking up the stairs to our apartment. "Okay, Anna-Marie," I say. "You can stop the hard sell. I'll do it. I'll apply to be an extra."

She lets out a little squeal and hugs me so hard I nearly fall down a step. Anna-Marie doesn't do things halfway, even enthusiasm. "It's going to be So. Much. Fun," she says, emphasizing each word as if I'm either hard of hearing or she's trying to brainwash me into believing it.

And maybe the brainwashing works. Because when I repeat the words "So. Much. Fun" back to her in an exaggerated Valley-girl accent to make her laugh—which works, as me doing that accent always does—I can't help but think maybe it really will be.

FOUR

I've been dropping Anna-Marie off at work on Lot C of Sudser Lane (the nickname for the studio where four of the major daytime soaps are filmed) for nearly two weeks now. Today, however, I'm actually parking and walking in with her on the way to my *own* job, which is an admittedly surreal experience.

She smiles and waves at various people—mostly crew members, though we spot a few of her co-stars. She's been telling me stories about these people for weeks, but even an LA-born-and-raised cynic like me feels a bit star-struck when I spot the legendary Bridget Messler in the flesh, chatting with a slender blond woman wearing a crew member baseball cap. Bridget's been on *Passion Medical* since the show started, I'm pretty sure. I have a few memories of seeing her on it when I stayed home sick from school as a kid—or at least walking in on my mom watching the show. She always quickly blamed our housekeeper for leaving it on, even though I'm pretty sure sixty-five-year-old Ingrid had about as much an idea how to work our complicated TV setup as she did NASA flight controls.

Back then, Bridget was part of this soap super-couple that everyone loved—she plays Sondra and the guy is . . . Sam? Simon? The name escapes me. I realize I don't remember seeing him the last few times I've watched the show with Anna-Marie.

I suppose I'll have a chance to find out where he's gone (perhaps into witness protection, waiting to reappear as an evil twin?), now that I'm working on the same set as these people. I still can't believe I passed the initial—and, as it turns out, only—test for becoming an extra at *Passion Medical*, which consisted of a twenty-minute-long Skype conversation with a bored-looking bottom-tier casting assistant. I'm guessing Anna-Marie's recommendation spared me an actual screen test of some sort, but maybe not. Extras are fairly expendable, after all. If one you hire sucks, you can probably poke your head into the commissary Starbucks and find twenty more to replace her.

I hope to at least collect one day's worth of wages before this happens.

Anna-Marie gives me a quick tour of all the locations for the *Passion Medical*'s fictional town of Hartsburg, Oregon. We walk through three-walled sets of various homes (which in typical soap opera fashion are comprised of mostly living rooms and, of course, bedrooms), the local coffee shop where gossip is slung and faces are slapped over Hartsburg's finest brew, and of course, Passion Medical itself. She practically bursts with pride as she points out the hospital room where she shot her first scene and where within days her character Helena both deflowered the teenage son of *Passion Medical*'s town villain and framed him for murder. She's been busy.

Though I've never been a regular fan of the show like Anna-Marie, I admit that it is pretty cool stepping onto these sets in real life after having seen them on TV. I pick up a stethoscope from a cart and wonder for a brief moment if it's the same one Dr. Katarina Gunn recently used to playfully examine Hot Doctor when he complained of heart palpitations being around her. Right before they—

"I asked for more instruments for this cart, but I don't see any," a female voice with a crisp British accent says from behind me, causing me to jump and drop the stethoscope with a clatter onto a metal tray. I whirl around, hoping my cheeks aren't as red as they feel. Unfortunately, my embarrassed flushes never resemble an attractive glow as much as a sudden patchy rash.

The woman standing behind me raises an eyebrow. She's the tall blonde I saw speaking with Bridget Messler earlier. With her high cheekbones and delicately pretty features, I might have mistaken her for one of the show's stars if she wasn't wearing the black baseball cap labeled "crew" in big block letters under the *Passion Medical* insignia.

"You're with props, right?" she asks, as I look around for Anna-Marie, who has abandoned me for the craft services table to chat up the actor whose character she deflowered in this very hospital bed.

"Uh, no, sorry. I'm a new extra."

Her lips purse in brief irritation, and she swears under her breath, but then she shakes her head. "No, I'm sorry. I think props is trying to repay me for making them redo Ryan Lansing's bedroom set four times. He's supposed to be a doctor, not a bloody bordello owner." She flashes a quick smile, which I'm sure is meant to be reassuring, but mostly just makes me feel uneasy. "But that's not your fault, is it? I'm Sarah Paltrow, no relation to Gwyneth, though I appreciate when people think it."

She sticks out her hand and I shake it. "Gabriella Mays."

"Well, Gabriella, I'm the director's right-hand woman. Good luck with the new gig."

"Thanks," I say, starting to warm to her a bit.

"A word of advice to sticking around that I tell all the extras. Keep your hands off the props. And the actors." She stalks off without another word, her shiny blond ponytail bobbing down her back with each step.

"Yikes," Anna-Marie says after Sarah storms past her, yelling for someone named Mark. "What did you say to her?"

"I'm not sure."

"Oh, well, don't sweat it. She's not called The BB for nothing."

"The BB?"

"British Bitch. Here, have a cronut. I've only ever had a bite of one, but it's amazing."

I taste the proffered pastry. It's no Breakup Tub, but it's pretty good.

A voice over the intercom starts calling off names needed for the first scene to be shot, and while Anna-Marie's is not among them, she practically dances with giddiness. "Time for makeup and wardrobe! And we've got to find the wrangler."

"The wrangler?" I didn't realize the show featured cowboys. Then again, anything is possible in soap opera land.

"The extras wrangler. He'll tell you what scene you're in, get you set up."

I'm not sure how much I love needing a "wrangler" and the comparisons to being cattle that it brings, but I am surprisingly eager to get started on my new job. The lure of TV stardom is strong, even for one who has resisted it as long as I.

Anna-Marie shows me the makeup and wardrobe areas, and seeing all the racks of gorgeous clothing—one marked specially with her name—I can understand her love for this particular room. Who doesn't love what essentially amounts to free high-end shopping on a daily basis? Not to mention having a professional do one's hair and makeup. I find myself hoping that extras get their turn in one of those chairs as well.

Just before she disappears to become more gorgeous than she naturally is (oh, the unfairness of it all), we find the extras wrangler. His name is Clint, and he actually does look like a cowboy who went through a mid-life crisis and fled the ranch for a lifestyle exactly opposite. He is big and burly, and instead of the ubiquitous crew member black baseball cap, he wears a wide-brimmed Stetson, black and crisp as if it'd just been pulled out of a hat box. His neatly trimmed brown mustache comes down past his mouth as if it means to become a goatee but can't cross the gap of chin in between. I expect a guy like Clint to be carrying a beer and speaking with a Texas drawl, but instead he's drinking a VitaminWater and speaks like he's from somewhere in the upper Midwest, nasally and fast.

"Gabriella Mays, huh?" He checks his clipboard and makes

a mark. "You're in group A today, the hospital team. I'm sure your friend told you about the extras massacre from last week? We lost another yesterday because he kept looking straight at the camera. Stick to your assigned task, don't try to be a star, and you'll do great. Maybe even get a line someday." He says this with enough significance that I assume this is the carrot ever dangled tantalizingly before extras—be a good little extra, chat silently and inanely in the background, don't draw attention to yourself, and a chance at actual stardom may someday be yours!

I think I prefer my Mom's old Halloween candy tactic. Regardless, I have no intentions of trying to upstage any of the actual actors, so I smile and nod. Clint smooths his mustache and points me toward Group A, my comrades in my first scene.

A tall Black woman about my mother's age approaches me. "Your first time?" she asks.

I nod, and she lets out a little relieved sigh.

"Me too. I was afraid I'd be the only one," she says. "Ian McKellen over there"—she points her chin at an older, white-haired gentleman who does somewhat resemble the actor, if at least in being old and white—"has been doing this for two months. And be careful about talking to him. He's all full of himself because he once played Hamlet on London's East End."

"Well, I played a lost boy in my fourth-grade production of Peter Pan," I say. "And I was told by my teacher that I was more convincing as a boy than a girl. So just let him try to intimidate me."

The woman blinks as if unsure what to make of me. Then, with a suddenness that makes me jump, she barks a loud laugh. "Just let him try!" She grins, and her whole face lights up with the energy of it. "I'm Karen," she says.

"Gabby," I return.

Before I can say anything else, though, Clint comes back and the attention of all the extras snaps over to him. With him is another crew member, a girl about my size and age and overall aspect of plainness. Clint eyes us briefly for a moment. "You,

you, and you three," he says, pointing to the once-Hamlet, an attractive Asian man, and a young Hispanic woman with two kids who appeared to be about twelve, "are patients. Lisa here will get you some street clothes."

I'm curious as to why the street clothes they're currently wearing won't work, but before I can think much on it, I feel Clint's dark eyes weighing me. I stand up straighter and suck in my stomach automatically.

"You and you." He points to me and Karen. "You'll be receptionists. You other two, nurses. Lisa will put you in some scrubs. And Lisa, remember, the light blue not the dark blue. B—, uh, Sarah says the dark blue scrubs draw the eye, and I'd rather not have my balls in a sling."

Lisa grimaces, whether at the lovely image or the thought of disappointing Sarah, I'm not sure. She nods. "Sure thing. Come on, everyone."

Karen grips my arm enthusiastically. "Receptionists. We won the background jackpot." She says this quietly, but I notice envious glares from some of the others in Group A.

"The jackpot? What do you mean?"

Even though she looks absolutely nothing like Anna-Marie, I can see my friend mirrored in that incredulous look at my cluelessness. "The actors almost always stand near the reception desk when they're filming a hospital waiting room scene. We'll be in practically every shot!"

"Oh. Yeah, cool." I try to put some excitement into my voice, because one of the "nurses" looks like she might shank me with a pen if I don't appreciate the honor I've been given. Mostly, though, I am suddenly nervous, and not about my fellow extras.

Practically every shot? On camera? I imagined the camera might catch a shot of my elbow, or at the most me walking briskly past. This whole plan seems bound to backfire horribly. Why did I let Anna-Marie talk me into this?

"Paycheck, paycheck," I murmur to myself, ignoring Karen's odd look.

Lisa takes us to the back of the wardrobe room Anna-Marie glowingly showed me earlier. I half-hope to see some of the other show's stars there (Hot Doctor, maybe?) but all I see are fellow crew members like Lisa scurrying around carrying outfits and purses and pulling racks. Of course. The stars themselves would never need to come to wardrobe. Wardrobe comes to them.

She eyes both Karen and me up and down. Karen's a little broader in the hips, but I'm bustier up top. Lisa opens a drawer marked "Scrubs – M" and fishes out two sets in a pale blue. We are directed behind a curtain to change, where we are soon joined by the nurses. I am reminded of my days in high school gym lockers as I face the wall and hurriedly disrobe. My sister Dana never had a problem waltzing around the locker room naked, but then again she'd been a size four through the better part of her life and popular, to boot. Whereas I was neither and had a bad case of bacne that is only now in my twenties beginning to fade.

The scrubs fit loose around my hips and tight across my chest, which I suppose is not a bad thing. At least Anna-Marie would probably say so. Karen's scrubs are the other way around and she eyes my boobs a bit warily, as if afraid they'll steal her spotlight at the reception desk.

Then we are ushered to makeup and hair, where a man with a bored cast to his mouth mutters to himself while dabbing powder on my face. He then squirts some gel into his hand and runs it through my hair before pulling it into a ponytail.

"Next," he announces with all the joy of a DMV worker.

I pat my hair, my fingers coming away sticky. Apparently extras don't warrant the full hair and makeup treatment, which I remind myself is fine. I'm not supposed to stand out. And looking in the mirror, at my neutral eyeshadow over brown eyes, my short, stubby (even with mascara) eyelashes, and my slicked-back hair, the shade of which is most colorfully (and accurately) described as "dishwater blond," I see what I see when I look in the mirror pretty much every day. Someone who won't draw attention.

And thus, someone who may just be perfect at this job.

FIVE

We are directed to the hospital waiting room set and shown our places. It looks pretty accurate to most hospital waiting rooms I've been in, if you can ignore the gaping black maw where the fourth wall should be. Within that maw, Sarah Paltrow stands talking with a rotund, bearded man with round John Lennon-style glasses. He is sitting, pointing at things while he speaks to her, and by the way she briskly nods at everything he says, I guess that he is the director, Bernard Penn. Anna-Marie told me he used to direct sitcoms, but got caught sleeping with the husband of a producer. And then later the son of the same producer. So it sounds like *Passion Medical* is where Bernard belongs, after all.

The patients are placed in the various plastic seats lined up along the waiting room. Some are given a magazine to flip through. The others are to just sit there and stare at the pictures on the wall showing how to most effectively wash one's hands, I suppose. The nurses are given stethoscopes and held off to the side (they are the ones who will be walking by in the background), and Karen and I are situated behind the reception desk, which I am pleased to see is high enough to cover the taut fabric across my chest.

Clint hops up onto the set with us, surprisingly light on his feet for such a bulky man.

"Bridget Messler and June Blair—better known as Dame Sondra Hart and Lucy St. James—will be arriving on set shortly. These ladies are pros, so this should be a one take. Provided none of you screw it up." His words are belied by a friendly smile that seems genuine enough.

He hands Karen the phone receiver from the desk. "You'll be taking a call during the scene. Hang up partway through, press some buttons and make another call."

He pulls an orange folder from an inbox and pushes it across the desk to me. "You'll be typing notes from this file into a computer. When she," he points to the nurse extra who looked ready to kill me earlier, "walks over to you with a clipboard, you hand her the file. Got it?"

Seems simple enough. My nerves have turned into a kind of fluttery excitement, buoyed by the palpable energy around me.

"I type, I hand over the file. I think I've got it."

"Good girl."

He hurries off to deliver more last-minute directions, and with each one I expect him to reach into a treat bag and toss out little bits of lunch meat for good performances.

While we wait for the stars, and crew members scurry around adjusting boom mics and props, I survey our desk. A computer monitor with Microsoft Excel pulled up on it faces me. At first I am surprised the computer works at all, but I suppose they want to cover all their bases for shots. Which I guess means I won't be playing Spider Solitaire on this thing until I know for sure which directions the cameras will be pointing.

Also on the desk is a cup holder filled with pens bearing the hospital logo and a stack of orange files like the one Clint handed me. I flip open the one on top and find sheets of old scripts inside. At least they recycle. Next to the phone that Karen is practicing punching numbers into (has the woman never used a phone?), post-it notes are stuck to the desk with tic tac toe games drawn on them, along with one very obscene-looking stick-figure. Before I can determine exactly what action is being depicted on the note, a cheer raises from all around me, Karen among the loudest. Bridget Messler has stepped onto the set.

The woman who is one of the most beloved icons in soaps for the last thirty years accepts the praise graciously, with a chuckle and beauty-queen-ready wave. Her short silver hair curls around her ears and the age lines on her face are etched just enough to indicate the maturity and wisdom of older years. She wears a glittery royal blue sequined gown (her character having come to the hospital from some gala or another, I guess) with a modest short matching jacket. (Though, seriously, even at seventy-something, this woman could probably pull off going sleeveless.)

The awe at her arrival is palpable among the extras. Karen lets out a tiny shriek and gives me a wide-eyed "OMG" expression that she drops when she sees how mine doesn't quite match her excitement. I mean, it's definitely cool to be within fifteen feet of Bridget Messler, but really. She's a soap star. We expected this, right? It's not like the pope just walked in ready to run lines.

I don't think I'm doing a great job of staying on Karen's good side.

The second actress in the scene receives far less open fawning. She's been on the show for a while, but hasn't reached the legendary status of the matriarch of *Passion Medical*. Lucy St. James—June Blair, I think Clint said her real name is—is a short dark-haired woman with overly thick eyebrows and a too-sharp nose, beautiful but in a rare, striking way not often seen in Hollywood. She, too, is wearing a gown, a red mermaid-style number so tight that wardrobe might need to use the jaws of life to get her out of it.

While Sarah talks quietly to June—who shoots a glare at Bridget while she's shaking the hand of one of the fawning "waiting room patient" extras—I lean over to Karen.

"So whatever happened to Sam?" I ask.

Karen's eyes briefly flick over to me, then back to Bridget. "Who?"

"Or, um, Simon. You know, Sondra Hart's husband? Is it Stedman?" I frown. "No, wait, that's Oprah's guy."

Now Karen fully turns to me, her eyebrow raised. "You mean Cedric? Cedric Hart, Sondra Hart's five-time husband and true love? Of the 1987 fairytale Cedric and Sondra wedding that the Franklin Mint made commemorative plates of?"

Okay, so I was a little off on the name. "Yeah, him. Wow, five times?"

Karen shrugs. "Well, it is soaps. They can't just *stay* married."

I imagine she's got a point there. "So is he still on the show?" I pause. "And please tell me you own the commemorative plates."

She eyes me dubiously, like she's trying to size up whether I'm mocking her. Or maybe just having a hard time believing there's someone who doesn't know the entire history of Cedric and Sondra Hart's epic love story. "Frank Shale, the actor who played Cedric, died six years ago."

"Really? How did he die?" I'm picturing something tragically mysterious involving a boating accident in the Caribbean.

"Liver disease."

"Huh." I guess playing a major soap opera star doesn't guarantee you a soap opera-dramatic death. Anna-Marie will probably be disappointed by this revelation, if she hasn't had it already.

Karen considers me a moment and seems to decide I'm taking this seriously enough to keep talking about it. "Frank and Bridget were actually married in real life, too. At least until—"

She cuts off when Sarah calls out to be ready on the set, so I don't find out what happened to Bridget's real-life marriage. And honestly, I care a whole lot less about celebrity gossip now that the cameras are about to roll and my nerves are back on high alert. I'm not the only one—Karen puts the phone to her ear and affects a look so full of concentration I wonder if she pictures the person on the other end needing her to help defuse a bomb.

I take a pen and open the orange folder in front of me, my heart beating a quick rhythm against my ribs.

All I have to do is stay in the background. Type, hand over file. Not get fired.

"Take one. Action!" a voice shouts from the gaping maw of blackness, and suddenly we're being filmed.

Sondra Hart (Bridget) and Lucy St. James begin speaking in dramatic tones about a car accident and how they worry that someone named Oliver (Sondra's grandnephew, I think?) won't pull through. I, however, am far less concerned for Oliver than I am about appearing appropriately studious at checking my file.

Then I remember I'm supposed to be typing something into the computer and have a brief moment of panic that I have no idea what to type into this random Excel spreadsheet. I haven't actually used Excel since high school and even then never really got it.

Just type something, idiot, thinks the practical part of me that is sick of having to look for new employment. And I do, typing the exact same words written in the old script in front of me.

I start to get in the zone, typing and checking and typing some more, satisfied that I am managing to actually look like someone who is adept at data entry.

And then I hear a tiny clearing of a throat. The angry nurse extra is glaring at me over the top of the reception desk, clipboard in hand.

I have no idea how long she's been standing there waiting for me to hand her the orange file. I summon the dispassion of every medical receptionist I've ever been forced to wait for while checking in and slowly close the file and hand it over like I have all the time in the world.

She swipes it out of my hand and walks out through the "hallway" in the back of the set. I hold my breath, hoping against hope not to hear the director yell at me for ruining the scene like Peter Dryden did so many times.

He doesn't. The scene goes on.

I feel strangely victorious until I realize that the scene going on means that they are still filming, and Clint didn't give me any further directions. Karen is on at least her third phone call by now, mouthing silently and nodding occasionally.

I decide to jot a note down on a post-it. *You're very convincing. Do you talk to yourself often?* I add a smiley face to soften the tone and slide it over to Karen. Her eyes dart down and then back up again, and I notice only the slightest quirk upwards of her lips before she continues her pretend conversation.

"And cut!" yells the same male voice as before, deep and booming. "Well done, ladies. No need for a second one." The tension of the scene that I totally missed while typing away on my ridiculous Excel spreadsheet dissolves. The other extras and off-set crew members chatter lightly.

Karen smacks my shoulder in a friendly way, like Anna-Marie often does. "You nearly had me laughing out loud! You better watch yourself in our next scene. I've got your number now." She brandishes the phone at me, and I grin, glad to see we really will be able to get along, despite my lack of basic soap opera knowledge. After all, we might be working together quite a bit, unless I still manage to get fired after my slip with the file hand-off today.

Clint cues us back up for two more hospital waiting room scenes, and we shoot them in quick order. One involves Lucy St. James and an attractive young man playing her son, which they also get through in one take. The next scene involves three other actors, one of which is Anna-Marie, dressed in a slim purple sheath dress. She smiles and waves at me before the scene plays out. A few of the other extras look at me with a kind of respect, while others appear wary, like my personally knowing one of the stars makes me a threat somehow.

Angry Nurse still looks angry.

I try to disregard them all as the scene starts. I'm in this for the paycheck, not the bizarre social politics of soap opera stardom. By this point, I'm pretty confident in my file checking and typing routine, and am able to pay attention to what the actors are actually saying. Anna-Marie has summoned tears that she appears

42

to be bravely holding back. I'm impressed. It wasn't so long ago that I walked past her room one night to see her staring into a mirror saying "Cry, dammit. Come on, Anna. Dead puppies. Dead damn puppies!"

The thought of dead puppies may not have worked, but she'd apparently found something that did. She wipes an escaped tear from her cheek as she speaks of the terror she'd felt when the car crashed, of how she realized in that moment that her life, which was almost cut tragically short, was being wasted in her petty schemes.

She probably has a point, since all her character appears to have done since returning from boarding school is to sleep her way around the hospital and frame some poor kid for murder. But now that I can actually pay attention to the lines, I'm surprised (and somewhat impressed) to realize it isn't a run-of-the-mill car accident that everyone's been talking about. The car crashed into the gala itself, taking out not only Sondra Hart's grandnephew but half the brass section of the band as well.

I really need to start watching this show.

While Anna-Marie monologues to a hot blond guy in a tuxedo, one of the car crash survivors is wheeled by on a gurney by some nurses in the background. I can't help but notice the excellent makeup work on the patient's bloodied face—which leads me to wonder what other wounds he sustained, before I remember that he's an extra just like me and they aren't likely to bother creating wounds that won't actually appear on camera. Still, it would be cool if they showed a bloody stump or something. I try to pay more attention to my file than nonexistent car crash wounds, and soon enough the scene is over, ending with Anna-Marie's character apparently already getting over her regret of a wasted life by flirting outrageously with blond tux guy.

"Cut!" The director yells from his seat of power. Light reflects from his small round glasses, but I can see little else of him. "Let's run that again. And this time, people, I want emotion!

43

Raw, sexual energy! I've seen piles of bricks display more passion than I just saw from you, Miss Halsey. Again!"

I flinch for Anna-Marie, but she doesn't seem fazed. They run the scene again, and a third time. I can't really tell the difference between the various takes—buried as I mostly am in my files and Excel spreadsheet—but she apparently does well enough after the third go-round that the director mutters something and declares it time to move on to the hospital room.

Actors are summoned from the intercom, and Karen and I are ushered unceremoniously from the set with the other extras. Clint waits for us with his clipboard and yet another VitaminWater.

"Good work, team," he says. "You're done for the day. Courtney will call you to let you know the day and time of your next scene if we need you again. Paychecks for today will be sent to the address you emailed her."

Courtney is the bored-looking casting assistant who interviewed me via Skype, I remember.

"Head back to Lisa to turn in your scrubs," Clint continues, scratching at his cheek just beside his moustache. "Maybe I'll see some of you around." His tone indicates that his life won't be made any better or worse regardless of if he does. There will always be more extras to be found in Los Angeles. He turns and lopes off without another word.

Clint's calling us a team is definitely a stretch at this point. We change back into our clothes, hand in our scrubs, and give each other falsely friendly good-byes, even though most of the extras are eyeing each other like if they don't get a call it'll be because one of other extras stabbed them in the back. I receive a full-on pursed lip fume from Angry Nurse when I tell her I hope I have a chance to hand another file to her someday.

"She sure looks like she's got a stethoscope up her ass," Karen says when Angry Nurse stalks away, her black ponytail swinging behind her like a pendulum.

I laugh. "Hey, anything can happen at Passion Medical."

"Isn't that the truth!" Karen grins. "By the way, I do own those plates—the complete set of five." She gives my arm a quick squeeze. "I hope we see each other at the reception desk again soon, girlie."

I grin back. "I hope so, too."

SIX

Before leaving for the day, I try to find Anna-Marie. I'm her ride, after all, and I need to find out when to come back to get her. But mainly, I want to make sure she's okay after getting chewed out by the director, and to see if I embarrassed myself too terribly in my attempt at extra-dom. The nice thing about Anna-Marie is that if I sucked, she'll tell me. And then commiserate with me over wine. That's what real friends are for.

She's getting ready to shoot her next scene at the most popular hang-out in Hartsburg outside of the hospital waiting room: The Brew, *the* place to go in soap opera land to pick up organic free-trade coffee and hatch a diabolical plot to steal your arch-nemesis's baby and pass it off as your own. Apparently, it isn't a place frequented by hospital receptionists, because no one on the reception team is being used for that one.

I find Anna-Marie talking with (or rather being talked *at* by) the BB herself.

I grimace and head over to the craft services table to wait. And grab another one of those cronuts while I'm at it. I pass Bridget Messler, surrounded by a gaggle of fawning extras—including Karen, not surprisingly. Bridget's signing glossy black and white 8x10 photos of herself with a slim purple Sharpie and smiling at them in a benevolent cult leader-type way as she passes out the headshots.

I notice June Blair standing not too far away, her eyes narrowed as she watches. When Bridget notices and gives a little wave—the smugness nearly dripping from her well-manicured fingers—June takes a giant swig from her coffee mug. Either the coffee has long since grown cold or that mug contains something else entirely.

Yikes. There are definitely some issues *there*. Fortunately, however, nothing that involves me.

It's a little past noon, and the pastries at the craft services table have been long since picked over and replaced by triangle-cut sandwiches, but I spot one remaining cronut hiding by a jelly-filled Danish, both lost and forgotten to the side of the veggie platter.

I take a bite. Good, but a bit on the dry side after sitting out all morning. I can practically hear my mom scolding me for eating a breakfast pastry at this hour of the day (apparently in her view, a late-night bit of pot is fine, but god forbid we abuse carbohydrates.) Thinking of her reminds me of her most recent text message: *Dana will be over this weekend and we are having a family dinner. You will be there Saturday, even if I have to send a driver to come get you.*

Even though my family can no longer afford to send drivers to do so much as go to the store and grab us a pint of ice cream, I assume the threat is legitimate. When mom digs in her fashionable heels on something, there isn't much that will stop her.

"I get angry when they replace the good stuff with cucumber sandwiches, too," someone says from behind me.

That voice. My heart forgets to beat.

Will Bowen. Here, at *Passion Medical.*

Drawing in a surprised breath, I start coughing on too much inhaled powdered sugar. He pats me on the back awkwardly. I'm not sure whether he's trying to dislodge any cronut in my throat or console me for my apparent inability to eat like a normal person.

"Sorry again," he says. "I seriously don't mean to keep scaring you. I might need to start wearing bells."

"No, no, it's fine," I say, slightly hoarsely. The powdered

sugar has clumped up somewhere in my esophagus. "I was just lost in thought. I should know better than to try to think and eat at the same time."

He grins, and that dimple appears. The tightening in my throat now has very little to do with stray pastries.

"It's a refreshing problem to see, actually. Too many people around here don't do enough of either. But seriously, what brings Gabby Mays to *Passion Medical*? Community education acting class one week, soap opera stardom the next?" I don't know if he tilted his head just enough to catch the set lights, but his green eyes actually sparkle mischievously.

Fricking hell. That's only supposed to happen in romance books, right? Or do cute guys have eyeballs that somehow defy the laws of basic anatomy? Regardless, my stomach flutters at the sight.

"Hardly stardom," I say. "I'm not cut out for acting. At all. Just an extra."

"Ah. Fresh chum."

I raise an eyebrow.

"For the sharks," he clarifies, rather unhelpfully.

"I got that. I'm just not sure who the sharks are supposed to be."

He nods toward the live set where Hot Doctor is taking time from saving Oliver Hart's life to sweep a gorgeous Black actress into a passionate embrace. Since the doctors are always busy having sex or getting involved in mafia schemes, I'm guessing the nurses of Passion Medical must be pretty damn good or nobody in Hartsburg would still be alive.

"Hot—I mean, Ryan Lansing?"

Will loads his plate with one of the aforementioned cucumber sandwiches and throws on the last remaining pastry for good measure. I hope he's not doing that just to make me feel better about my noon cronut. Then I remember the Swedish Fish.

His eating habits don't seem to be much better than mine, a thought that makes me unreasonably happy.

"Among others," he says. "But Ryan's the one to watch out for. He likes to make his rounds with the female extras."

I wish I could pretend he's saying that because he'd be jealous, but I'm far too much a realist. This is, after all, a guy who once fired me.

"So I hear," I say dryly, remembering Anna-Marie's tale of the hair-pulling girl fight which opened up my current job opportunity. "But I think I'll manage. So what are *you* doing here? Do they just keep you in some dark closet somewhere until it's time to warn the new batch of extras about predatory actors?"

His grin widens, and I'm glad to see he caught the playful note in my tone. I'm proud that I can still carry on a relatively normal conversation with him, despite how standing so close to him makes me feel both giddy and also a bit empty, like I'm missing something important.

Like I'm a poorly drawn toucan without a top hat.

"You're right about the dark closet," he says. "It's called the writer's room."

"You're a soap opera writer?"

I don't mean to sound incredulous, but he winces. "Yeah, right? It's hard to believe someone is actually paid to write this garbage."

"That's not what I meant. Weren't you working on a novel? I just thought . . . I mean, *Passion Medical* is great. There've been some good storylines lately, what with the car crashing into the gala, and . . ." I try desperately to think of anything else that's been happening on the show and come up awkwardly short. So much for any pride I had in my conversational skills.

"Don't bother. Our storylines have sucked lately, big time."

"To be honest, I don't watch the show much, so I can't really say. But Anna-Marie's loved it this last year."

"Anna-Marie?" He pauses in between bites of jellied donut. A bit of raspberry sits on his chin, and somehow manages to look charming. "Oh, the new Helena. She's your friend?"

I nod. "My roommate. And she has some pretty discerning taste. She has all the boxed DVD sets of Joss Whedon shows arranged in order of awesomeness, and I agree with most of her choices."

This unintended shift of topic puts me back in my usual groove when talking to cute guys, steering the direction of the conversation toward my much hotter friends or sister. I realize this could be what really shoots me in the foot when it comes to dating. Once they realize my gorgeous friends are also cool and smart, then they also realize that they don't need to settle for personality over looks. But the truth is, they're going to find out eventually.

I know it doesn't matter, since Will is way out of my league and really wasn't ever all that into me, but I suddenly wish I hadn't said anything about Anna-Marie.

"Hmmm," he says. "And which choices don't you agree with? Please tell me she doesn't have *Firefly* lower than the top three. Otherwise I may have to give her some truly terrible dialogue as penance."

I laugh. "No need on that one. *Firefly* is firmly in second place, which means we can have a respectful relationship. But *Buffy* season four behind *Angel* season one? And *Dollhouse* season one before *both* of them? The girl is insane sometimes."

"Well, she's an actress, right? Isn't that part of the deal?"

"For writers, too, I hear."

"You don't know the half of it."

I wait for him to make some seemingly offhand comment to indicate he'd like to be introduced to Anna-Marie, but instead he surprises me with, "You remembered that I was working on a novel?"

My cheeks warm, and I turn to stare at the veggie platter, as if intently searching for the perfect stick of celery. "I remember you spending lunch breaks doing an awful lot of typing. I guess I just assumed."

This is a lie. I remember perfectly the excitement in his voice

50

the one time I'd actually gotten up the courage to ask him about his writing. A customer had come in before I could ask him what the novel was about, and I hadn't wanted to interrupt his writing groove again afterward.

The next day I set the microwave on fire. The day after, he fired me. I hope against hope that he wants to talk about that incident as little as I do.

"Are you still working on it?" I say, before he can reminisce too deeply about our short mutual past.

When I glance back at him, he is considering his cucumber sandwich with a strangely wistful expression. An expression that disappears so quickly I wonder if I imagined it. "Not for a long time." He shrugs. "I guess priorities change. You know, that needing to pay the bills conversation we already had."

"Well, I hope you get back to it sometime."

"Maybe." His lips quirk back up in a warm smile. "But how about you? Gabby Mays, Joss Whedon fan and soap opera extra extraordinaire, what is it you really want to do with your life?"

I blink and notice my pulse thrumming. I don't know if it's the deep, pine needle-green of his eyes or the weirdly serious direction a conversation at the craft services table is turning, but I take a step back, and suddenly all I want to do is keep taking steps back.

Back away from Will, back away from this table and this set and most especially this question.

"You've got jam on your face," I blurt out, cringing inwardly at his confused expression. "I mean, well, not metaphorically or anything, but actual jam. It's okay. I need to get going. It was great seeing you again. Again."

Without looking back to see the scene of my strange social meltdown, I walk with as much dignity as I can out to my car. Anna-Marie can text me when she needs a ride.

I only realize as I get in that I am still holding the plastic plate with half a pastry on it. With a groan, I toss it into the passenger seat. The pages of the community education brochure stick out from between the seat and the armrest, forgotten since last week's humiliating attempt at acting class.

"What do you want to do with your life, Gabby Mays?" I ask myself in a mocking copy of Will's oddly serious tone.

It fails. I have spent tens of thousands of dollars on a marketing degree I don't care about and will never finish, and have been let go from jobs a fifteen-year-old could excel at while texting and vlogging simultaneously. I've avoided seeing my family for months even though they live barely an hour away. My phone sits heavy in my pocket, my mom's last text practically burning its way through the denim.

The only one worth mocking here is me.

"So what is it exactly that we're doing here?" Anna-Marie asks, raising an eyebrow at the clump of buttercream balls that are supposed to resemble a spray of rosettes on the small cake in front of her.

"I would think that's pretty obvious." I add another clump to my own cake with my frosting bag, hoping for at least one to turn out more like a flower than a sad little snowman turd.

The teacher strolls around the class, making brief, encouraging comments to the students. She is a round, cheerful woman with wisps of hair escaping her jaunty little beret. In short, she is everything I envisioned a woman teaching a community education cake-decorating class would be.

Anna-Marie rubs her nose and sighs when she realizes she's just smeared frosting on her face. "I mean, what are we really doing here? This isn't about what that writer guy said, is it? I know you said he's cute, but asking someone they barely know what they want to do with their life? That's weird. And he fired you, right? Which makes him both weird and an asshole."

I bristle inwardly at her saying that about Will, though I would have said the same thing had our situations been switched. "This sounded fun."

"In all the time I've known you, you have never expressed a desire to decorate cakes. Ever."

"Aren't you the one who's always trying to get me to be more adventurous?"

She shoots me a flat look, made more humorous by the fact that she missed some of the frosting on her nose. "Um, yeah. Adventurous. Like rock-climbing, or dating someone who owns a piercing parlor just to get a free nose ring. Not taking a class in cake decorating."

"And yet here you are with me."

"Because best friends don't let best friends take up tragically lame hobbies alone."

My grin lasts only as long as my next squirt of frosting. "Damn. I can't even get one. This is ridiculous. Are we sure we didn't sign up for the master-level class by accident?"

The lanky fellow in front of me, who might have taken exception at Anna-Marie's labeling of cake decorating as 'lame,' turns and says, "This class just started last week, ladies. Rosettes are for beginners." The sneer on his face suddenly drops when he sees who he's talking to. Not me, obviously, but Anna-Marie. "Oh my god," he says, dropping his frosting bag on the table. "Are you Helena Hart? From *Passion Medical?*"

Anna-Marie flashes the shy smile that pretends at embarrassment at being recognized. It's definitely part of the act. Inside I know she does a little happy dance every time someone asks for an autograph. She'd wear a sign around her neck every day that says "I'm a star on a hit soap opera," if it were socially acceptable and the sign were fashionable enough. Frankly, I don't blame her. She's starting to achieve her dreams. Some of us aren't even sure what our dreams are.

As the students around us begin to fawn over Anna-Marie, I wrinkle my nose and poke at one of my "rosettes," as if that will magically turn it into the lovely swirl it is meant to be. It only leaves a fingertip-shaped crater.

"You were amazing when you seduced Diego," gushes the guy in front of us. "What was it like kissing him?"

"Forget Diego," a pretty Asian girl with bright purple eye makeup says, pointing her frosting bag for emphasis. "When is Helena going to get with Trevor Everlake?"

Several students around us nod. At least two make an "mmm-mmm-*mmmm*" sound like they're picturing covering Hot Doctor with frosting.

Suddenly I am, too. It isn't an unpleasant train of thought. Frosting goops from the tip of the bag I'm clutching too tightly, and the lanky guy snickers.

My cheeks heat up like I'm a fifth-grader in a maturation class, instead of a twenty-three-year-old woman who . . . okay, is still technically a virgin, but has rounded every base but home plate. Not to mention that I've read all five books of the latest best-selling erotica series, *Sultry Sins*. If I hadn't known twenty-one different ways to describe a man's throbbing member before, I certainly did after chapter two.

"I can't reveal anything from the latest script," Anna-Marie demurs, "but I can assure you, you'll definitely want to—"

"And what's going on over here, class?" The plump, rosy-cheeked teacher makes her way into the small crowd forming at the back of the classroom with us at the epicenter. The students hurry back to their own tables as if she'd been tapping a cudgel against her palm and scowling instead of merely smiling like the living embodiment of Mrs. Claus.

"Sorry," Anna-Marie says, "but I don't think I'm cut out for cake decorating." She gestures at her cake, which is only slightly less pitiful looking than my own.

"Nonsense, dear." The woman whips out a small set of silver tools from her apron. "See this one here? You almost had it. Make a little swipe here and here—" she does something I can't really see with what I can only describe as a frosting scalpel, "—and look. Perfect."

Anna-Marie and I peer at the cake. An unsightly blob of

frosting has become a lovely little flower.

"And you did half the work yourself," the teacher continues. "Not too bad for a beginner."

Half the work seems a bit of an overstatement, but Anna-Marie beams.

The teacher digs a card out of her pocket and hands it to Anna-Marie. "I don't just teach classes. I also run a catering service, so just in case the food on set at *Passion Medical* isn't up to snuff . . ." She trails off.

"I'll, uh . . . I'll look into it," Anna-Marie says.

The teacher smiles that grandmotherly smile and walks past me, barely glancing at my cake. "Too much frosting, dear," she says, her tone much less sickly-sweet than it had been for Anna-Marie. "And ease up on your grip on the bag. You're making rosettes, not milking a cow."

The guy in front of me coughs in a suspiciously laugh-like way. I want to throw my frosting bag at the back of his head.

By this point it is clear to me that a career in cake decorating is not in my future. Not only because I obviously have no inherent skill at working with a bag of frosting, but because it's not nearly as fun as all those romantic comedies with female leads who own a bakery make it seem. I should have known this one, honestly. I've never had an artistic bone in my body. The misshapen mugs I'd bring home from elementary school art class looked like something created by a drunk Salvador Dali compared to my sister Dana's at the same age. My parents didn't even bother pretending to be impressed by the time my papier-mâché monstrosity of a Venetian mask came home, nor did they bother hiding it when it went straight into the garbage the next day.

I'm not sure how many more free trial classes the community college will let me have before they decide I'm running some sort of scam, so I should probably rule out any art-related ones in the future. And stop bringing Anna-Marie. Because it'll probably only take one more attempt at finding a "fun new hobby" before she realizes I'm using a community education brochure to figure out what I want to do with my life, and I'll never live that down.

The teacher begins discussing fondant textures, and Anna-Marie appears to be paying even less attention than I am. She picks drying frosting from her newly-manicured fingernails.

My phone buzzes in my pocket. I don't recognize the number, which is a relief, since I more than half-expected it to be my mother.

I duck out into the hallway to answer.

"Gabriella Mays?" a bored-sounding female voice says.

I hold in a sigh. After a short, failed stint as a telemarketer myself, I have an inability to just hang up on them like any other self-respecting person. "Yes?"

"This is Courtney with casting at *Passion Medical*. Clint wants you back for another few scenes on Monday. Are you available?"

I hold in a squeal of excitement that is out of proportion to my actual joy at being asked back. I liked being an extra (and cashing a paycheck far higher than what I deserved for a few hours of doing not much more than existing), and seeing Anna-Marie's glamorous work life is undoubtedly fun. But something tells me that's not the main reason I'm looking forward to going back.

I try not to think about Will's smile. Or the way whenever I talk to him I feel like the rest of the world doesn't exist except as background to *us*.

"Yeah! Uh, yes. I'm pretty sure I'm available."

"Great," she drawls with a level of enthusiasm indicating she's about as thrilled with my acceptance as she is about cleaning out the workplace fridge. "Check in with Clint at seven AM."

"Definitely. Thanks, I—"

Before I can finish, she hangs up. I look back at my phone and see that I missed a text from my brother, Felix.

Mom's losing it. She says to tell her you're coming to dinner.

I groan. I should have responded to one of my mother's dozens of texts about the family dinner, so she wouldn't resort to making my brother in New York City hassle me about it.

Yes. I'm coming. You can tell her to leave you alone.

Like that will work, he texts back.

At least someone in my family gets it.

Still, I'm going to put off thinking about having to deal with my family as long as possible. Right now is for being excited about another paycheck. I head back into the class and sidle up next to Anna-Marie.

"I got a call from *Passion Medical.* They want me back again," I whisper.

Anna-Marie squeals loud enough to interrupt the teacher's latest bag-squeezing demonstration, but it's Anna-Marie, so no one seems to mind.

My rosettes continue to suck, but I find myself humming quietly as I make them.

SEVEN

I pull into the long driveway leading up to my family's house in Brentwood just after 5 PM. Dinner's at six sharp, but I'm pretty sure I've already pushed it with my mom by ignoring her texts for so long. I don't need to risk making it worse by dropping in just as the food hits the table.

My sister Dana's fully-loaded black Lexus sits in the driveway next to my father's red Mercedes Benz, the only car he has left after selling his other two. The way he talks about it, selling those cars was a personal tragedy rivalled only by those who have experienced plague or genocide.

I have Anna-Marie calling with an "emergency" if I can't make it away from these people by nine.

I jingle the car keys in my hand as I walk to the door. I'm being unfair, perhaps, acting like my family should be avoided at all costs. I do love them, though generally better from a distance. My brother especially has always been someone I could confide in, though since he's been away at school, our sessions of complaining about the rest of the family have been few and far between. Which is too bad, because he can do a seriously fantastic impression of my mom chewing out our gardener Luis while she and Dad are on their way to attend a gala to support immigration reform.

They may be pretentious enough to think my attendance

at UCLA will harm the family reputation, and I often feel like I belong among them as much as that last cronut among the cucumber sandwiches, but I *am* part of the family.

Besides, it's not like I haven't suffered through these family dinners all my life. I'll put in my time, spend the evening listening to my parents gush about the achievements of my siblings (and themselves). Then when the inevitable pointed questions about my lackluster life come up, I'll wish I was a better liar and could convincingly invent both an astronaut boyfriend and a job offer from Bill Gates himself. Or that Bill Gates is my boyfriend and *I'm* going to be an astronaut.

At the very least, the food will be good.

I pull open the Italian wood doors (special-ordered from Naples after the neighbor had hers redone) and walk right in. Dana must not have arrived much before I did, as she is crouching in the marble entryway, trying to wrestle the shoes off her two-year old son, Ephraim, as he kicks and yells.

"You could help me, you know."

At first I think she is speaking to me, but her husband Paul pokes his head out from the library just long enough to say "Ephy, be a good boy."

Ephraim sees me first and stops fighting. His round, currently red face brightens. "Aunt Gab-Gab!"

"Hey, big E." I grin down at him. My nephew is the lone bright spot in our family dinners—possibly because he seems to be the only one to notice me for anything other than criticism. I've always thought his name was a bit formal for a kid, but apparently he's named after Paul's Jewish grandfather, who was a prominent research scientist as well as an accomplished classical pianist.

No pressure *there*, Ephy.

Dana manages to slip off the final shoe just before he bounds toward me. I wrap him in a big hug and plant a kiss on top of his mass of brown curls. The hug doesn't last long. Seemingly realizing he's finally free of his mother, he wriggles away from

59

me and takes off running down the entryway into the kitchen.

Dana sighs. "Hi, Gabby. Glad you came this time."

Her words sound pointed, but her tone is too exhausted to back it up. I haven't seen Dana this tired since she was pregnant with Ephraim and simultaneously working on the project that would eventually earn her that big industry prize I can never remember the name of. Possibly not even then. Stress always energizes Dana.

Now, noting the dark circles settled in under her blue eyes, it appears there might be some kinds of stress that can unhinge even my powerhouse of a sister.

"It's only been a month or two," I say, but do some quick mental math and grimace. *Or four.*

Have I really managed to avoid my family for four months? I am simultaneously proud and disgusted with myself.

Dana gives me a hug that is all surface, not the tight grip of true affection her son gave me. She smells like Chanel No. 5 and diaper rash cream, and I force my nose to unwrinkle before I face her again.

"So where's Mom, anyway? After all the texts, I kind of expected her to be perched out by the roadside with binoculars, waiting for me."

Dana opens her mouth to answer, but an unexpected male voice chimes in from the direction of the kitchen. "She was planning on it. I hid the binoculars."

Our brother Felix strides toward us with that careless, relaxed gait of his, a slumped teenage walk he never quite grew out of but somehow made into his own. Like Dana, Felix was lucky enough to inherit Mom's slimmer build and airy blue eyes instead of the cow-brown I share with Dad. I've been told Felix is a serious hottie by more of my friends than I'd care to admit, a fact Felix has taken full advantage of.

"Felix!" I only belatedly hope Dana doesn't take any offense at how enthusiastically I'm greeting him as opposed to her. After all, Felix hasn't been home in over a year, wisely choosing to spend both the summer and holidays with his friends in New York. And also, I've always been closer to him.

Who am I kidding? Dana will take offense, and I don't care enough to do much beyond feel slightly guilty. This is the kind of oil on which our family runs.

He hugs us both—me with more gusto than Dana, I am secretly happy to see—and steps backs with a grin. "I'm glad you came."

"So that explains your sudden concern with Mom's dinner plans. But what are you doing here?"

"And in the middle of the semester?" Dana asks. Trust her to be concerned with the toll a home visit might take on Felix's academics. Of course, maybe I should be, too. It *is* Juilliard, after all, and probably much more difficult to blow off than my former classes at UCLA.

Felix cocks his head to the side and looks just past my head, not quite meeting my eyes. "I needed a break, I guess."

"In the middle of a semester?" Dana repeats, horrified. "Isn't that what, you know, winter break is for?"

I want to pinch her like I used to as a kid when she would get all high and mighty with me. Doesn't she see how Felix's smile isn't quite right, how his eyes are skipping over our faces and never quite landing?

Something is wrong, and I'm afraid to find out what it is. Felix isn't supposed to have big problems, and for that matter, neither is Dana. These are the two who had everything figured out from the cradle.

"Yeah," he says with a fake laugh. "Maybe."

"Well, I'm glad you're back." I give him a playful shove. "Now I don't have to deal with Mom alone." This I say in a low voice that hopefully won't carry across the marble to where Mom is lurking.

Hurt flickers in Dana's eyes, more than I would have expected, and I feel bad. But it's the truth—Dana never dealt with Mom. Dana was the poster child of Mom's brilliant parenting, the two of them always thick as skinny WASPy thieves. Whereas Dad's favorite kid has always clearly been Felix.

This leaves me as the favorite of neither parent, but honestly I don't mind the lack of constant attention that my siblings receive for their shining efforts.

Felix grins back at me, but there is still something missing, some piece of my brother that appears to be have been left in New York. Or maybe lost there.

The click of heels signals my mother's arrival, and she sweeps into the entryway like a grand dame of old Hollywood, though with less bouffanted hair and a Bluetooth clip glowing from behind her ear.

"I see you've found my little surprise," she says, placing her hand on Felix's back. He stiffens noticeably. "You all say I can't keep secrets, but this one I managed quite well, I think."

The way she says that makes me realize that Felix didn't just fly back today. How long has he been home? Why? He squirms under the suddenly suspicious gaze of both Dana and me. I try to relax mine. He's my brother, and he's home to visit. That's all that should matter.

"Where's Dad?" I ask, to relieve Felix.

"In the library with Paul," Dana says, making a dismissive motion, as if both Dad and Paul could stay there the rest of the night for all she cared. "Dad's showing him some new investment opportunity he's got up his sleeve."

I cock an eyebrow at Mom, whose lips have pressed tightly together. They'd lost a fortune back when the recession hit California like a ton of Adjustable-Rate Mortgaged bricks, though for a long time they'd somehow managed to keep our family's lifestyle pretty much the same. It wasn't until it was about time for me to go to college that I started hearing phrases like "we need to economize" and "she'll be fine with a Hyundai."

Judging by the paintings and statues missing from the entryway, I'm guessing Dad's latest money-making schemes haven't been doing any better than those he started working on back then. I wonder how empty the house will have to get before Mom and Dad decide to downsize and move into a condo like sane people.

Very, very empty, most likely.

"Come, dear," Mom says, grabbing my elbow, "You can help me chop vegetables."

Normally this is a task she assigns Dana, because I have cut my finger enough times "helping" that the family has learned to keep knives well away from me. But Mom is nothing if not deliberate, which means she has very specific purposes for wanting to discuss something with me alone. I hope it doesn't involve getting chewed out for my terrible texting response rate.

Ephraim comes running back, and so I don't see whether Dana is bothered by my taking her vegetable chopping spot in the family tonight. Felix just watches me with a look of sympathy and huddles further into himself, like he wants to disappear into the tall potted plant next to the door.

The once-state-of-the-art kitchen appliances still gleam like they're brand-new, and the granite countertops are spotless. I know Mom can't afford to hire the usual housekeeper anymore, but I'm guessing she had a maid come over just before dinner tonight. There's no way my mom scrubbed down that sink herself, unless things have taken a drastic turn for the worse in the last few (four) months.

The scent of brown sugar glazed ham wafts from the oven, and my mouth waters. Cooking was never something Mom hired out, at least not for weekend family dinners. She isn't domestic in much, but the woman can cook, and despite her obsessive need to keep up with designer trends, she never succumbed to fad foods. She just always made sure to carefully restrict how much of the good stuff we'd be allowed to eat.

I straddle a stool and pick up a knife, eyeing the bell pepper.

"It's not going to jump at you, Gabby. Just cut it." Mom tucks into an onion with swift, practiced strokes.

63

I do, and she nods. "So you must have been very busy at the boutique lately," she says.

Damn. I knew she'd start about the unreplied-to texts. I also knew I didn't want to tell her I'd been fired.

"That and other things. I started a new job."

"Mmm-hmmmm."

Normally this would make her ears perk up, but she is focusing on the onion like I'm not even there.

"Mom? Is everything all right?"

Chop, chop, chop. The knife thunks into the cutting board several times before she says, "Your father and I are getting a divorce."

Despite my tendency to drop whatever I am holding when startled, I keep a tight grip on the knife. Maybe too tight. "What? Why? The money thing?"

She narrows her eyes at me. "Don't gape, dear. You'll catch flies."

"Is this why you flew Felix home? To tell us all?" A thought occurs to me, and though I likely deserve it, I am annoyed. "Am I the last one to know?"

"Nonsense. I told you first."

"Before Dad?" Despite all my parents' issues, I'd never known them to talk about divorce. They'd always said it was such a cliché.

"I'm not going to dignify that."

"Okay, but why? And why tell me?"

"To the first, it was just time. And to the second . . . you're more *flexible* than the others. If you're fine with it, Dana and Felix will come around too." She beams at me, the same smile she gave me when bribing me with Halloween candy, the same smile she always bestowed when I could make life so much easier for everyone involved by just going along with it.

Normally I do. But this . . .

"It's just *time*?" The knife quivers in my fist, and I set it down. "Did your marriage have an expiration date on it you just noticed?"

"Honey, you're still important to both of us. This has nothing to do with you." She sounds like she's reading from a pamphlet made for comforting second-graders.

Of course it doesn't have anything to do with me, I'm never around, I want to say, but I also don't want to swing her ire in that direction.

"It's not that, I just . . . This is insane."

"Do you have any friends with parents still on their first marriage?" she asks, one cool, perfectly penciled eyebrow arched.

Truthfully, I don't actually have many friends besides Anna-Marie, and her parents are divorced. But I get the point. This is LA. First marriages are as disposable as last night's sushi.

But my parents had always been different. Like their two perfect children (with me being an invisible outlier), they had always had a perfect marriage. They rarely fought, they took walks together in the mornings, and they cuddled in front of the television at night.

I'd never felt like I could attain any of the levels of success that the rest of the family had, but their marriage was one thing I'd actually aspired to. This one thing that didn't require talent or a genius-level IQ, but just happening to find someone who fit you like the perfect pair of jeans.

Not that I'd ever had great luck finding perfect jeans.

"Don't tell me you cut your finger again," Dana says, strolling into the kitchen with Ephraim on her hip. He wriggles, but she holds him tighter. "Because that would be sad, Gabby, even for you."

Against my mother's advice, I gape some more, unsure of how to act around my siblings now that I know this new information. I stare down at the bell pepper, only two strips cut into it after all the time I've been sitting there.

"God, Dana, leave her alone," Felix says, following her in. He likes to jump to my defense, as if he's the older sibling of the two of us. I appreciate it, but it inevitably makes me feel worse. Especially now.

How could my mom say that it was just *time* to get divorced, as casually as one decides it's time to change the upholstery?

"She knows I'm kidding," Dana says. "Unlike you, Gabby has a sense of humor."

"Well, I'm glad to see you can all still bicker like you're twelve again." Mom takes the pepper from where it sits uselessly in front of me and starts doing my job. She gives me a significant look, but I'm not sure what it's supposed to mean. Don't tell them yet? Please tell them so I don't have to?

My mom and I are rarely on the same wavelength enough to make non-verbal communication anything but a comedy routine gone wrong. We have proven this countless times playing charades on family game nights of days past.

I pretend I don't see her watching me.

My mind reels as they all make small talk until dinner is ready and then more small talk once we're all seated. Dad praises Paul's latest promotion and Dana's latest prestigious trade journal publication and even Ephraim's ability to identify all fifty states and half of their capitols. (Which, damn—can't at least one other person in this family be average?) Mom praises Felix's mastery of some super-complicated classical piece he was chosen to perform for some of New York's elite. She also praises her own ham, and we echo the sentiment as expected. I toy with my (admittedly delicious) food and make faces at Ephraim to elicit giggles.

Through all this, Felix sits too still, not really looking at anyone. Does he know? He's been here a few days, apparently. Maybe Dad told him, or he saw something that clued him in. I wish I could talk with him alone. Or that Mom would just drop the bomb on everyone so I wouldn't have to deal with the information all by myself.

Then again, she expects me to somehow make it better for everyone else, and I don't have the faintest clue how to do that.

"Gabby," Mom says. "You said something about a new job, didn't you?" She stresses the word job, though I have no idea why. Am I supposed to transition the conversation to divorce somehow?

"What happened to the boutique?" My dad pauses with his fork loaded with potatoes halfway to his mouth. He appears to notice my presence for the first time, which isn't anything new. Maybe if I had money to invest, I'd have been invited to hang out with him and Paul in the library.

"What happened to your college education is the real question," Dana says, not quite under her breath.

I ignore her. We've had this argument before, and she doesn't understand that college just isn't for everyone. It must be easier for her to be so pro-university when she had a major she actually cared about.

I plaster on a forced smile. "It didn't work out. But get this— you know my roommate Anna-Marie?"

"The pretty one? From the country?" Mom, of course, would classify her this way.

"The wannabe actress," Dana clarifies. Her tone reflects her very poor opinion of anyone wanting to be an actress.

"Exactly. So she got hired as a regular on *Passion Medical*—"

"The soap opera?" Mom's eyes widen. She is impressed. Eagerness to share my own tiny slice of the glory swells in my chest.

"Yes, and—"

"At least it's a regular paycheck, even if it's only a stepping stone," Paul offers, as if he is so well aware of Anna-Marie's goals and dreams. "Like commercial work."

"It's not at all like commercial work. She's an actual character on the show."

No one appears to have heard me.

Dad points his fork at Paul thoughtfully. "We could look into commercials, I think. I have a few contacts from the studio that have gotten into that line of work. They might be interested in the ideas I've come up with."

Mom slams her fork down on the plate and we all jump.

"Can we please have one meal in which I don't have to hear about how you will lose more of our money?"

If I'd been able to process anything other than shock, I might have taken pleasure in the fact that even Dana gapes unattractively. We all stare, even Felix, who hasn't made eye contact with anyone since dinner began. Mom doesn't have loud outbursts. She makes her digs with the passive-aggressive flair of a professional LA debutante.

Dad is the only one not shocked. He chews, takes a swallow of wine, and then stands up to leave.

"Do not leave this table. We have all our children here, finally." Mom's voice fights for firmness, but trembles anyway.

"Exactly." Dad sounds deceptively calm, but his eyes narrow. "And I do not need you harping on my financial decisions in front of them."

"Financial decisions you make alone."

"Because you want to pretend our problems don't exist!" He explodes then, and I want to crawl under the table, maybe also take Ephraim, who stares up with wide eyes and a quivering lip.

Now that Dad has started, he isn't inclined to stop, even when Ephraim's lip quiver becomes a whimper. "You want to pretend we still have enough money to afford this house, to still go to charity events in a new designer gown, to go to lunch with those parasites you call friends, to do all this and pay for flying back and forth to New York and Felix's rehab and—" He cuts off, seemingly realizing what he's said by how ghost-white my mother's face has gone.

"Rehab?" Dana asks in horror. I wish I could judge her for her tone, but it is exactly the same way I said it in my mind.

My stomach has dropped to somewhere near my knees. Not Felix. He was always a good kid. No drugs, barely even drank alcohol. Music was his drug, he always said. Music was his life.

Will Juilliard let him keep his scholarship if he was caught with drugs? Will they even let him stay at the school?

How long has he been home?

Felix blinks too quickly and then stands up and leaves the table. My heart goes with him, wants me to go talk to him, but honestly, I don't know that my brother wants to talk to anyone right now.

Ephraim clearly doesn't know what's going on (hell, I'm not even sure), but as soon as Felix leaves the room, he starts crying. Paul takes Dana's not-so-subtle pointing and mouthing "take him" clue, and picks Eph up with a quiet, "Hey buddy, let's go play in the library."

Mom glares daggers at Dad. "Do you really think now was the best time to bring that up?"

Dad groans. "No, I don't think now is the best time, but this family damn well better start actually talking to each other at some point, shouldn't we?"

"What does that mean?" Dana's eyebrows draw together suspiciously.

"They're getting divorced," I whisper.

And for once, everyone hears me. Dad clears his throat, and Mom flushes, her glare turned toward me, as if I, too, need to take lessons on bombshell-dropping timing.

"What the hell?" Dana asks. "And how does *she* know this?"

Worry lines form in Mom's forehead. Disappointing Dana is high on her list of things to avoid doing. "Honey, I wanted—*we* wanted," she interjects with a motion towards Dad, who snorts, "to bring this up in a calm family meeting, discuss what's going to happen. It's not really going to affect anything—"

"Like hell it's not." Dana sounds like a petulant five-year-old with a penchant for swearing. I realize I must have sounded the same when I first heard the news, but the divorce thing has taken second priority to me all of a sudden.

"What about Felix? Is he going to be okay?" I ask.

"He'd better, at fifty grand a month," Dad grouses.

"Fifty grand we could have had if you hadn't lost twice that on your last ridiculous scheme." Mom's jaw clenches so tight I think her cheeks might crack.

I can't take it anymore. My chest is squeezing in, and it's getting hard to breathe. "I'm done," I say.

Dana lays into my parents some more, but Mom's eyes follow me as I leave the room. I can feel their weight even after I round the corner into the hall. Tears burn behind my eyes.

How did all this happen? My family had issues—my parents' focus on designer clothes and cars and material success at the exclusion of almost anything else comes to mind—but we are the Mays family. A unit, one that even I, with my utterly mediocre abilities, was somehow a part of.

A unit that until today I didn't think could come cracking apart.

I head to the door, wanting nothing more than to just be back in my apartment, or even better, at Fong's All-American nursing a double heaping of the Breakup Tub. I pause with my hand on the doorknob.

I can't leave yet. Not without at least trying to be there for Felix. I head upstairs to Felix's room.

His door is closed. I knock, but he doesn't answer.

"Felix?" I lean my forehead against the door.

Still nothing.

"Hey, look, I get that you don't want to talk. That's cool, or whatever. I'm taking off now. Just . . . just call me if you want, okay?"

He doesn't respond, but the cello sounds, low and strong. It's Johnny Cash. I listen for a minute or so, and then head back to my apartment.

EIGHT

We drive to Sudser Lane so early the sun hasn't even crested the mountains yet. My check-in time may be seven, but Anna-Marie is scheduled earlier, and being an actual star, she gets more time allotted for hair and makeup.

Despite driving a compact Hyundai, there's a few moments as we sip our lattes on the way to set where I feel like a TV star myself. It's not a bad feeling. I can sort of see why people in Hollywood are so willing to sell their souls to keep it around.

It's almost enough to make me forget my family problems. Almost.

"It's like my whole family imploded overnight!" I start all over again. "Well, not overnight, I suppose, because who knows how long Felix has been in rehab."

"I know," Anna-Marie murmurs in response to my family drama, but her heart isn't in it. It was there most of the weekend as I babbled nonstop about it. I take this as my cue that I am stretching the bonds of best-friendship thin.

I decide it's probably better for both of us if I just immerse myself in the soap opera world until I can figure out a way to think about my family's new issues that doesn't make me crazy.

Which may be a long time.

"So today's the big day, huh? Helena gets it on with HD,"

I say.

"HD?"

"Hot Doctor. Trevor Everlake."

Anna-Marie gives me a sidelong look. "We don't get it on, really. Just a passionate kiss outside The Brew before his brother—my boyfriend—catches us." Despite her attempts to downplay excitement, her lips twitch at a smile. She knows what a man-whore Ryan Lansing is just as much as everyone else on the set of *Passion Medical*, but it would take a woman with a libido of stone to not be eager to share a kiss with HD.

I remember what Will said to me about being chum for the sharks. I'm not proud of it, but HD is one shark I wouldn't mind circling around me. Just a little, of course.

Yet when I try to picture locking lips with Hot Doctor, I find myself imagining Will's face pressed against mine.

"A *passionate* kiss, huh?" I say, trying to clear my head before I let that particular image go any further.

"That's the script talking, not me," she says.

"Uh-huh. Well, from what I've seen, Hot Doctor doesn't have any other way of kissing. Just don't let yourself get mauled by any jealous extras after the cameras turn off."

"Those are the risks that come with being a star, dah-ling," she says with an exaggerated Old Hollywood accent and a grin.

Despite the ridiculously early hour, *Passion Medical* is already bustling. Crew members move from set to set, arranging and re-arranging props, adjusting lights, barking out orders that make absolutely no sense to me, like "Kilgrow to R4, down to L11."

My stomach knots when I see Sarah Paltrow turn and glare at me, until I realize that she's actually glaring at Anna-Marie. She taps her watch and turns back to the terrified-looking crew member she was previously gesturing angrily at.

"Are we late?" I look at my phone, still surprised at the num-bers there. I normally go well out of my way to get jobs that don't require my presence for at least another four hours. "How can we be—?"

"We're not late. She's just got to find something to jump up my ass for. The woman's a monster." Anna-Marie grits her teeth, then lets out a slow, loud breath I remember Peter Dryden having us all do before each scene in that sham of an acting class. Though purposefully breathing like I have bad asthma and a nasty sinus infection didn't do much for my calm then, it seems to help Anna-Marie now. She beams. "Off to the daily grind."

"Is that what everyone calls their scenes with HD?"

She snort-laughs, which is the one thing even Anna-Marie can't manage to do charmingly, and blushes, looking around to make sure no one else heard her before heading off to her glamour squad.

I stand around for an awkward moment, then mosey over to the catering table again. I am uncomfortably disappointed that Will isn't there, but at least this early in the morning, I have the full glory of the breakfast buffet for my choosing. I grab a cronut and some orange juice, then add a couple of carrot sticks to my plate to at least maintain the illusion I'm not trying to OD on sugar first thing in the morning.

A few others mill around the buffet table, and judging by the snippets of their conversation—spoken in a hush, like they know they don't belong here anymore than I do—these are also extras who have arrived way too early. I guess I'm not the only extra who may have been helped into her job by being the means by which a star or crew member got to work that morning. I don't recognize any of them from before. I wonder if I'll get a chance to work with Karen again.

"Ms. Messler is a treasure, an absolute treasure," an attractive middle-aged woman opines while brandishing a jam-slathered English muffin.

"I've heard she's taken extras under her wing before," a younger woman, maybe a year or two older than myself, says in a reverent almost-whisper. "Advice, informal training, that sort of thing. Even getting them lines."

"Well, I imagine if Dame Sondra Hart herself wants someone

73

to have a line, it'll happen," the first woman agrees.

Two others standing with them—a Hispanic man with streaks of gray in his well-coiffed black hair and a petite woman with skin so porcelain-white she looks like she might crack at the first smile—nod aggressively, like enthusiasm alone will make them Bridget Messler's chosen one.

I debate actually eating one of my carrot sticks rather than just having them placed there for show, all while priding myself on having no desire to earn Bridget Messler's mentorship, or even a line.

The carrot stick dangles uncertainly in my fingers while I imagine myself actually being a soap actor, even for the brief moment of one on-camera line, one "Your triple venti soy no-foam latte is ready, Ms. Hart."

No. Somehow it would go horribly wrong. And I need to keep this gig as long as possible, not throw it away for the chance to bungle the words to a complicated coffee order.

"Of course, I'm guessing Ms. Messler regrets having been so charitable with June," the middle-aged woman says with a pointed look around the table. The others murmur in agreement, and the Hispanic man shakes his head, though it seems to be in sympathy. With Bridget?

I think of the smug looks and the glares I've caught passing between the two soap actresses, and it's hard to picture the word "charitable" applying to their relationship.

"What do you mean?" I ask.

They all look over at me, and for a moment I feel like the new kid in school approaching a full lunch table, looking for a seat.

"Ms. Messler once took on a mentorship role for June Blair when June first joined the cast, fourteen years ago," the middle-aged woman says. She takes a delicate bite of her muffin, then continues. "Lucy St. James was initially written as a small part, meant only for a storyline about Cedric and Sondra's extortion by the mafia. But—"

"But Bridget worked with June and convinced the show

heads that the character of Lucy St. James had lots of potential for other stories," cuts in the younger woman, still in an almost whisper, though an excited one. The woman with the muffin narrows her eyes, though I'm not sure whether she's more mad at being cut off or that the other woman dared call Bridget by her first name.

"And we all know how that turned out," the porcelain-skinned woman says. Her eyebrows are tweezed into a bit of a high arch, and she looks permanently startled.

"We do?" I look at the others, hoping that at least one of them is as confused as I am.

None of them appears to be.

The woman with the muffin clears her throat, retaking the conversation. "There was a storyline where Cedric Hart and Lucy St. James started an on-screen affair. Wasn't long before Frank and June took that off-screen as well. Ms. Messler divorced him soon after."

"Poor Dame Sondra," the younger woman whispers sadly.

"And June just carried on with him for years," Muffin Woman continues. "Blatantly throwing her betrayal in Ms. Messler's face, up until the day Frank died. Downright disgraceful, her acting like that, and I'm not afraid to say it."

I somehow doubt this woman would be so confident in her badmouthing if June Blair herself—or any of the show regulars— were actually standing at the table with us. But I can definitely see why there might be enough bad blood between Bridget and June for a whole Taylor Swift album.

Still. It kind of feels like Frank Shale should take the bulk of the betrayal blame, having been Bridget's husband and all. But maybe being part of the legendary super-couple of Cedric and Sondra and, well, *dead* lets him off the hook with the soap fans.

I'm about to—possibly unwisely—bring this up when movement in my peripheral catches my attention, and I see Will standing by Sarah, who is flipping through the pages of the day's script. He is waving at me and grinning. I wave back, my mood lightening just by seeing him. I don't want to think too hard about that.

Will makes a very deliberate chin-tipping gesture, like "Look behind you." I do and see HD approaching the craft services table. Despite everything I've heard about HD making his way through female extras like they're an escort delivery service the soap provides just for him, my heart rate accelerates at the mere sight of that perfectly chiseled jaw.

Damn biological imperatives.

I am not the only one affected by his oncoming presence. The three women all standing with me become visibly flustered. Even the lone man shrinks back under the glare of HD's veritable glow of attractiveness.

"Please tell me you ladies are new series regulars," HD says, without any preamble.

The nervous giggling that erupts at Trevor Everlake speaking is grating, more so because I have to fight from joining in. I stuff a Danish in my mouth to prevent any pathetic outbursts.

HD clearly loves the reaction. His blue-gray eyes, framed by long dark lashes, focus with laser-beam intensity on each of the three women now gathered around him. He doesn't appear to notice me yet, but I am across the table and have a large pastry obscuring most of my face, so I don't blame him.

"You seem like you'd have an excellent bedside manner," HD says to the muffin-eating woman, giving her a wink.

Barf. Seriously, if this guy was any less hot this woman would probably file a police report. And yet . . . damn if I don't kind of wish he'd comment on my potential bedside manner.

I look back behind me at Will, who is, embarrassingly enough, still watching us. He raises the back of the script he's holding, upon which he's drawn a shark in red ink, its fin poking out over hastily scribbled waves.

Watch out, he mouths, his eyes wide in mock horror.

I grin behind my Danish, and he holds up his finger in a "wait" gesture, then scribbles some more on the picture. When he holds it up again, I almost choke on my pastry trying to hold in a laugh.

The shark now wears a top hat and a monocle.

I give him an approving nod, hoping the way my heart is doing little back flips in my chest isn't super noticeable in my expression. Sarah looks up from the page she was reading and sees the picture. She glances over at the table and Will says something to her. She doesn't look amused. She glares in my general direction and stalks off. Will runs a hand through his shaggy hair, watching her leave.

The backflips trail off uneasily. I hope I didn't contribute to him getting in trouble. How much control over the writers does the director's assistant have?

"I've seen you around here before, haven't I? Stand-in for Katarina Gunn?"

For the briefest of seconds, I think HD's caramel-smooth voice is talking to me, and I flush at the comparison to the gorgeous Dr. Gunn. Then I turn and realize he's holding the hand of the young whispering woman who wanted to be Bridget Messler's protégé. She looks like she might die of pure joy.

It is curious how well HD does this. He glides from adoring woman to adoring woman, blatantly flirting with them all and yet somehow managing to make them each melt under his gaze like she is the only woman in his world.

The Hispanic man has wisely stepped away from the table. He stands no chance of making any inroads with the ladies while Trevor Everlake holds court. I lower the Danish and move closer to the table. Might as well get this over with.

I brace myself to stifle my giggle reflex, as HD's gorgeous face swivels to me. He stares at me rather blankly for a moment, then: "Are you with catering? If you guys can cut the carbs a bit, that would be great. Maybe some green smoothies, something with kale?"

"Kale?" I blink stupidly.

"You use organic, right? Make sure you do."

"I'm not—" I start to say, but he's already turned back to his admiring flock.

"Well, ladies, I've got to get to hair and makeup, make this mug presentable." He somehow manages to wink at each one of them. The super pale-skinned woman flushes brighter red than the veggie platter's cherry tomatoes.

HD saunters away, leaving me feeling strangely defeated. I re-check my outfit, seeing if anything I'm wearing screams "don't flirt with me; I'm with food services." Jeans, a plain lavender t-shirt, sneakers. I'm not ready to go on the runway, but I don't think I look like I just emerged from a garbage heap, either.

It bothers me how very much this bothers me. Why should I care if HD didn't flirt with me like he does with apparently every other breathing woman alive?

The other women are still giggling to each other like HD's attentions have bonded them into a small sisterhood. I don't think they realize that those very same attentions will eventually lead to hair-pulling fights and losing their jobs. I am embarrassed for my gender. I am even more embarrassed for myself.

"That was weird," Will says, making me jump. The Danish drops onto the table with a sugary thump.

I spin around and see him right behind me. If he wants to stop startling me, he should really stop lurking there.

He winces. "I think the ten second rule can be expanded to at least twenty-three seconds if you just drop it on the table."

I pick up the Danish and take a big bite, making a show of considering. I swallow and nod. "Yep, still good. I think it picked up the sugar from a dropped cookie or two."

"Well, it appears you escaped being chum. For the time being, anyway."

"For the time being? So you didn't hear our enchanting exchange. He thought I was with craft services. He wants more organic kale, by the way."

Will looks as if he can't decide whether to laugh or look at me with pity. He does a strange mixture of the two.

"It's more than okay," I say, perhaps a little too hurriedly. "I actually prefer not to be hit on creepily by strange men. Crazy, I know."

"Makes sense to me."

"And he's not exactly my type, anyway." Why on earth am I saying this to Will, of all people? He certainly doesn't need my awkward defense of my inability to attract male attention.

"Oh yeah? Handsome television stars don't cut it for you?"

"Too common. Like finding a penny on the street out here. And not a lucky one."

He nods as if I'd said something deep. "So what kind of guy would be like finding, say, a quarter? Or even a Susan B. Anthony?"

"One who knows who Susan B. Anthony is, for starters," I say, a little proud that this at least falls near the ballpark of flirting. Will raises an eyebrow, and I panic a little and add, "Also, someone who wears flannel shirts unironically, because he's really a mountain man who spends his time chopping trees and befriending wolves."

This is total BS. Although book number five of the *Sultry Sins* series did feature a gorgeous lumberjack on the cover that I kept face-up on my nightstand well after I'd finished reading the book.

Will smiles. "Wow. LA does not seem like the best place to find this feminist-leaning mountain man."

"Damn. I suppose I'll have to settle for a life that doesn't revolve around finding a man." Saying this makes my inner feminist proud. I only wish it hadn't come quite so soon on the heels of my inner idiot being disappointed that HD hadn't hit on me.

He nods. "Good call. If writing for *Passion Medical* has taught me anything, it's that romance usually leads to jail time for murdering your evil twin. You were a student at UCLA, right? Still there, or did you graduate?"

He picks up on the wince I try to conceal, a reflex every time I think of how much money and time I have wasted on college.

"Touchy subject, huh?" he says.

This time I'm the one being weird. Asking someone if they're in college is nowhere outside the realm of normal social interaction. I just hate talking about it. Or thinking about it.

"Neither. I didn't finish. I just . . . "

Couldn't figure out what to do with my life. Couldn't figure out if I *had* a life to do anything with.

" . . . ran out of money," I say.

"Ah. The need for food and shelter outweighing your dreams. I understand that all too well."

But he doesn't, apparently, because he imagines I have dreams, passions I had to sacrifice for survival, like every other normal person. Something I shine at, other than making people look good in comparison.

Not that I want him knowing any of this. I like having him think I have secret dreams of opening an art studio or running my own Fortune 500 company. I don't want him to know I spent yesterday afternoon at another trial community education class, "Beginning Metalsmithing." And I definitely don't want him to know about how I accidentally used the small soldering torch a bit too close to my class materials packet. Between that little incident and the microwave fire of years ago, Will might start to think I'm an arsonist.

Classes involving fire—clearly a pass from now on.

"So this novel of yours. What's it about?" I ask, hoping that by steering the conversation towards him I can pretend to be the person he thinks I am for a little while longer.

He hesitates.

"If you don't want to talk about it—" I start.

"No, no, it's good. I just haven't told anyone about it in a long time. It's my Great American Novel. Only, like, the science fiction detective noir version. You know, layers of my musings on social justice cleverly concealed by chapters full of whisky-swilling ex-cops and spaceship battles."

I am legitimately impressed, not because his dream book sounds particularly good, but because I can tell he isn't feeding me BS like I did about my perfect man. Will has an openness about him, a kind of uncynical sincerity, that is . . . nice. And all this talking to him is turning my insides all kinds of gooey. I'm starting to return to images of that tropical honeymoon with birds in top hats and monocles that I'd convinced myself long ago could never happen (and probably couldn't because surely there are animal rights groups that don't approve of clothing wild animals).

"I know, right?" he says, and for a split second I think I've said the honeymoon thoughts out loud. But no, he's referring to his novel, and his lips curve into a smile that doesn't reach his green eyes. "Sounds horrible. Thank god Sarah convinced me to use my powers for . . . well, not good, not by a long shot, but for something that actually pays the bills."

"No," I say hurriedly, hoping whatever expression was on my face didn't contribute to the snuffing out of his dreams. "It doesn't sound horrible, it . . ." I trail off, realizing what else he said. "Sarah?"

"Sarah, yeah." He gestures over to where Sarah Paltrow is picking through the surgical equipment on a cart, her lips pursed like she's deciding which instrument she could use to stab the person who set the cart up so haphazardly. "She's my fiancée."

My mouth goes dry, and those gooey-turning insides congeal into something rock-hard in my stomach. He's *engaged*?

To *her*?

Will watches her with an expression I can't quite read. When he turns back to me, he looks wary. "I know her reputation around here, the British Bitch thing and all, but she's really not like that."

I get the feeling he spends a lot of time defending her. Maybe even to himself.

I open my mouth to say something, ideally "maybe you

shouldn't be marrying someone you have to defend constantly against claims of bitchiness" or, more likely, "no, she seems really cool," but the buzz of a voice on the intercom calling for "five minutes to scene one," relieves me of having to lie or step way outside my comfort zone.

Will grins again, that dimpled, wide smile that makes me a little light-headed.

Jeez, Gabby, enough. The man's practically married.

Oh, god. How obvious was my flirting? BB or not, Sarah is gorgeous and accomplished and probably amazing in bed. And he is all hers.

"Well," he says, "I'd better get back to the writer's dungeon. We've got to figure out how to cure Lucy St. James's selective amnesia."

"Lucy St. James gets selective amnesia?"

He makes the motion of locking up his lips and tossing away the key, and I can't help but smile. Though as Will grabs a pastry and holds it up in farewell, I look down at my half-eaten Danish.

I toss it in the trash and head to find Clint to check in to work.

NINE

Today I am not a receptionist in the hospital. Today I am a regular citizen of Hartsburg, Oregon, taking a stroll through a sound-stage park filled with fake pine trees that smell like dust and plastic. I am reading a book as I walk, slowly crossing the stage once for each re-take of the scene. Despite my fear that I'll trip over one of the mics or lighting cords only partially buried under fake grass, I manage to both walk and appear to be reading while doing so. I don't draw attention to myself, and though the director, Bernard, is on the warpath today, yelling swear words in combinations I've never heard, he says nothing at all to me. I might as well not even exist.

Anna-Marie is right. I am good at this.

The scene taking place while I'm walking past in the background is between June Blair (Lucy St. James) and her on-screen son, an actor who plays Diego. Anna-Marie's Helena slept with him her second day back from boarding school, I think. He is no HD in the looks department, but holds his own in the realm of soap opera attractiveness.

Today, instead of her gala gown, June is wearing a fashionably cut business suit and wide gold hoop earrings that keep catching the light, causing Bernard to put some poor girl from wardrobe in tears. Earring gaffe aside, they seem to be doing just fine to me, though Bernard makes them do five separate takes. June Blair stalks off after the final one, muttering to herself. Looks like Sarah isn't the only one considering stabbing someone today.

Thinking about Sarah Paltrow—who stands beside the director, all slim and pretty and glaring as if she can earn protection from Bernard's wrath by mirroring it herself—reminds me of the pit in my stomach that never quite left after my conversation with Will.

"Good work for today," Clint says to me and the one other extra in the scene, a blond woman in a sports bra and yoga pants who jogged past just before I made my star-turn of walking while reading. Clint takes a swig of his cherry VitaminWater, which leaves droplets on his mustache. "You can go check out with Courtney."

"That's it? Just one scene?" I am torn between being happy I can go home and crawl back into bed and annoyed I got up so early just to walk across a set five times.

Clint chuckles. "Pays the same, sweetheart. Count yourself lucky. I wish I could go home this early—my boyfriend would sure as hell appreciate it." He starts calling for the next group of extras.

Clint may have a boyfriend to spend an early day off with, but sadly, I do not. I pull out my phone to text Anna-Marie, whose scenes have gotten pushed back for another hour, and tell her to call me when she wants me to pick her up.

Then I check out with Courtney, who shows no sign of recognizing me or caring about life at all. While she's briskly typing notes into her iPad, I stare straight ahead, forcing myself not to look around and see if Will is anywhere about. It doesn't matter anyway. He's probably back in the writers' room gossiping about how obviously into him I am, and how he had to casually drop his fiancée into conversation just to get rid of me.

Except he didn't mention her for a long while, even though

he clearly had the opportunity. And Will doesn't seem like the type to be gossiping about anybody. In fact—

"Gabby!" he shouts, just as Courtney is done with me. I wheel around. Will is standing there looking slightly out of breath, and I can't help but hope that he knew I was leaving and raced out here to catch me. He runs a hand through his hair in what appears to be an attempt to look casual. "I was just going out to grab coffee," he says. "Want to join me?"

I stare at him. Bookstore Employee Gabby would have killed for this invitation; hell, even the person I was earlier today would. They're both turning cartwheels—something I've never been capable of in real life—and cheering for me to say yes.

But the current version of me is questioning why on earth he's asking. I mean, he's got a gorgeous (if bitchy) fianceé he could take out for coffee, and a whole host of fellow writers if she's too busy chewing out the extras to make time for him.

And maybe that's it. Maybe Will is so starved for company that doesn't come with a cloud of anger and resentment vibrating around it, waiting to lash out at the nearest target. But no matter how much pettiness I want to wallow in, that thought doesn't bring me any satisfaction. It just makes me sad, and hopeful it isn't true.

Sarah has to be a better girlfriend than that, doesn't she?

"Okay," I say. "I'm done for today, but I can ride along for a little while."

Will smiles and looks almost relieved. We walk out to his car, which surprises me—there are two Starbucks right here on the studio lot within walking distance. Will sees my confusion.

"There's this little mom and pop coffee place I like to go to," he says. "I like to get off the lot sometimes, and this place—I don't know, it's kind of nice to go somewhere that's not a chain, right?"

I wonder if he'd love Fong's as much as I do, then mentally chide myself for the thought. Going out and grabbing mid-day coffee with a coworker is one thing. There's no way he's ever going to end up across a poorly-lit booth at Fong's with me on some Saturday night, just the two of us, sharing a plate of Moo Goo Gai Pancakes.

We get in his white Toyota Corolla, which looks about as well-cared for as my Hyundai—which is to say, not very, though his backseat clutter is more stacks of old scripts and uncapped, likely dried out highlighters, while mine is my college marketing textbooks I keep meaning to get rid of and a couple of old In-N-Out bags. We cruise down Sudser Lane in awkward silence. I'm searching for something to say that isn't "why on earth are you dating *her?*"

I finally settle for, "So how long have you and Sarah been together?"

Will lets out a slow breath, like he's trying to remember. "Almost two years," he says.

I nod. So probably they weren't together yet back when I worked at the bookstore with him. Not that it matters. "And is the engagement thing new?"

He shrugs. "Six months, give or take."

"Do you have a date yet?"

I'm hoping to discover that theirs is one of those engagements that is just a polite way to tell their grandparents they're living together, but instead he nods. "In a year."

Silence falls again, and I'm starting to feel a little invasive asking question after question about his personal life that he seems uncomfortable answering, even though he must get asked these things all the time, right? I should probably let the subject drop and switch to something safe like Ryan Lansing's latest conquests or what he actually does with all those old scripts in the backseat—fodder for his screenwriting classes? Building a huge script-and-blanket fort? But before I can do so, Will sighs.

"I know what you're thinking," he says. "Why would I be with someone like her, right? But she's not always like that. It's Bernard. He puts so much pressure on her—on *everybody*—for the show to be perfect. He treats us all like we're disposable, and I suppose technically we are. It's not an easy environment to work in, and it's hardest on Sarah."

I'm not sure I agree with that, after seeing the way Bernard talks to his actors, but I get what he means. "Yeah, it's probably easier to be tucked away out of sight in the writers' cave."

"Not that we don't hear it sometimes. Believe me. But Bernard would have to actually know which of us wrote a given line to single us out, so he mostly threatens to fire us en masse. There's a lot less of a chance he'll follow through with that. He does need someone to write his show, after all."

"I don't know," I say. "It might be hilarious to watch him try to write and act all the parts himself." I'm more than a little amused thinking of him in one of the skin-tight dresses they make Anna-Marie wear. Just watch *him* try to exude "raw, sexual energy" while wearing six-inch heels in a hospital waiting room.

Will smiles as if he's picturing the same thing. "Don't think he hasn't threatened it." His smile drops. "And Sarah gets the worst of it. If anything goes wrong, he blames her, and she's the one who has to fix it. It puts her on edge."

That makes sense. "So what's she like when she's not at work?"

Will is quiet for a moment. "It's the kind of job that follows you home, I guess."

We arrive at the coffee place, so I'm spared having to react to the awkwardness of that pronouncement. The coffee shop doesn't appear to have a name, unless it's "Fresh, hot coffee," which is scrawled with paint on the window. Inside, it's small but more well-lit than Fong's, with each table having its own lamp that appears to have been scavenged from yard sales and thrift stores—which kind of reminds me of Anna-Marie's and my apartment. The coffee shop walls are lined with bookshelves filled with tattered paperbacks and remaindered hardcovers, as well as stacks of old board games. A couple of women who appear to be in their fifties sit at a table, sipping their coffees and playing what looks like an intense game of NCIS: Clue. I would think this coffee shop is going for a hipster vibe, but there seems a distinct lack of mention of anything "organic" or "fair-trade."

Even with there only being five different types of coffee on the menu—one of which is just called "Normal"—I can definitely see why Will likes this place.

Will steps up to the counter and orders six coffees to go—which makes sense, really. He wasn't asking me out so much as looking for someone to ride along with him, and I just happened to be the one he passed by on his way out. In a hurry. Because they were having some sort of coffee-related emergency?

Then he turns to me. "What do you want?"

I stammer out an order and Will pays for the whole thing, then gestures to a table and sits while we wait for our order to come up. I resist the urge to tell him I can pay for my own coffee, since he very clearly offered and is apparently buying coffee for all of his colleagues.

But are they paying him back?

We sit down across from each other and Will rests his elbows on the table. Between us is a lamp with a base that looks like someone just glued a big conch shell to it and called it home decor. "What about you?" he asks. "Are you seeing anyone?"

This morning's me does one last cartwheel before I shove her right out of my mind. He doesn't mean anything by this. It's just a topic of conversation. "Oh, you know," I say. "I'm between relationships."

Will nods, as if he can imagine this. "Happens to the best of us."

I'm eager to turn the conversation back to him, before he wants to delve into the details of my last relationship, which was with a guy obsessed with curling (the sport, not the hair process) and who shortened every word relentlessly ("Should we order some apps to go with our 'za?"). I haven't exactly set a high bar for the whole boyfriend thing.

"So how did you and Sarah meet?" I ask.

Will smiles. It's genuine and much better than his frequent winces every time she's mentioned. "We met at a wedding, actually," he says. "One of my roommates was marrying one of her roommates, and we both ended up in the wedding party. The wedding was on this cruise to Cancun, but the bride and groom disappeared on an off-ship excursion. Sarah and I spent six hours searching for them. Turned out they'd been arrested for soliciting underage prostitutes."

I gape. "Are you serious?"

"It was a total misunderstanding—they'd thought these teens were offering a tour of some local ruins. I didn't say either of them had a ton of common sense," he says with a laugh when I raise an eyebrow. "And they had clearly had too much to drink, which didn't help their case with the local police. Anyway, it took them three days to sort it out, so Sarah and I were frantically making calls to the US embassy and we all missed the second half of the cruise entirely. And neither of us speak a bit of Spanish. I took German in high school, and she took Latin, of all things." He shrugs, still smiling, like he's remembering this all fondly, which I suppose he would. "It was a total mess. But she was great, just so determined, and . . . well, fearless."

Something clenches in my gut, hearing him say that in an almost awed tone. Fearless. Determined.

Two words that have never been used to describe me.

"We got it all figured out, though," he continues. "And in those three days we spent a lot of time together, just hanging out and talking, you know? And, okay, doing our own fair share of drinking."

My gut is twisting even deeper, thinking of them spending long nights on a beach or in some cantina, drinking and laughing and learning about each other's lives. It's much easier to imagine their time in Cancun consisting of Sarah scowling and blaming everyone within a ten-mile radius for everything not going exactly her way. I'm guessing some amount of that happened, too.

"At least something good came out of it, then," I manage. "Besides your friends' wedding, of course."

"Including that," Will said. "They lasted six months before the divorce."

Now it's my turn to grimace. "Yikes."

"Yeah." The barista—an older woman who may actually be the "mom" of this "mom and pop place"—calls out our order, and Will goes to pick up the cardboard tray. I'm about to stand to join him when he brings the whole tray of coffees back to our table and hands mine to me. He takes the seat across from me and rests one hand on the table, taking his own coffee with the other one.

I guess we *are* going out for coffee, not just picking it up.

"So are you going to get married on a Mexican cruise?" I ask, taking a sip of my coffee. It's pretty good, dark and rich, though I admittedly miss all the flavor options of Starbucks. "To relive the magic?"

"God, no," Will says. "We're planning this formal thing at a reception center in Anaheim. Or, I guess, Sarah's planning it. Another reason she's so stressed. The wedding is a year out, but I guess all the decisions have to be made well in advance. I'd help, but, you know, she likes things done a certain way." He shrugs again.

I bet she does. My mind reels with questions from how he feels about being left out of the plans for his own wedding to whether he wants to be marrying Sarah at all. But instead I take another sip of my coffee and steer us back toward safer waters. "Does she like her job?" I ask.

"Yes and no," Will says. "Ultimately, she wants to direct, but there are so few female directors, even in soaps. Bernard is kind of . . . the thing she has to do to get there, I guess."

I smile. "Not literally, I hope."

Will cracks a smile again. "God, I hope not."

I set down my coffee cup and find that our fingers are resting only inches away from each other on the table. We've spent all this time talking about Sarah, and yet I feel closer to him, like I'm getting a glimpse into what his life is really like. And maybe I'm just imagining things I want to be true, but he seems . . . lonely.

I look up at Will and I realize he, too, is staring down at our

90

hands. His fingers twitch, and my heart thuds as I wonder if he's going to reach out and take mine.

Then he clears his throat and puts his cup back in the cardboard tray. "I should get these back before they all settle to room temperature." He smiles at me. "You ready?"

"Sure," I say, taking my own cup. And I know I should be glad nothing happened. I don't need to get involved with a man who's practically married to a girl who could get me fired for looking at her wrong. I should be glad he's taken, so things won't be awkward when I lose this job to whatever the equivalent of the microwave fire will be.

But I'm not.

TEN

Three days later, I'm back on set again, checking out the craft services table. Between my family mess—especially worry for Felix, who isn't responding to any of my texts—and the boulder in my gut that appears whenever I remember that Will is engaged, I want to spend my time before check-in aimlessly stuffing my sorrows with carbohydrates. Instead, I decide to hang out with Anna-Marie while she gets her hair and makeup done, as if maybe attaching myself even more to her enchanted life will rub some of that enchantment off onto my own.

I turn to head toward the stars' dressing area and find Will looming unexpectedly behind me. I let out an undignified shriek.

"Sorry!" he yells, holding up his hands as if he's afraid I'll react to my surprise by delivering a blow of self-defense to his Adam's apple. "I didn't mean to—"

"Um, hi," I say. "Hi, Will."

We both make an effort to look casual, and I'm afraid mine fails as badly as his.

I feel a swelling of panic. He knows how I feel, how I've daydreamed about what would have happened if he *had* held my hand at the coffee shop. Maybe he's even somehow figured out about the honeymoon I used to imagine and the little birds in top hats and now I've made things impossibly awkward. I'm trying to figure out how to extract myself from this conversation so I can slink into a corner and quietly die, when Will clears his throat.

"Oh, hey, I know this may be weird, considering how little we know each other and how you're anti-LA guys and all—"

What? "I never said I was anti—"

He cringes. "Would you be interested in a blind date with my brother?"

My eyes widen. "*What*?"

"My younger brother. He's twenty-four, not a serial killer, employed, and while he's not a flannel-wearing mountain man, I think he's camped on occasion and not hated it."

My chest feels all too tight. "I, uh, I'm not sure. Blind dates . . ." I trail off, trying to think of a gracious way out of a blind date— which honestly, I've avoided for the past twenty-three years of my life and have hoped to avoid for the next eighty more—with the brother of a guy I am way too inappropriately attracted to.

"Look, I know, they suck. But my brother is a good guy, and the women he dates, well . . ." He makes the "so-so" motion with his hand. Like "the women he dates are all bimbos" or possibly "are all gorgeous but arrogant Brits."

Okay, so that last thought isn't exactly fair.

"But you're cool," he continues. "Real. I think he'd like you."

My mouth works for a moment without sound coming out. I don't think I'm currently doing any justice to his opinion of me.

Will tramples right over my hesitation, kind of like I often do through awkward silences. "I was just thinking about our conversation the other day," he says. "Thinking about how lucky I am to have Sarah. I was drifting before I met her, you know? Completely directionless. And then she came along, and suddenly my life made sense."

I gape at him, not sure whether to be more stunned by the fact that he thinks he had no direction before Sarah—I remember, after all, how deeply committed he was to that novel back in our bookstore days, when he worked through all his lunch breaks, typing away on his laptop—or that he's noticed how very directionless I am and has decided that the answer is . . . his brother?

"I mean, I know you're not looking for a man to solve your problems," Will says quickly, clearly having realized that's exactly what he implied. "What with your passion for rural feminism and all. But Sean is a great guy. Real, kind of like you. I think you would get along."

My brain stutters. Will keeps saying I'm *real*, and I'm hoping he means I'm down to earth and not that he's merely noticed that I am a person, and not, in fact, a wardrobe mannequin who comes to life just for improv classes and breakfast pastries.

"Think about it," he says. "I'll be around." Then he walks off, possibly not realizing that as an extra, there's a chance I *won't* be around after today.

"What the *hell* just happened?" I say to myself, glad I am actually still verbal when I'm alone at least, as I make my way to find Anna-Marie.

The dressing area for the stars at Anna-Marie's level is roughly the same as the one for the extras, with rows of mirrors and makeup kits and the pervasive smell of hair spray. But here everything is nicer, and the makeup and hair people seem more into their job, or at least not treating it with the level of joy you'd find in your average postal worker.

Anna-Marie is sitting in her chair, scrolling through something on her phone, waiting as the hairdresser works on another actress a few chairs down.

"Finding any good deals?" I ask, assuming she's shopping for shoes, though there's about an equal chance she's on some forum for that zombie shooter video game she loves. I look over the dozen (at least) makeup brushes of different sizes and shapes on the table, next to a stack of eye color palettes and mascara tubes. I pluck one strange-looking tool from among the brushes. It's basically a tightly wound silver coil with little handles on either end. I squeeze it like it's some sort of tiny exercise machine to buff up my palm muscles. "What's this for?"

"I always find good deals. It's my superpower," she says with a smile, confirming my shoe-shopping guess. She snatches the coil thing from me. "And that removes facial hair."

I give her such a skeptical look that she sighs and puts it up to her upper lip and twists the ends. "See?"

I doubt she had any mustache for this thing to actually remove, but I pretend to be impressed. I could probably stand to do a bit of mass tweezing myself, but something like that seems better left to professionals and not someone who once ripped out half the lashes on her left eye with a rogue lash curler.

"So Will just asked if I wanted to go on a blind date with his brother."

Anna-Marie's eyes widen. "*Really.* That's . . . awkward."

"Is it? I mean, I don't see why—" I cut off when I see her pointed look back at me in the mirror. I haven't brought up Will much to Anna-Marie since the cake decorating class—which makes a part of me feel guilty, keeping something that has occupied so much of my thoughts from my best friend. But apparently she's figured me out anyway. I sigh. "Fine. Yes. It's awkward."

She opens her mouth like she's about to say something, but then her eyes begin tracking something behind us. I don't have to turn around to see, because as soon as he enters our mirror-view, he grabs my attention, too. Hot Doctor, laughing at something Sarah says as she holds up an admittedly douchebag-looking shiny purple men's dress shirt. She is smiling, too, a wide grin that lights up her whole face. It's the first time I've seen that expression on her. I am both irritated that I haven't seen her look that way at Will, her fiancée, and validated to see that HD's power of attraction is so great it can even coax a genuine smile from the BB.

That makes me feel a little less terrible about how much I still kind of wish he'd flirt with me. Just a little. A wink, even, or a friendly nod I could pretend meant something more. My feminist-lit professor would be horrified by these thoughts.

"Do you and HD get it on today?" I ask, watching Anna-Marie watch him. I recognize the predatory gleam in her eyes, and think that Helena might not be the only one of her personalities on the prowl.

"Almost. His girlfriend walks in on us."

"Trevor Everlake has a girlfriend?"

"Trevor Everlake *always* has a girlfriend. What he doesn't have is a tendency to say no." Anna-Marie grins. "And I'm looking forward to exploiting that."

"You, or Helena?"

She dabs on some more lip gloss, though the makeup artist had already applied plenty. "Helena, obviously. I'm done with guys like Ryan Lansing. All looks, no subst—"

Her comment on HD's lack of substance cuts off when June Blair stomps by behind us, her tall heels snapping against the floor as she storms over to Sarah. HD takes a step back at June's approach, nearly falling into the rack of clothes.

"You need to do something about this, Sarah," June demands, holding up a wad of black fabric. She lets part of it drop from her fist, and as one long strip unfolds, I can see that it's a pair of pantyhose.

Sarah's smile from before is long gone, replaced by her usual scowl. And some amount of confusion. "Your underwear? I think you need to talk to wardrobe if you want—"

"I've talked to wardrobe," June says, her thick eyebrows drawn tightly together. "I've told that new girl there over and over that I will not continue wearing these cheap hose, that they give my legs a rash. And yet who gets a stack of new pantyhose direct from Bloomingdales? Bridget! While I have to make do with wardrobe patching this dollar store nightmare until there's more clear nail polish than fabric!"

Sarah's lips tighten, and she lets out a little breath. "June, let's talk about this somewhere more private, shall we?" Sarah shoots a pointed look over to us at the hair and makeup station, and Anna-Marie and I make an undoubtedly unconvincing attempt to look like we're super busy staring at her phone and definitely not paying attention to June's pantyhose rant. The other actress and hairdresser two chairs down appear to be doing the same thing, studying various cans of hairspray.

"Let everyone hear, I don't care," June says archly. "Maybe they'll learn that June Blair won't put up with being treated like a second-class citizen by Bridget's minions. Not anymore! I've held my tongue for years, because I am a *professional*, but I think it's time my importance to this show is acknowledged."

"Everyone knows how important you are to the show," Sarah says, keeping her tone calm, which is admirable given how worked up June is. "Just last month, we had that party celebrating the anniversary of Lucy St. James's first episode—"

"A party that was nowhere near as extravagant as Bridget's," June snaps. "She had waiters serving canapés, for god's sake! Canapés!" She shakes the wad of pantyhose in Sarah's face. "What did I get? A six-foot *party sub!*"

Sarah's cheeks are turning red. "June, please calm down and—"

"Bridget's not the only one with fans, you know. I have fans! Legions of them," June says. "Lucy St. James is vital to *Passion Medical*, and they all see it. I won the *Soap Opera Digest* Reader's Choice for 'most tearjerking moment' four times in the last year—four! And don't get me started on the number of charities that are begging for me to headline their causes—"

There's more to June's cataloging of her importance, but HD has extricated himself from the clothing rack next to Sarah and is walking over to us. It's kind of hard to pay attention to June with HD approaching, his black hair carefully swept back and gleaming under the make-up bulbs.

"Hey there, gorgeous," he says, and my heart palpitates, even though it's Anna-Marie's shoulder he squeezes. "I'm looking forward to our scene today." He's clearly trying to break the awkwardness of Sarah and June's drama in the background, and judging by the way Anna-Marie simultaneously flushes and brightens, it seems to work.

"Of course you are. Helena's the only one in Hartsburg Trevor hasn't ruined yet," Anna-Maria tosses back flirtatiously.

"From what I've seen, Helena may be the one to ruin Trevor."

If by "ruining" they are referring to sex, that ship has sailed for both characters long ago. Still, Anna-Marie seems to be enjoying the banter plenty for a girl who just claimed to be over guys like HD.

I look behind us again. Sarah seems to be saying something that is having a mollifying effect on June, who has her arms folded across her chest and has stopped shouting, at the very least.

I think of the way the extras talked about June back at the craft services table. I don't have a ton of sympathy for the woman's lack of party canapés or her sub-par nylons, but it must suck to live in Bridget's shadow constantly, having it suggested that her years-long relationship with a man to his death bed was motivated only by spite. Then again, I can't imagine being Bridget and having to work every day for years with the woman who slept with my husband, even if he was clearly the one more at fault.

"Ryan, have you met my roommate, Gabby?" Anna-Marie says, gesturing into the mirror at me. "She's working as an extra."

HD stares at me blankly. "I don't think so," he says, extending his hand. "Pleasure to meet you."

I decide not to remind him of the fascinating kale conversation we've already had the pleasure of. "You too." His hand is weirdly cold and his handshake weaker than I'd expect.

"Well, off to see if they can make this mug presentable," he says, grinning that million-dollar (or maybe just hundred thousand? We're talking soap opera money, not movie money) grin at Anna-Marie in the mirror.

She returns it, then giggles as soon as he's out of hearing distance.

"I'm guessing by that eye roll of yours, you've also caught that he uses that same lame line every time he leaves?" she asks.

I'm glad it's not just me who has noticed this. "God, yes.

Does he expect us to contradict him or something? Does his ego really need that much stroking?"

"I don't know about his ego, but he sure thinks *something* does."

I laugh, looking behind us again. Sarah and June are both gone from the dressing room as well.

"God, that was intense," I say. "The whole June thing."

"Seriously," Anna-Marie says. "And who wears pantyhose anymore?" She shakes her head and lowers her voice. "June puts the bat-shit in crazy. Everyone says she's been having these little meltdowns on the regular for a while now. Sarah figures something out to keep her happy for a month or so, and then it starts all over again."

It makes me feel a little bad for Sarah. And worse for Will, who has to put up with the ripple effects.

I glance at my watch. "Well, I'd better go check in with Clint."

Anna-Marie arches an eyebrow. "And maybe make some time to have another craft services rendezvous with Will?"

"Shhhh!" I hiss, looking around furtively. Sarah may no longer be in eyesight, but I still don't trust she won't just pop out from behind the racks of business suits. "There's no rendezvous. He's engaged. To . . . *her*."

"Engaged isn't married. Hell, this is LA. Married isn't married." Her eyes narrow at her phone, and I'm not sure if this is directed at LA's fidelity woes or at a shoe deal she missed out on.

"You've been on a soap opera too long. Besides, he's not into me. Not that I'm into him. I mean, he fired me once, and since then we've only talked a few times. *And* he wants to set me up with his brother."

She frowns prettily. I'd never understood that expression until I met Anna-Marie, but there it is. "What are you going to do about that?"

"You know my feelings on blind dates."

"I also know your feelings on spending the last five months' worth of Saturday nights alone with your Netflix account."

"I happen to like my Netflix account. It hasn't broken up with me yet. And it recommends I watch more Nathan Fillion." Still, she has a point. It's been a long time since I've worn anything other than my (admittedly super comfortable) Garfield flannel pajamas on weekends. I'm about two binge-marathons of *Castle* away from becoming a complete hermit.

"Whatever you say," she says. But she smiles with actual understanding. "Maybe this weekend we should go to Vegas and drink enough Mojitos to forget about family and men entirely."

I'd personally prefer to hit Fong's and forget those things in a Breakup Tub, but I've already been there twice since family dinner. If I come there again this week, they're going to put my picture on the wall for some kind of ice-cream-eating world record and I don't think I'm ready for that to be my only success in life.

"Maybe," I say. "But I'd better go see if they can make this mug presentable." My imitation of HD is pretty darn good, actually. Take that, Peter Dryden, star of *Cuffs*, who said my acting mastery was limited to "breathing in a fairly realistic manner."

Anna-Marie laughs, and I wave at her reflection before heading to the extras pen (a name only I use, but it seems to fit well with Clint being a "wrangler.") I do sneak a peek at the craft services table as I cross the studio. Will isn't there.

Not that it matters. I have no plans for any kind of rendezvous, especially the kind where he tells me more about how in love he is with his fiancée. And I still don't have an answer about the blind date.

I head toward the area where the extras gather, waiting to be assigned roles.

"Hey, girlie!" a familiar voice calls.

"Karen!" I grin at my fellow hospital receptionist from day one. Seeing a familiar face that actually knows who I am is a treat. Even Clint still doesn't seem to recall having hired me three times now.

"I guess we knocked it out of the park last time at reception," she says.

"Purely based on your phone-miming skills, I'm sure."

Her laugh is loud enough to startle the other extras, some of whom have the same nervous expressions I'm sure I had my first time here. I love her laugh. Most people I know—or at least on this set, in particular—have a kind of cynical, self-conscious titter of a laugh. Karen's is infectious. It reminds me of Will's somehow, though the two sound absolutely nothing alike.

"You two were reception before?" Clint, despite his girth, is a sneaky fellow. I'd think stomping around in those cowboy boots would give him away, but I never hear him coming. He flips through a stack of papers on a clipboard.

Karen nods. "Best damn reception team *Passion Medical* ever had."

His mustache twitches in amusement. "Then you're both hired again. Head back to your desk."

Karen can barely hide her glee and lets out a "whoop!" the moment Clint has finished assigning the others.

Even though I've only been at the reception desk once before, I feel strangely at home being back there in front of the same computer, staring at the same open excel sheet. Someone has typed long rambling nonsense sentences on it since I've been there, and I resist the desire to erase it all.

Clint gives us a few basic commands like before and Karen and I are left with a few minutes to chat while crew members fiddle with props and lights.

"So how long have you been an extra?" I ask.

"That other day was my first time on *Passion Medical,* but I've been doing this for years." She wipes the handset of the phone down with a wet wipe from a little packet she must have snuck into her scrubs pocket. I don't remember her doing that last time. Maybe she, too, wants to erase any trace of other extras doing *our* jobs at the reception desk.

"Years? Wow." Given how excited she was at every star who walked on set, I would assume she was a newbie, like me. "Are you looking to become a real actress? I mean, not that this isn't acting." I hope I haven't horribly offended the only work-friend I have besides Anna-Marie. (And Will? Does he count?)

She chuckles. "Nah. I love the shows and all, but I'm not the actress type. I'm the 'my kids are at school, and I've got lots of free time' type."

"I hear you. I mean, not about the kids. But the free time."

She eyes me. "Free time? I thought you were doing this to pay for college or something."

"Or something," I say with a sigh.

She raises an eyebrow, and I imagine this is the same look she must give her kids when she suspects they've hidden their report card or sneaked a second dessert. It is remarkably effective.

"I dropped out of college," I fess up. "And I had just lost my job, so this was . . . I don't know, something to do in the meantime."

"In the meantime?"

"Until I figure out what I want to do. With my life." The force of her no-BS mom-stare is so great I almost launch into how there's a community education catalog in my purse that I'm using to try to figure it out, but she drops the intense look and smiles warmly.

"You'll figure it out," she says, squeezing my arm. "Besides, you look like a risk-taker."

"A risk-taker?" I have been called many things in my life by many different people—various former bosses in particular— but that has never been one of them.

"It's a good thing. Trying out new jobs, new experiences. That's how you find out what you really want." She grins. "And hey, maybe soaps are your true calling. You look like you really belong."

"Maybe it's just being a hospital receptionist that's my true calling. I can't argue with the uniform." I gesture down at my scrubs, and she laughs.

Her words stick in my mind, though. Risk-taker. New jobs,

new experiences. This is a new job, but I've had more of those than any one person should have by twenty-three. New experiences? Does cake decorating and terrible improv count?

Am I really taking risks, or just trying things that feel different, but still safe?

I think of Will at the coffee shop, talking about the things that attracted him to Sarah: that she was determined. *Fearless.*

Before I can chide myself for caring so much about whether Will could ever think that about *me*, Bridget Messler is announced, ending any further navel-gazing on my part. She steps onto the set with all the pomp and grandeur and applause of the first day. What must it be like to have that kind of reverence and adulation every time you set foot in the studio?

Tiring, probably. For all that I complain about being invisible, I don't think I could handle the constant worshipful gaze of everyone around me. Anna-Marie might think differently.

The scene is a dramatic one, with Sondra Hart learning of the mugging of Lucy St. James (her former best friend and current arch-nemesis—apparently both on-screen and off). Sondra also learns about Lucy's subsequent selective amnesia. I want to tell Karen smugly that I already knew about Lucy's amnesia, that I had an insider tip even my star roommate didn't know until yesterday. But I worry this might somehow get Will in trouble, and also, I kind of like the knowledge that he gave me information he probably shouldn't have. I like it enough that I want to keep it to myself.

Karen and I do our parts, typing and phone-miming and handing medical charts like pros. Which means no one notices us, with everyone mesmerized by Bridget Messler. As it should be. And really, Bridget runs the scene beautifully, choking up just enough with fear that Lucy will have permanent brain damage and hidden guilt that she herself set up the mugging. There's a reason she's the level of star that she is—she's incredible. Though I do find myself distracted by wondering how often real hospitals get amnesia cases. Definitely not at the rate soap opera hospitals do, I'm sure. I kind of want to Google real-life amnesia and find out how all that actually works and how it's treated, and—

My fake typing has slacked off, and I pull myself back into the scene. I cannot get fired because I'm too busy thinking about the medical accuracy of a show where the hospital has the word "passion" in the name.

With a big event like Lucy St. James's mugging, there are several scenes that need to be shot in the hospital, a few of which are at her bedside, which they'll do later. Karen and I are receptionists for four scenes, with nine takes total, before Clint comes with his big "Great job, you two. Go check out with Courtney."

I'm sort of wishing he would mix it up a bit, throw in a wolfish grin and a "You lived to die another day," but I guess everyone gets stuck in their ruts, even in soap opera land.

As I am leaving, I see Will. He's standing behind the assistant director's chair, though Sarah is nowhere to be seen. He waves at me, and I curse the eye contact we've made for keeping me from pretending I don't see him. I also curse it for the tingly feeling it gives me. He doesn't move towards me—is he giving me space to flee if I'm still not ready to answer him about the blind date? Very considerate if true, but possibly he's already forgotten all about it. Something I wish I could do.

Still, I can't stop thinking about what Karen said about taking risks, or thinking about desperate weekend mojitos with my roommate, who would do something as stupid as dragging me to Vegas just to get me to have something of a life, even for a weekend.

I've never gone on a blind date before, certainly never with the brother of someone who gives me thoughts worthy of a *Sultry Sins* novel. But obviously, the things I'm doing aren't working, neither in the romance department nor in general life. Hence the whole reason I've been piling up trial community-education classes like a hoarder, only with bizarre skills rather than broken toasters and empty coke bottles.

I breathe in through my nose, straighten my posture ("strength comes from your core" is a phrase that leaps to mind—from a yoga class I once tried? A late-night core reformer infomercial? Who knows) and march over to Will, trying not to feel like I'm walking the Green Mile.

"Not a serial killer, right?" I ask, before he can say something charming enough to convince me this is a really bad idea.

Confusion knits his eyebrows together.

"Your brother," I clarify.

"Ah, okay. No, he's not. At least, not that I know of. But he's not someone I'd describe as 'quiet, keeps to himself', so I think we're safe."

I realize my life sounds perfectly suited for serial killing.

"Then if you want to set us up, I'm game." *No, I'm not game, that's a phrase I'd never actually use in real life, it just sounded flippantly casual enough* screams a little voice in the back of my head.

"Great!" His tone sounds incredibly pleased, but there's something in his expression that makes me think he's forcing his enthusiasm. Though why would he? He was the one who came up with this blind date thing. "I'll tell him to wear flannel," he says. The dimple puckers with his wide smile. Maybe his brother has a dimple, too. Maybe his brother is a slightly-less attractive version of Will, funny and charming and not engaged and more in my league.

We swap phone numbers so he can get his brother—whose name, he tells me, is Sean—to call me with the details.

Sarah steps down from the set and hurries toward us. Her face is oddly red, and at first I think she's jealous at seeing her fiancée trading numbers with one of the extras, but when she reaches us, she doesn't even spare me the courtesy of a side-eye glare.

"Damn actors," she growls. "June won't run any scenes with Bridget now. Says the woman is an 'energy vortex.' What the hell does that even mean?"

Will clears his throat, and Sarah appears to notice me for the first time.

"This is the girl I was telling you about," he says. "Gabby. I'm setting her up with Sean."

Sarah's icy blue eyes sweep over me and sum me up in less than a second. "Fabulous," she says without any emotion. Then she turns her whole body to Will, effectively shutting me out from the conversation. "I'm going to convince Bernard to shoot Ryan's scenes with the new Helena next. Ryan may be an idiot, but he's a professional, at least. I can't handle any more divas today. Meanwhile, take the script back to the dungeon and get me a new scene that doesn't require Sondra Hart and Lucy St. James to talk to each other."

She turns to me then, her pretty face pinched tight. "And not a single word of this—or anything you heard earlier—will find its way online, are we clear?"

I nod, squirming under the wrath threatened in that gaze. "Um, definitely. Definitely clear."

She storms away without another word, and Will cringes. "Sorry about that. When the big-name actors don't do their jobs, Bernard takes it out on her."

"Yeah, no, I get that."

He hefts the script that now needs revising with a sigh. "Off to go make my masterpiece."

There is a hint of something—a longing, a weary dissatisfaction—in his voice that resonates in me.

"You'll still do your novel someday, right?" I ask, though I'm not sure why. Maybe not having dreams of my own makes me realize how precious they are. "This is just a stepping stone."

His lips quirk up, but only a little bit. "Some days it feels more like a road block." He shakes his head, as if to clear it. "Anyway, I'll let Sean know."

I nod and start to walk away.

"Gabby," he says, and I turn back. He opens his mouth to say something, then closes it, then tries again. "Hope to see you back again soon."

ELEVEN

I slide into my usual booth at Fong's All-American, comforted by the familiar crackle of the worn faux-leather seats. Anna-Marie was horrified that I convinced Will's brother—Sean, I remind myself, I should probably start thinking of him as Sean—to meet me here for our dinner date.

She was unmoved by my insistence that if I was going to be eating dinner alone with a complete stranger, I needed to do it somewhere the waitstaff knew me well enough to read any silent distress signals I'd send out.

"That's what cell phones are for, dummy," Anna-Marie had said, while lathering my hair with some kind of anti-frizz serum that smelled like grapefruit. "If he mentions that he drives an unmarked white van or tells you stories about his seven cats all named Fluffy, then you call me under the table and I'll extract you."

"Which will be easier to do when I'm just down the street at Fong's."

She wrinkled her nose at me in the mirror. "Just don't order the ice cream thing, or he'll be the one making an extraction call."

I refuse to pretend I subsist on celery and cigarettes like too many other women around here, but I see her point. Gluttony isn't my most attractive quality, and should probably wait until at least the third date.

Su-Lin approaches, that big smile on her face. Her black hair hangs down past her shoulders in two braids, both of which are tied off at the ends with neon lime green . . . pipe cleaners? I think the girl actually has pipe cleaners in her hair, and yet somehow it works for her. She hands me the menu and eyes me up and down, at least the part of me she can see over the table. "You look so nice tonight!" she says in a voice as bright as her hair accessories.

"I'm meeting someone." I tug self-consciously at my silky red shirt, the only thing of Anna-Marie's that would fit me. On her, it is practically a circus tent, though she still manages to pull it off with leggings.

She raises an eyebrow. "New boyfriend?"

"Not yet he isn't." This comes out sounding more confident than I feel. Much more. I'm worried I'm already sweating through the silk on this shirt, extra-strength deodorant be damned, but there's not really a way to check without being so obvious about it that the waitstaff of Fong's will be talking about my pit stains for the next week.

I consider fleeing before he arrives, but it's too late. Just as I start planning the quickest exit, a tall blond man walks in, and I know instantly that this is Will's brother.

A wide smile stretches across his face when our eyes meet, a wider smile than I'd expect from someone at seeing me waiting for them. Maybe Anna-Marie is right. Maybe a little make-up and attention to valuing clothing for other purposes than "this looks comfy to eat a bucket of popcorn in" bumps me up to a reasonable level of social attractiveness. (The "reasonable" part is mine. What she actually said was "There, see? Gorgeous!" But she's also an actress, so I don't trust her not to lie to me before a blind date.)

"Gabby Mays?" He extends his hand, and I shake it. Unlike HD, Sean has a solid grip. Just like I imagine Will does.

"That would be me. And I can tell from the family resemblance that you are Sean."

We make some small talk, with Su-Lin watching us

unabashedly from where she slouches over the rickety hostess table. When she sees I've caught her staring, she gives me an encouraging grin and a thumbs-up.

Maybe I should have picked a different restaurant, after all.

Sean looks quite a bit like Will, but I can tell the differences in personality right away. Sean is more gregarious, filling the booth easily with a booming (though not annoying) laugh and funny stories about his job as a contractor to the stars. He doesn't have Will's self-conscious shrug or his way of watching people like an anthropologist fascinated by the quirks of an alien culture. Or his habit of asking overly personal questions.

A relief on a first date, and yet I find I miss those things, even as I laugh at Sean's tale of a reality show star who insisted on adorning her toilet tank with rubies because she thought they'd aid in digestive health.

We eat Mu-Shu Pork Chops and french fries (a "surprisingly edible combination" Sean says after the first bite) and I find I am actually enjoying myself. On a blind date. And better yet, Sean seems to be enjoying himself, too.

"Will tells me it's even crazier in the soap opera world." Sean takes a pull on his Corona. I usually drink Diet Coke with my Chinese/American food combos, but I followed suit and ordered beer this time. It brings out the saltiness of the pork chops and makes my head buzz pleasantly.

"Than rubies on a toilet tank? I don't know about that. Maybe I haven't been there long enough yet. But there does seem to be a lot of drama off set. Not exactly the same kind of evil-twin drama as on the show, but not all that different."

"Had any run-ins with Sarah yet?"

I freeze with my fork halfway to my mouth. A glop of sauce slides off and splats onto my fries. "You mean, um, your future sister-in-law?"

He makes a face. "Don't remind me."

The easy banter from before suddenly seems miles out of my reach. I'm not sure how to respond. I don't like Sarah much, and

I gather that he echoes the sentiment, but it feels like a betrayal of Will to openly discuss with his brother our mutual feelings on Will's frosty fiancée.

And yet, I can't think of a way to naturally change the conversation. "We've spoken a bit. She seems . . . good at her job."

"Making my brother her doormat? Yeah, she's good at it."

I clear my throat, and Sean points the top of his beer at me. "I know, I know, it's my brother's fiancée, I should probably make an effort to like her."

"Probably. Family reunions will be awkward otherwise."

"Just like I made this dinner awkward?"

I look up from where I'd been subconsciously poking my fries with my fork. Sean is smiling, and it is so open and genuine (another part of him that reminds me of Will) that I return it. "It wouldn't be a blind date if there wasn't some awkwardness, right? You were just getting it out of the way."

"One of us had to. Will was right, you are amazingly easy to talk to."

I feel my cheeks warm. Amazingly? Will said that? And Sean agrees? "Well, apparently good conversational skills run in your family, as well."

"You only say that because you haven't met our dad. I think Will and I talk so much because someone in the family had to."

"If that's what leads people to be good conversationalists, it's a wonder I can talk to people at all. Because my family never shuts up." A pang hits as I think of that disastrous family dinner. I've texted Felix at least a dozen times but still haven't heard anything back. Is he in rehab again? And if so, where? I should probably call my mom or Dana, but I can't bring myself to take that step.

Su-Lin brings out another beer after he makes a motion for one. She attempts to wink at me subtly, but it ends up looking like a rapid-fire blinking, like she has a clump of mascara in her eye.

"Would you like our dessert menu?" she asks. She's never

asked me before, or at least not since the first several times I ordered the Breakup Tub without even eating dinner first. I had completely forgotten this place even had a dessert menu.

"Absolutely," Sean says. "You're not one of those always-on-a-diet LA chicks, right?"

"Nope. You're not one of those guys who pretends to hate the always-on-a-diet LA girls, but secretly only dates swimsuit models, right?"

He grins. He does not, I notice, have a dimple like Will, which is slightly disappointing.

"Not at all."

We order a slice of chocolate cake topped with crushed fortune cookies and Red Hots (even I think Fong's is trying too hard on that particular combination). It is no Breakup Tub, but this one comes with fortunes jutting out from odd angles of frosting. The one he picks reads "Success is around the corner." The one on my side of the cake reads "You will find love soon," but with the soon crossed out and "tonight" written above it. I glare at Su-Lin, who is wiping down a table and still managing to watch us, but she just widens her eyes in mock innocence.

I tell him mine says I should get a real job, and he laughs.

"Extra-ing isn't all you dreamed of?"

There's that word again, dreams. So commonly tossed around that I must truly be the only one who doesn't yearn for something specific in her life.

"It pays well, and it's kind of fun. Which puts it above most jobs I've had." I pause, looking for any sign on his face that he knows his own brother had fired me from one of those previous jobs. But I see no flicker of pity or guilt or anything like that. Maybe Will never told him that part.

Maybe Will no longer thinks of me as the girl who started a microwave fire in the break room.

The pause has gone on too long. I clear my throat. "But I can't go on forever just hoping *Passion Medical* will call every day."

"So what are you going to do?"

I resist the urge to look at my purse, where the community education course booklet is stuffed. Last night I'd tried out another class, Beginning Samba. I was pretty sure dance wasn't my thing—effortless grace never being something I've been accused of having—but it sounded fun. And it had been, until I'd been paired with a beefy balding guy who, after one dance, demanded the teacher give him another partner, someone who "doesn't think tempo is a suggestion."

I'd been flipping through the community education course list again before I left the apartment, though I keep telling myself to just throw the damn thing out.

Floral arranging. Beginners Spanish. Gold mining for fun and profit. I should say any of these things to Sean, anything that makes it seem like I have a direction in life rather than just "stay afloat."

But instead I go for honesty. "I don't know yet. I haven't quite gotten my life figured out."

He nods sympathetically, but judging by the passion with which he spoke of contracting, even while complaining about the less savory aspects of dealing with celebrity ego, he doesn't really understand. "You'll get there."

There is such surety in his tone that I allow myself to forget, for the moment, that he doesn't actually know me.

I'll get there. I'll eventually have a *there* to get to.

Su-Lin brings the bill over, and I reach for my wallet, but he waves me off. "Nonsense. You introduced me to true Asian-American fusion cuisine. I've got this."

His gallantry is welcome. Being an extra pays pretty well (though infrequently), but I managed to glance at the bill before he grabbed it, and the Fortune Cookie Cake wasn't cheap. Which reminds me that I should probably start looking for another regular job soon. I can't keep myself afloat by sitting by the phone waiting for Courtney's next disinterested call.

But I don't want to think about this now. I have a handsome date, with a pleasant personality, and I've managed to not think about the completely unavailable Will for several moments at a time, even while I'm sitting across from his doppelganger. I will enjoy this while I have it.

I can hear Su-Lin speaking rapid, excited Mandarin to the bus boy before the door swings shut behind us, and then Sean walks me out to my car. He places his hand on my back for a few steps before I reach the Hyundai. I like the pressure of his hand. It feels solid, comforting.

In the yellow haze of the streetlight, his eyes are dark, velvety brown, losing that hint of green I saw in the restaurant. His smile is broader than Will's, his lips a tad fuller.

Not that I've been studying Will's lips.

"This has been an unexpected pleasure," Sean says.

The way he says it sounds so old-world chivalrous, not like the standard (at least for my dates) "See you around" date ending, usually while barely taking their eyes from the phone in their hand. One guy I was pretty certain was actually texting his next date while ending ours.

"Quite," I return, feeling like it wouldn't be out of place if I offered my hand for him to kiss, like in a Jane Austen novel.

Instead he reaches in and kisses me full on the lips, stealing my breath and every thought of Jane Austen or previous bad dates. Once the initial shock passes, I respond to the kiss, to the prickles of warmth spreading throughout my body, sparking in my vision like fireflies.

All too soon, he pulls back with a smile. I wish I knew the kind of words Anna-Marie might say, the words that would bring a man like this back to our apartment to keep kisses like that coming.

But my mouth betrays my brain, fumbling out, "Okay . . . well."

"Yeah, well." Amusement crinkles the corners of his eyes. "I'll call you?"

I like that he makes it a question, as if seeking my approval.

"That would be great."

"I think so, too." He gives me one final grin, turns and heads off down the sidewalk, rounding the corner past Fong's and out of my sight.

I get my car door open and melt into my seat. That was beyond amazing. A movie kiss, but in real life. In *my* real life, of all things.

Is this what kissing Will is like?

Before my treacherous thoughts can lead me further down that path, I turn on my radio and blare Katy Perry. My lips still tingle, all the way back to the apartment, and I do something I never do, even alone in the car with no one to hear me: I sing along.

I am still singing—though quietly—as I walk up the steps to our apartment. The words die on my lips when I reach the landing.

Sitting on the floor, leaning against the door with his head propped against his knees like he's sleeping, with a large cello case at his side, is Felix.

TWELVE

couldn't take it anymore." Felix's hands wrap around the warm mug of coffee I hand him, but he doesn't drink, just breathes it in and sets it down.

"Mom and Dad's problems aren't your fault."

He shrugs. "Maybe. But I'm making them worse."

I've never seen Felix like this. His skin is pale and drawn, eyes red-rimmed and drooping. A red mark stains his jawline, as if he cut himself shaving like he used to as a teenager. His clothes are rumpled, slept in. From what I can tell, all he has with him is his cello. No matter what, he'd never leave that behind.

"Are you still using . . . whatever you're using?"

He gives me a baleful look and tugs at his long sleeves until the edges cover his knuckles. "No."

"Well, that's good." I can't tell whether to believe him. He looks like hell, but could that be withdrawal? Though wouldn't that have taken place at rehab, whenever that was? There's too much I don't know, too much I'm afraid to ask. "You're welcome to stay with Anna-Marie and me, but you know Mom and Dad will figure out where you are." They probably already have. As soon as I get Felix settled in on the couch, I check my phone to find a dozen missed calls and texts from Mom.

"I know. Whatever, right? They'll probably just be glad I'm

not in jail again."

Jail? Again? I work to hide my dismay. Felix needs someone on his side, and I'm not going to get there by freaking out like our parents would have. Still, I can't help my curiosity. "What happened, Felix? I mean, last I heard, everything was great. New York was great, Juilliard was great. You really need to find a new adjective to describe things, by the way."

He drums his fingers on our cheap thrift store coffee table. Despite looking like he spent most of the week on a park bench begging for spare change, his fingernails are meticulously trimmed and clean. He always keeps them that way, never willing to touch his precious cello with anything less.

"Got in with the wrong crowd, I guess," he says, but I don't buy it for a second. Felix used to hang out with the wrong crowd plenty in high school, unbeknownst to our parents, but he was never tempted by the drugs and binge-drinking that fueled their fun. He was like a laser pointed at Juilliard, at musical greatness, and nothing got in the way of that focus.

Except something had, apparently.

"Felix, I—" I am cut off as our apartment door opens and Anna-Marie sweeps in, a smile stretched so wide across her cheeks her face looks about to split.

"Okay, don't judge me, but . . . Oh, hey." She stops, her coat halfway off her shoulders, blinking between Felix and me.

"Anna, this is my brother, Felix. Felix, Anna-Marie."

He glances up, but only long enough to return a mumbled "hey," before returning to studying the coffee mug. Felix has flirted confidently with friends of mine almost as gorgeous as Anna-Marie, but right now he looks drawn into himself, a lost child waiting for his parents to claim him at the mall security office.

Anna-Marie's blue eyes widen.

"I'll get you something to eat," I say to Felix, though he doesn't appear to be paying attention. "I'm sure we have chips or something." I'm not actually sure of this. Anna-Marie went shopping last, and her snack indulgences are unsalted almonds.

She follows me into the kitchen, which is only about six steps from the living room, but is separated by a wall.

"What's going on?" she asks, as soon as the wall blocks Felix from view. "Is he high?"

"Of course not," I snap, though really, I have no idea. But I don't like her judgy tone. "He needs to get away from our parents. He'll just crash on our couch for a day or so."

She bites her lip, and I can see she wants to say something but is holding back. Finally, she gives me a small smile. I dig through our snack cabinet. Just as I feared—almonds, rice cakes, the crappy kind of trail mix that doesn't even have M&Ms. I really need to go shopping with her next time. I settle on the rice cakes, which at least are supposedly cheese flavored.

"I . . . Uh, I might not be here for the night," Anna-Marie says, leaning back against the counter a little too casually.

"Really? And whose place will you be at?"

She picks at her fingernail polish, a bright cherry red that matches her lipstick. Which I now notice is smudged. "Ryan Lansing."

"HD?"

"Seriously, his name's Ryan."

"And seriously, I thought you were over guys like him. All looks and no substance and all that."

"Substance can be overrated."

I sigh, but I can't really blame her. It is HD, after all. Even after knowing what a tool he is, even after tonight's amazing kiss with Sean, I know I'd still get a little weak in the knees if HD ever paid me the slightest bit of non-kale-related attention.

"If you need me to stay, though, I can."

It's nice of her to offer, but I shake my head. "It'll probably be easier on Felix if it's just him and me for tonight, anyway."

"So I take it the blind date didn't go well?"

Of course Anna-Marie would assume that. When she has a blind date that goes well, she's never home by 10 PM, unless the guy gets brought home with her.

117

I twist my lips, considering how to answer. "Actually . . ."

"You kissed him! Oh my god, Gabby!"

"Should I be insulted that my kissing a guy warrants you having a heart attack?"

"What about your two-date minimum rule?"

I blush, thinking of Sean's lips on mine, his hand pressed firmly against my back. "Two-date minimum rules can also be overrated."

Anna-Marie looks impressed. "Nicely done. Well, I expect to get all the details tomorrow."

"Likewise," I say, though I'm not actually sure I want *all* the details of Anna-Marie's night. *Sultry Sins*-level narrative becomes more awkward when you actually know the people whose genitalia are being described.

"Here, you deserve better than rice cakes to celebrate with." Anna-Marie opens a lower drawer full of pot holders we never use since we never cook, reaching underneath to withdraw a half-eaten bag of Spicy Nacho Cheese Doritos.

"Anna-Marie, you are a devious little minx."

"We all need our vices," she says with a wink. "And since I'm off to indulge in my other vice, you might as well enjoy this one. Have fun with your brother."

She grabs a sweater from her room, and though she tries to make it seem casual, she locks the bedroom door behind her, something she never does. I try not to take it personally. She doesn't know Felix, doesn't know that he would never steal anything.

Would he?

I bring the bag of Doritos out to the living room, ready to use as much delicious high-fructose corn syrup as necessary to pry free more information about what happened in New York, but Felix has fallen asleep sitting up on our couch. One of his arms hangs over the side, his hand resting on his cello case like it's a teddy bear, a comfort to ward off nightmares.

I bring an extra blanket out from my room and cover him

with it, moving Anna-Marie's Xbox controllers off the other cushion so he can stretch out later. I leave a note on the coffee table saying that he can stay as long as he needs to. Then I text my Mom, telling her that Felix is fine and with me. Before I turn my phone off to avoid the inevitable freak-out replies, I notice I have a message from a number that is becoming welcomingly familiar: Courtney from *Passion Medical* is telling me to report back in on Monday morning.

I stuff the Doritos back in Anna-Marie's hiding space (after stifling a brief desire to ransack the rest of our kitchen to see if she has any other secret stashes she's been keeping from me) and decide to make it an early night. I pull out the community college course guidebook, flipping through the pages I've dog-eared with possibilities. Tomorrow afternoon I have a CPR class I signed up for last week, a three-hour certification course I actually had to pay for. It seemed like a good idea at the time, actually learning something medical-related, given all my time in a fake hospital. I sigh, imagining how I'm going to bungle this next one. One more thing to be terrible at.

You'll get there, I hear Sean tell me, and in my mind his face is a strange mixture of his own face and Will's. Sean's lips and Will's dimple. Sean's boisterous laugh and Will's intense green gaze.

I fall asleep dreaming of the best kiss ever, not sure which of them it is I'm actually kissing.

Felix is gone when I wake up, though he has scribbled a note of his own on the bottom of mine: *Thanks for the couch, see you tonight*. I have no idea where he's gone, but his cello is gone with him. I hope that's a good sign. Maybe he's out auditioning for a local orchestra or even just enjoying a sunny day in the park, playing for passers-by. I'd much rather imagine that than him spending the day passed out in some rat-hole somewhere, surrounded by needles.

I consider calling my mom, seeing if she'll tell me the whole story, but I can't get caught back up in their drama as well. I know too well how this works. Mom will barter information about my brother to get me to convince my dad that he's wrong, or to get me to call Dana and make her apologize for yelling at my parents.

I'm done being their emotional errand girl.

Besides, Felix will talk to me. I know he will. He just needs more time, needs to remember how we used to stay up late and share everything, even when we were in high school and it wasn't super cool to be best friends with your sibling.

I turn on my phone and see the replies from Mom: *Is he okay? Tell him to call me. Gabby, call me when you get this. Just Mom, checking again to make sure Felix is fine. Tell him he should come home. Your father is thinking of calling the police.*

Among these expected replies is one very welcome and unexpected one, from Sean: *Hey, I had a great time last night. Maybe we can do it again next weekend?*

It's enough to make me smile despite Mom's threat of calling the police on my brother. It's enough to make me sing in the shower and put on a nicer t-shirt than usual, even though I'm going to be spending the day at the community college learning how to save the lives of mannequins.

A guy like him—cute and smart and possessing more than the most basic level of social competence—actually likes me. Actually kissed me and wants to see me again. My whole opinion of blind dates has reversed dramatically, along with my view of what kinds of guys would be attracted to me. Maybe I am not invisible. Maybe I am not an extra in everyone else's life movie. Maybe I have a movie of my own.

This sunny outlook only lasts until about forty-five minutes into my CPR certification course.

Once again held in the now all-too-familiar community college (which I'm starting to feel more at home at than I did at UCLA), there are about fifteen other people here with me, a more motley assortment than even in the world of extras. The instructor is a brisk woman who appears to be in her late fifties or early sixties, and who wears a too-tight polo shirt bearing some sort of accreditation logo for saving lives. Her thinning red-dyed hair hangs in wisps around her face, and her dark eyes focus intently on each of us one by one as she speaks about how these next three hours could be the most important of our lives.

I'm all for learning the Heimlich in case someone at Fong's eats their Kung-Pao Pizza Rolls too quickly, but I somehow doubt my life's turning point will occur in a community college multi-purpose room. Then again, if there's not at least the chance of that, what the hell am I doing at all of these trial classes? After all, my blind date taught me that maybe I should give things more of a chance.

Be a risk-taker.

So I listen intently to several stories from her days as an EMT, which are admittedly pretty interesting, if a bit filled with descriptions of various exposed organs. I pay close attention to the video she shows about the Heimlich maneuver and CPR, both adult and infant. I take dutiful notes and manage not to snicker with my classmates at the terrible acting and questionable fashion choices in the video.

This will be better than cake-decorating or acting class, I determine. This is quantifiable. I learn the techniques, I do them, I get my certification. It seems gloriously easy.

And then we are asked to find a partner to team up with. Much like in high school gym class, everyone seems to naturally drift to each other, leaving me standing there clutching my notebook to my chest and praying that just one person notices I exist. I hate the sick feeling that settles in my stomach, the reminder that one good date hasn't changed my inherent invisibility.

No. I am a grown damn woman, not a high school wallflower anymore. Drawing a deep breath in through my nose, I spot a younger Hispanic girl standing off to the side by herself. She looks about seventeen, wearing shorts with ripped hems and a thin hoodie printed with some anime character I don't recognize. Her dark hair is cut in a pixie style with a green streak on one side. Probably some teenager being forced to take this to keep her regular babysitting gig. She hasn't looked up from her phone a single time the entire class, from what I can tell.

"You want to be my partner?" I ask, trying for a cool nonchalance.

Her eyes flick up to my face just long enough to coat me with disdain. "Whatever."

I take that as a yes.

We are given a dummy that is basically a vaguely male head and torso and nothing else. I suppose arms and legs aren't really part of the CPR process, but I'd feel better about being able to save an actual human being if my dummy was more than just a rubber chest.

I practice chest compressions, checking and re-checking my notes for the proper intervals. Steve—the name I've given our torso—is in good hands. Not my partner's, who still hasn't bothered to look up from her phone or do more than murmur "yeah, sure" when I ask her if she's paying attention. It probably shouldn't bother me that she isn't, but the teacher is right. Someday we could save someone's life with this, someone who is more than a rubber torso and creepily unformed face.

There's something so concrete, so methodical about the motions. I can do this, and a bit of pride blooms in my chest.

"One more time," the instructor announces. "And then we'll move on."

I start again, determined to get this one thing right, this one skill learned. My phone buzzes in my pocket. I pause, unsure whether I should take the call. It could be Anna-Marie, needing rescue from HD's lair of sexual conquests. It could be my mother, ready with a high-powered guilt trip. It could be Sean.

The teacher isn't watching, and heaven knows my partner isn't, either. I pull the phone out just as the "missed call" signal flashes. It wasn't from any of them.

It was from Felix. Felix, who never calls, who only rarely texts. Felix, who could be in god knows what kind of trouble right now.

"Your patient is dead." The instructor's voice is flat and somehow right beside me. Apparently they teach ninja-level stealth in EMT school.

"Ah, no, I just . . . Steve's fine." I should shove the phone back in my pocket, but I can't. I need to call Felix back, make sure everything's ok.

"Steve?"

"The, ah, the patient. Sorry, my brother just called, and—"

"Oh, no problem. Of course if your brother calls, you should take a break from saving a life. Please, call him back." The sarcasm is so heavy I am offended on behalf of comedic subtlety itself.

"I did the compressions. Several times. Correctly. I have notes." I look to my partner for some kind of support, but she just watches us with wide, innocent brown eyes. Her phone apparently *can* detach from her hand, because it is now jutting out of the tiny shorts pocket as if it has been there all along.

"So I only now just happened to look at the very moment you decided to play Candyville on your phone?" The instructor's nostrils flare out. They are incredibly wide from this close and towering above where I kneel beside the dummy.

"Candy what?" My anger is rising, flushing out the shame and humiliation I felt at the improv class under Peter Dryden's judging eyes, at the cake-decorating class while I stared at my deformed beginner's roses. At the university classes I barely passed, at the high school I walked through unnoticed in the shadow of my bright-burning siblings. "I told you, I did the CPR. I followed every direction. I told my partner to call 911."

The instructor turns to face my partner, who shrugs. By now, the rest of the class is silent, everyone watching us. Dummies are dying fake deaths all around us as hands freeze in the act of doing CPR.

Before the instructor can speak again, I stand up. "Screw

this. Screw you."

She blinks, clearly taken aback. She is used to being the god of her little community education world, like the rest of them, and having no one protest. And maybe she doesn't deserve this. Maybe I could just have apologized and asked to re-do it and all would be fine. But she has become Peter Dryden, the cake-decorator lady, my snide samba dance partner, my parents. And I'm sick of apologizing and asking for re-dos that don't ever help. That don't ever make me worthy.

As I grab my purse from where it rests against the wall, I see the community education guide sticking out. I pull it out and drop it on the ground, the pages fluttering ungracefully as they fall. "You can keep this. I'm done."

"You won't get a refund—"

"It won't be the first time I've quit early. Feel free to commiserate with my parents." I wave at my dead dummy. "Good luck, Steve."

Then I stalk out of the classroom to call my brother.

THIRTEEN

I grip the steering wheel of my car so tight as I race down the streets that I start to lose feeling in my fingers. I force myself to ease up a bit, both on the steering wheel and the gas pedal. The last thing I need right now is to get pulled over. What would I say? "Officer, the reason I'm going sixty in a forty zone is because my music prodigy little brother who I recently found out has been in jail on some drug-related charges needs my help right away. I don't know for what, but I promise to check his cello case this time and make sure he's not smuggling a cello-sized amount of cocaine and guns in there and taking over the south LA drug syndicate."

Okay, I'm clearly overreacting. But thinking of it that way—Felix as some *Breaking Bad*-type drug lord—is keeping me from thinking of it in the way that truly terrifies me. That he's been beaten half to death in some deal gone bad. That he's overdosed and dying. That if either of those things haven't happened yet, they will.

Gabby, I need your help, he'd said, in that oh-so-brief phone conversation just outside the room of my failed CPR training. *Please, I just . . . I messed up. Please.*

He sounded either on the brink of tears or at the tail end of them. And though I'd pressed for more information, all he would tell me was the address of where he was, a solid forty-minute drive from the community college even with me risking a speeding ticket.

Forty minutes of imagining the worst possible scenarios. Forty minutes in which I start to feel some actual pity for my parents, who have known about Felix for much longer, who have had to fly to New York to bail him out of jail.

And then I'm there, my phone's GPS telling me I've reached my destination in such a soothing voice it's almost as if she's been leading me this whole time to a day spa rather than some seedy city backstreet lined with liquor stores and tattoo parlors. I park in front of a closed-down discount furniture outlet, get out and look around, squinting in the sunlight.

I'm about to pull out my phone and try calling him again when I spot him further down the street hunched over a garbage can. I'm afraid to know what on earth he's doing.

"Felix!" I call out, and he jerks his head up, wiping his mouth on his sleeve. As soon as I get within ten feet of him, I can smell why. Judging by the splatters on the sidewalk, he didn't quite make it to the garbage can before he started.

"Felix," I say again, as if I just need to confirm that this is actually my little brother and not some ragged doppelgänger in last night's clothes, reeking of vomit and stale smoke.

"Hey Gabby." He straightens just enough to not be hunched over the trash, but still maintain his signature slumped shoulders. One of his fists opens and closes, again and again.

And suddenly, I am furious. "Don't 'Hey Gabby' me! When you called like that, I thought you were lying bleeding in some alley somewhere! I nearly ran over a half-dozen nuns at a street crossing trying to get here before you died!" This isn't entirely true. I'm pretty sure it had actually only been a couple of street performers putting on a sidewalk version of *Sister Act*, but I'm not about to tell him that.

He glares at me. "You sound like Mom."

"*Not* the way to get on my good side," I growl back.

He scuffs the toe of his sneaker against the sidewalk, in one of the lone patches around the garbage can not littered with chewed gum, cigarette butts, or, more recently, puke. "Sorry," he says, so quietly I can barely hear him.

With my outburst, the anger has subsided a bit. At least enough for me to notice the way his hands are shaking. "Come on," I say, putting my hand on his arm and guiding him away from the trash can before the smell makes me follow his example. "Let's go back to my place, and we can figure this out. I'm sure I have some clothes you can borrow, especially if you don't mind Garfield pajama pants and—"

"No," he says quickly, pulling his arm away. "No, I . . . I need your help here. I need you to help me get my cello back."

My eyes widen. His cello? It's gone? It occurs to me that nothing about Felix—not the bloodshot eyes or the shaking or the pale face—makes him look more unlike the brother I know than not having that cello case attached to his hand. I think part of me always imagined him in New York carrying that cello everywhere he went—the laundromat, on dates, buying a second seat for it at the movies. That's practically the way he was when he lived at home.

And yet now, looking around, I don't see it anywhere.

"What do you mean, get it back? Did someone steal it?"

He sniffs, and I can't tell if it's because he's about to cry or because he snorted a line or two of something before I got there. I hate that I even have to wonder this about my brother. His gaze falls to the sidewalk, and his fist starts opening and closing again.

"Felix," I say. "What happened? You're using again, right? That's what this is all about. Were you passed out in some drug den and someone took your cello? Like your dealer or something? Did you owe money to the wrong people?"

He gives me a slightly disdainful look, which I suppose I've earned, trying to speak about street life and drugs like I have any idea what I'm talking about beyond what I vaguely remember from cop shows.

Maybe Peter Dryden would remember enough from his *Cuffs* days to know what to say to Felix, but sadly he's not here and I am.

"Felix—"

"Yeah, okay? Yeah. I . . . I did some. I needed it, like . . ." He shakes his head and stares down at the sidewalk. "I just needed it. But Mom and Dad took away all my money, and I couldn't . . . I wasn't thinking right."

"Obviously," I say. "Otherwise we wouldn't be hanging out on a street that's one strip club short of the place where they find the dead hooker on *CSI*. What happened to you, Felix? Where is your cello?"

He sniffs again, and when he looks up, his eyes are watery. He blinks rapidly and then looks across the street. To a pawn shop.

I swear. "You pawned your cello?" I don't know why this seems so much worse than him getting mugged for it. Maybe because if there was one thing I could count on with Felix, it was that he'd sooner lose a leg than be parted with that damn instrument. It had been his life since he was ten years old. His future.

The thought that he sold it—to a pawn shop!—for a stupid fix . . .

"I told you, I messed up, okay?" His voice cracks, and he swallows. "I need your help, Gabby. I need to borrow some money to buy it back."

I have money, but not near what his cello is actually worth. "I—I don't have very much myself. I've only done a few days of work on *Passion Medical,* plus what's left in my savings, and I have rent coming up, and—"

"Please, Gabby. I fucked up my whole life already. If I have my cello back, I know I can get back to where I was. Please."

The sheer ache in his voice makes me want to march right over to that pawn shop and not only buy back the cello but chew out the shop owner for taking advantage of my little brother.

But if he's willing to sell his cello once, what would keep him from doing it again? What if this isn't rock bottom?

I eye the pawn shop. "How much is he asking for it?"

The grimace on Felix's face speaks volumes. "Ten thousand."

"Ten thousand! At a pawn shop?" I swear again. The real horror is that I know that's only a fraction of what Felix's cello is actually worth. It's also an amount I still technically have in my bank account, if I want to hand Felix the lion's share of my safety net. "Okay, and how much do you have left from what he gave you?"

Felix sighs and pulls out a few crumpled twenties from his pocket.

No, I correct myself when he hands them over. Not a *few*. Two.

"You only have forty dollars left? Out of—never mind. What about your phone? Could you get something for that?"

He pulls his phone out of his other pocket and I can see why he didn't bother selling that before his beloved cello. The thing is one of those old flip phones I haven't seen since I was in high school. I wasn't even aware they made those anymore. And it definitely isn't the top of the line one he was sent out to New York with.

He's back to staring at the ground again, and the sick sensation in my gut has nothing (well, almost nothing) to do with the pervasive smell around us. He has this phone because he already sold his other one for drugs. He probably sold everything he had that was worth anything.

Everything but the one thing none of us ever thought he'd part with.

Until today.

"How did this happen to you, Felix? You had everything. You—you knew what you wanted your life to be like since you were ten years old, and you were there. Why? Why did you start doing this?" I gesture vaguely at our surroundings, because maybe even now I can't bring myself to say the words out loud.

"It doesn't matter. I'm going to fix it. I'll go back to rehab and do it for real this time. Just . . . Are you going to help me?"

His eyes bore into mine, pleading.

I want to, I really do. He's my brother, and the one member of my family I can actually stand to be around for longer than twenty minutes. But the way his hand shakes, the way his clothes hang loose on his too-slender frame, the way his blue eyes look empty, devoid of the life and humor and quirks that make up my brother . . . I haven't been one for putting too much trust in what my gut tells me, as a general rule (since generally it just tells me I need more Breakup Tub). But this time I know in some way beyond my comprehension—like how dogs can sense their owners coming home long before they walk in the door, or how Anna-Marie can tell if a guy has an ass tattoo without even talking to him—that Felix isn't ready to fix anything.

And that if I help him now, I'll only make it worse.

"I'm sorry, Felix, I can't," I say. "For one, I don't have the money, and even if I did—"

His expression changes from bleak sorrow to fury so quickly I take a step back. The immediate guilt of lying is now making *my* hands shake. I'd give every penny I have to save Felix if I could, but I'm not going to hand it over for both of us to drown.

"Even if you did, you wouldn't, is that what you're saying?" His balled-up fists no longer look so much like a tic but more like a purpose, and my heart slams against my ribcage.

"Felix, I—you need help. And getting your cello back won't fix anything." I am tempted to take another step back, but force myself to stand firm. This is Felix. He won't hurt me.

Would he?

"I thought I could count on you!" He yells this so loud that a group of teens congregated in front of a liquor store further down the street all turn and look at us. "I thought that you, of all people, would understand. . . ." He shakes his head, running a hand through his greasy hair. "But of course not. Because you don't get it. You mess up all the time, and no one gives a shit, do they?"

His words are a punch to my gut.

You mess up all the time. No one gives a shit.

And the unspoken addition to that: *Because it's just what you do, Gabby. You mess up.*

"But me," he continues, pacing back and forth in front of me, trailing his sneakers through splatters of his own vomit. "I have to be the best, all the time. All the time."

The earlier anger is spiking in me again. "You don't *have* to be. You always *wanted* to be. You wanted Juilliard. You wanted to be the best cellist in the world. And you were getting everything you wanted!"

He scowls, tugging at his hair like he wants to rip it out of his head. Then he stops pacing and drops his hands to his side, where they tremble. "Right. Everything I wanted," he says bitterly.

"Felix—"

"Go away, Gabby. If you won't help me, then you can just stay the hell away from me." He puts his shaking hands and his crumpled money back in his jeans pockets and starts walking away.

I call after him, but he doesn't turn or even acknowledge me. I am hollow, watching him walk further and further away, not sure if I made the right choice, not sure he won't end up in a worse situation or even if this is the last time I'll ever see my brother.

I'm not sure of anything anymore. And maybe that's why I do the only thing I can think of when I get back in my car.

I call my mother.

131

FOURTEEN

I am exhausted when I pull into Sudser Lane the next day, and grateful that Anna-Marie stayed at HD's place and got a ride with him this morning. I am in no mood to report in extra early or to talk to anyone about what happened with Felix. Talking with my mom about it was bad enough, though because of that, Dad came and picked him up and brought him back home, so at least he's off the streets. I'm in no mood to go to work, either, but discussing Felix's monetary problems (clearly the smallest of his problems) also made my own painfully clear.

My meager savings will barely keep me afloat when this extra gig runs up. I can't buy my brother a new cello, and I certainly can't help my family pay for more rehab. I can barely afford to pay my car insurance. I'm fully aware I'm on borrowed time with this job. How many more calls from Courtney will I receive before the phone stops ringing? Before I'm back to another job I'll somehow manage to screw up?

I'm determined to make this one last as long as possible.

My stomach is growling when I enter (apparently having gotten used to breakfast on stars' call time rather than extras') and glancing at my phone, I see I have about ten minutes before I need to report to Clint. Enough time to hit up the pastry table.

On the way there, I see Anna-Marie stepping off the set for

the Hartsburg Country Club, wearing a cute little tennis outfit and carrying a racket. "Gabby! Hey!" she calls with a grin.

So much for avoiding talking, though I can probably keep the conversation on other topics than my druggie brother. "You're in a good mood this morning."

"I have a steady paying job on my favorite soap opera," she says. "Of course I'm in a good mood."

"And here I thought it might have something to do with having sex last night with Hot Doctor."

Anna-Marie shrugs, though her eyes gleam mischievously. "Maybe. Maybe it has something to do with having sex again this morning with Hot Doctor."

"Seriously? You had to be here at like five! How early did you need to get up to—Oh." I cut off, seeing HD himself over in front of the darkened, currently unused set of The Brew. He's wearing his doctor's uniform and talking close with a pretty girl in a crewmember cap. Really close. Like practically on top of her as he whispers something in her ear that makes her giggle.

I shoot a concerned look over at Anna-Marie, who has followed my gaze.

She rolls her eyes, but her good mood still appears completely intact. "Looks like I might be needing a ride home with you today."

"That doesn't bother you?" I ask. HD tucks a strand of hair back behind the girl's ear and I can actually see her knees go weak. "Him doing . . . that, when he just . . ."

"Did me?" She laughs. "God, no. We're not, like, together. This is Ryan Lansing we're talking about. Good to look at and good in bed. And that's it. Besides," she says, "the more time he spends with other women, the less I have to hear about the one-man play about the life of Charlie Sheen he wants to produce and star in."

My mouth drops open. "I have so many questions."

She groans. "Yes, it's called 'Winning.' No, he doesn't get that the nation has long since stopped caring about Charlie Sheen.

And more importantly, no, I did not know about this until *after* I'd already slept with him."

It speaks to how well Anna-Marie knows me that those were my main questions. "And yet you kept on doing it. Um, him."

"I have my ways of getting guys to stop talking. This comes in very handy with guys like Ryan." She grins again. "Anyway. Off to get changed for my next scene—which is in the hospital, so I'll see you there at the reception desk."

I haven't checked in with Clint yet, so I don't actually know that's where I'll be working today, but I like the idea that I have a place I belong here.

She squeezes my arm and heads off to wardrobe, while I head over to get my breakfast. I'm beginning to recognize the black-outfitted crew enough to smile and wave at several of them and only receive blank stares back from about half. I pick through the offerings on the craft services table with the confidence of someone who belongs here. A huddle of new extras watches me as if trying to suss out how I fit into the operations here, whether I'm someone important. It won't last much longer once they see me report in to Clint alongside them, but I try to enjoy it for the moment.

Anything to take my mind off of Felix.

"So, how was your weekend?" Will's voice comes from behind me, and in testament to my getting used to life here on set, I manage to neither choke on nor drop my cronut.

The fluttery feeling returns to my stomach. Because he looks so much like Sean, I reason. I gather he wants to know about a specific part of my weekend, and not the part where I tried to decide if I could save money by buying off-brand peanut butter (which was a mistake.) "I suppose if you wanted to supplement your soap writing income, matchmaking might help pay the bills," I say. "You appear to have a passable talent at it."

"Are you and Sean going out again?" He leans just enough against the table to look casual and not topple the thing. I have a feeling I would be able to do neither.

"Maybe. I mean, yeah, I guess. He wants to get dinner again this weekend."

Something flickers in his green eyes and is gone, a hesitation that precedes his smile. "Good. I figured he'd like you."

"Because I'm not . . ." I make the same "so-so" gesture he made when describing the type of women Sean normally dates. "Right?"

"Right." There it is again, that hesitation, a tension around his eyes. Or am I imagining it? Why would he have a problem with things working out with Sean and me? Isn't that what he wanted?

Isn't that what *I* want?

"How's the writing coming?" I ask, because the twistiness in my gut is confusing me, and I hope switching the subject from my dating life will eradicate it.

"Well, now that we have to limit the scenes between Bridget and June—"

"Not that writing, your novel. You said you'd try working on it again."

He looks uncomfortable, even in such a casual pose. "Ah, that. It's . . . I don't know, something's just not working about it. It's probably not worth the mess."

"Just 'cause you've got a flat tire doesn't mean you go slash the other three."

His eyebrows raise. I notice how his left eyebrow is slightly crooked. It should decrease his attractiveness (symmetry being the desired trait that it is), but it actually does the opposite. I wonder if Sean's eyebrows are symmetrical.

"It's something my childhood nanny LaRue used to say," I clarify, tracing my finger in the powdered sugar lining my plate. "Of course, she always followed it up with 'The only tires worth slashing are a cheating ex-boyfriend's.' But I think the overall message about not giving up because of one set-back is relatively sound."

He laughs. "I would very much like to hear more about your

childhood sometime. It sounds amazing."

A touch of panic sets in. Tell Will about my childhood? About my successful parents and brilliant sister and musical genius brother? About how my whole family is falling apart now, and I'm still capable of no more than just filling space in the background?

Like dating, this is another subject I choose to avoid. "And I would very much like to read your novel. So you'd better get past that flat tire."

"Well, I wouldn't want to disappoint my only potential reader." His easy grin is back, and I wish I didn't have to avoid any topics with Will. That I could just tell him everything and still have him smile at me like that. I find myself returning the grin without meaning to, warmed by the green depths of his eyes.

So much so I don't notice Sarah's arrival until she's standing at his side. I drop my eyes to my plate, too quickly. It looks guilty. For what? For talking to her fiancé? For encouraging him to follow his dreams when she just wants him to be at her side for hers?

It is neither of those things, and yet I don't want to focus too much on what it actually is.

"Aren't you running late?" Sarah says to me. "Clint's gathering the others now. You wouldn't want to lose that prime reception spot." Despite the words, her voice itself isn't as razor-threatening as usual. Her hand is pressed against Will's back, but the way her gaze flickers around behind me as if looking for something makes it feel less possessive than it might otherwise.

Of course, why on earth would a woman like her be jealous of me? If she's irritated I'm talking to her fiancé, it's probably because it might interrupt her fantasy of a soap opera set that runs without problems.

"She's filling me in on the date with Sean," Will says. "I'm sure Clint can wait another minute or so."

I wasn't talking about Sean at all, but I am unreasonably pleased he wants to keep the conversation going, even for just another minute.

"Damn it, Rosemary! If I wanted Lucy St. James dressed like she was going to a funeral at a strip club, I would have said so," she calls to a passing crew member toting a black dress with far too many slits to appear like it could actually stay on a body in one piece. I don't love Sarah's treatment of the crew, but I kind of have to agree with her on this one. "Sorry, love, I've got to go handle this." She squeezes Will's upper arm, and they meet eyes, and in that moment I know that my strange attraction to Will is entirely futile, no matter how many great conversations we have.

Despite their problems, he still loves her. I can see it in the way his gaze focuses on her, how he tracks her as she walks away, his smile softening in a way completely incongruous with the kind of guy who should be upset with his fiancée bringing underlings to tears on a daily basis.

It should make me like him less, but all I can think is that he must be an incredibly loyal guy to still see the girl he fell in love with. Still feel that, deep down, she's still whoever the girl is that he got to know while wading through international police bureaucracy and sharing drinks over their success.

Anyway, it doesn't matter. Sean's the one I actually like. And maybe, just maybe, he likes me back.

As if he can read my thoughts about Sarah, Will frowns. "You really should get to know her," he says. "She's not always like that. It's just the stress."

That's the dozenth time he's made lame excuses for her she has no compunction to make for herself, but I'm not going to be the one to point it out. "That would be cool," I say. Totally cool. The picture of cool. I would be on freaking Antarctica about spending more time with Sarah and really getting to know her.

I hate how much I have to fight even to think it.

And then I have an idea. "Why don't we all go out sometime?" I ask.

Will blinks at me. "What?"

"You, me, your brother, your fiancée. Why don't we all go

out to dinner? You guys do eat dinner, right?"

He seems stunned, as if I've just suggested that we take over the roles of Lucy and Sondra ourselves, excessively slitted dresses and all. "Y-yes!" Will says. He shakes his head as if to get a hold of himself. "Yes, everything you've heard about writers subsisting on their own tears is a myth, I'm afraid."

"Okay," I say. "So we'll all do dinner, and I'll get to know Sarah, and you can hang out with your brother, and everybody wins." My palms begin to sweat as I realize all the things that could go wrong with this plan. Maybe Sean doesn't really want to go out with me again, and now Will is going to be the one to break it to me. Maybe he can tell that I'm just doing this to spend more time with him, even though I am definitely more interested in his brother and definitely just trying to keep all this from becoming horribly awkward when Sean and I go on our honeymoon to somewhere not at all tropical and clothe some other kind of animal entirely based on an as-yet-undetermined but ridiculously adorable inside joke.

"Sure, yeah," Will says. "Everybody wins."

I'm afraid he can sense my panic, especially when I take a step back like a cornered animal. "Sarah's right, though. I'd better get going."

"Okay. But, um . . ." He frowns, scuffs his foot on the floor. "Hey, you'd really want to read it sometime? My novel?"

I blink. That's right. That's what we'd been talking about. "Of course," I say. I remember wanting to do so way back when we worked at the bookstore together. I find I want to even more now.

"All right, then."

"All right."

He takes a bite of cronut and smiles a shy powdery smile. "I'll talk to Sean. Set up dinner." And then he walks off at a stroll, not the full out run I'd assume he would break into if he knew even one of the many things going on in my head.

As I head to the extras area, trying desperately to think of anything other than how good Will's lips must taste right now, I see Sarah again, this time with HD. Her eyes are narrowed and she's shaking a script at him as she talks. I'm not close enough to hear the words, but I can tell he's getting it worse than poor Rosemary just did. His perfectly shaped lips are tightened as if restraining what he really wants to say back to her. It's nice to know that even the stars are afraid of Sarah's wrath.

I volunteered to go out to dinner with this woman?

"Good Lord, girlie, you almost lost out to that one!" Karen all but yells as I reach the extras pit. She points at a young man in glasses who shrinks back at the thinly veiled contempt in her voice. "I told Clint you'd be here, though."

"Thanks Karen. I owe you one. And maybe I'll get Clint a VitaminWater or six to make up for it."

"I prefer the pomegranate apricot, if you're just giving them out," Clint says, jotting notes in his clipboard as he steps out from behind a rack of nurses' uniforms.

"So I'm still in reception?"

"Today. But seven AM means six-fifty. Not seven."

"Noted." It's actually only six-fifty-eight, but I'm not inclined to argue right now. I've gotten fired for following such an urge to clarify before.

His lips pucker under his thick mustache as he considers me as if to check for sarcasm. Then he nods and gives us our marching orders for the day.

Hair and makeup go as quickly as usual, what with nurses and receptionists not needing much more than to not look like total crap. I tug on my scrubs, realizing that this is the most comfortable work uniform I've ever had. It sure beats all the skin-tight dresses and sky-high heels they always have Anna-Marie in. I'm dressed and camera-ready (or as much so as I'll ever be) and heading toward the set when I hear Bernard's booming voice traveling practically from one end of the sound stage to the other.

"Sarah!"

I turn around and manage to step aside in time to keep

from being run over as the director storms his way over to her with alarming speed for a man his size. I don't think he notices my existence at all, even though his elbow hits mine when he passes me.

Sarah's eyes widen. "Bernard, I'm working on it," she says. "I've talked to some agents, and we should have a new—" She cuts off when she sees me staring, her gaze sharpening to a deadly glare, and I start walking again, pretending an intense fascination with the lighting setup overhead.

"I don't want to hear 'working on it.' I want to hear that my problems are fucking fixed. Now." Bernard speaks in a tone that makes me want to hide behind the nearest boom mic operator. "Or I'll find an assistant who does their damn job."

I can't help but look back, and see Bernard storming off toward the hospital set, Sarah staring after him, her already pale face as white as the script paper. She blinks rapidly, her lips tugged down, and as she turns away from me, I see her wipe at her eyes.

Oh my god, Sarah is crying.

It's not my business, I tell myself. God knows she's made plenty of others on set cry. Keep walking.

But guilt pulls at me, and something else—sympathy. I know what it's like to feel not good enough. And for all that can be said about Sarah, the woman does work her ass off for this show. If Will loves her, there has to be *something* else under all that bitchiness.

Against my better judgment, I turn back and walk towards Sarah. She's facing away from me, her hand up over her face. I hesitantly reach out, though I can't bring myself to actually touch her hunched-in shoulder. "Hey, Sarah, are you okay?"

She spins around so quickly I lose track of my words under the anger in her ice blue (though clearly teary) eyes. Her face isn't stark white anymore so much as patchy red. "I'm outstanding," she growls.

"Um, great. Good." I should just run off right now and never look back, but she is Will's fiancée and Will is my friend, so I make one last attempt. "But if you need anything, you know, like someone to talk to or—"

"The last thing I need is some hair-braiding bonding session with an extra," she says, crossing her arms over her chest.

Now it's my cheeks flushing. I want to tell her she could at least try to be a decent person, that she could at least make the faintest effort to be worthy of a guy as incredible and kind and funny as Will.

But no. Their relationship is none of my business. God, I'm glad that Sean's the one I actually like.

So I don't say anything more to her, just turn and walk away, fighting to keep my head high. Fighting to keep from crying myself, though I have absolutely no reason to.

By the time they're ready for us on set, I've managed to push down all the shame and anger of my interaction with Sarah and am feeling somewhat better. I tried to be nice, and if she can't be nice back, that's her problem.

I worry, though, that this doesn't bode well for the double date I stupidly suggested.

Karen and I and all the other extras and actors are on set and ready to go when the action finally happens. Only this time, it's not the action that's supposed to be happening.

The scene is supposed to be Anna-Marie's character Helena (I give Anna-Marie a little wave before the camera rolls) and her current lover (in both the soap opera and real world) HD discussing the likely outcomes of the surgery her one-time lover Diego needed after being shot. Lucy St. James (June Blair) is also there for the conversation, fretting about her son's health, even though she doesn't remember that he is her son and thinks he's just a very nice young man who jumped in front of the bullet to save her.

Fairly simple, in soap opera plot terms, and Anna-Marie is doing a lovely job despite Bernard's occasional harangues about her "wooden stance." I do my typing thing and even get

141

to answer a fake phone call and receive a folder handed me by Karen, who has taken to trying to get me to laugh by putting post-it notes with hilariously accurate sketches of various cast members on top.

And then, as HD describes various organ traumas (which he is somehow able to make sound sexy), a shout comes from the darkness beyond the set.

"Arrest her! I insist she be taken into custody at once!"

Everything on set freezes. Everything except my fingers, which have become so accustomed to pressing keys that I end up typing for about ten seconds after the rest of the set has gone silent.

Bridget Messler, Dame Sondra Hart herself, steps onto the stage wearing a cream silk dressing robe and little else. Her hair and makeup are already done, and little gold and ruby chandelier earrings swing as she strides across the set toward June Blair, a long thin accusing finger outstretched.

June drops her character's vaguely confused concern and puts her hands on her hips. "What are you on about now, you crazy old bit—"

Bridget slaps her hard across the face with a resounding crack. Gasps sound, and Karen drops the phone in her hand onto the reception desk.

June stumbles back, her hand up to her now-red cheek, then launches herself with a roar at Bridget. Anna-Marie makes the noble but perhaps ill-conceived effort to place herself in front of the elderly acting legend and gets taken down in her stead. June and Anna-Marie are a tangle of arms and legs and beaded designer purses, and Bridget cackles like some fairytale witch.

I instinctively run out from behind the desk to help Anna-Marie, and pull her up and away from June, who is being held back from another lunge at Bridget by HD.

"Enough!" Bernard roars, as several crew members wearing matching black outfits step up to stand in between Bridget and June like they are forming their own diva protection brigade.

"My set will not be made into a circus!"

He should probably rethink that sentiment, this being a soap opera set and all. This is far from the craziest event this set has seen, though possibly the craziest real-life event.

"That woman is a criminal and needs to be arrested," Bridget says with a sniff, her haughty demeanor firmly back in place.

June's jaw drops, her botoxed forehead even managing a wrinkle. "She's insane!"

"What do you think June has done exactly, Bridget?" Sarah steps onto the set, her voice calm and hands outstretched like she's dealing with an escaped tiger at the zoo.

"She stole my Daytime Emmy," Bridget says.

Sarah stares at Bridget, eyes wide and mouth slack. A moment passes in which I think all of us are wondering whether someone is going to jump out and yell "You've been punked!"

This doesn't happen.

June lets out a crazed-sounding bark of a laugh. "You don't even have an Emmy! She's totally lost her mind!"

Bridget folds her long, slim arms across her chest, the very picture of calm and control now that the slapping is over. Though we all know June is speaking the truth, June's the one who looks crazy. "Obviously you've never heard of Taiwan's 'Most Resplendent Bubble-Time Star' awards, my dear. They copied it exactly after the Daytime Emmy trophy."

"Taiwan?" June attempts to push her hair back into the bun most of it has escaped from and somehow manages to make it look worse. "You all see she's insane, right? Why would I steal some knock-off Emmy?"

"Because you knew it was important to me. And because you wish you had even the slightest bit of the respect in the industry that I do. Unfortunately, respect doesn't come by mattress-hopping your way up the food chain."

Another round of gasps, along with a few titters. Anna-Marie coughs into her hand. She, too, has her brown hair askew and her dress twisted strangely around her waist, but manages to make it look like the newest fashion.

June scoffs. "Says the woman who can't even climb onto a mattress without activating Life Alert."

A murmured combination of shock and anger and a few more gasps sweeps over the assembled crowd.

"You just can't keep your hands off of things that don't belong to you, can you, June?" Bridget sneers.

"Damn, she went there," murmurs Karen next to me with no small amount of admiration, and I'm glad I've already been filled in on the whole Cedric/Frank aspect of the women's history. Because clearly they are no longer talking about a Taiwanese award.

"Maybe you should treat your *things* better," June snipes back, "so they don't all keep running away from you."

Another round of gasps and whispers follows this.

"Ladies, let's calm down and discuss this off the set and in private, please." Sarah also places herself between the two of them, a kind of sacrificial slapping lamb. Though I doubt even Bridget Messler would be able to slap Sarah Paltrow without some serious repercussions. "Unless you want all of this to end up in the *Enquirer* tomorrow."

I think the situation is already way too far gone for that. A crew member standing half-hidden behind the hospital room's fake fern slips his phone back into his pocket, and the only question in my mind is how much he'll make selling that video.

Bridget sniffs again, then turns and strides off the set with the regal air of a queen. Sarah gestures to June, who follows, grinding her teeth so obviously I imagine I can hear crowns cracking.

The set is quiet for a moment, uncertain, until Bernard shouts out, "Break for thirty. And someone better bring me a goddamn vodka!"

People start moving again. Anna-Marie turns to me, her face flushed and her blue eyes sparkling. "Did I mention how much I love this job?"

FIFTEEN

Since my first date with Sean was at my favorite restaurant, it seems only fair that our second date take place at his, an Indian restaurant in Fairfax. It's a hole in the wall kind of place like Fong's, which makes me like Sean even more, though a quick scan of the desserts listed shows there is nothing nearly so enticing as the Breakup Tub. Will and Sarah are apparently running late (typical, according to Sean, which makes me wonder how Sarah manages to maintain her conviction when she screams at anyone and everyone on set for being a fraction of a second late). This gives me some time to remember why Sean is, in fact, the one I want to be dating. He's basically the non-attached, non-complicated version of Will.

And, like Will, it turns out he's a good listener.

Sean grins at me over his beer as I spend a good portion of our wait describing the soap opera altercation that took place earlier that week. Normally I might be self-conscious monopolizing so much of the conversation, but really—who *wouldn't* want to hear every insane detail of the diva slap-fest of the century?

"I still can't believe she actually slapped her," I say. "That old lady packs some power, too. When I went back to work on Wednesday, you could still see the mark under the makeup on June Blair's face."

He shakes his head in amusement. "And here I thought my sub-contractor breaking his toe on one of those naked peeing boy statues would be the work-related injury of the week."

"Normally, yes. But apparently not when you're dealing with someone who works on a soap opera set." I take another bite of the appetizer Sean ordered us—patties of some unidentifiable vegetable substance dipped into mint chutney. Spicy, but not so much I'm regretting the restaurant choice.

As on our first date, the conversation flows easily. Something about Sean (like Will, I realize, a little guiltily) mutes the constant voice in the back of my head that calmly predicts complete and utter failure.

Maybe it's a family trait of theirs.

Speaking of which . . .

"You're just being extra polite listening to me tell you all this, aren't you?" I ask, pointing at him in mock-accusation with my fork. "Your brother probably told you about it already."

Sean shrugs. "Will and I don't talk that much anymore. We used to, but now we're pretty much down to the occasional text. Anyway, I'd rather hear it from you."

I wonder why he and Will aren't close anymore. Does it have to do with Sean's dislike of Sarah? I want to pry, but the moment I do I know Will and Sarah are going to materialize right behind me and Sarah is going to hit me over the head with her Burberry bucket bag.

"So other than some real-life soap opera drama, how has your week been?" he asks.

I normally would answer such a question with a basic "great," but Sean feels different. Like he really cares about the answer. And this is our second date. I don't want to spill all my family crazy out at once, but the way he laughs at my jokes and touches my hand across the table, it seems we'll be having more. I'd better start doling out the pieces now.

"A bit difficult, actually. My younger brother Felix showed up on my doorstep. He'd been fighting with my parents—"

"Sean!" Will yells, and I turn around to see him and Sarah approaching our table.

If I'd known he was going to announce his arrival so loudly, I would have pried.

Sean waves a disinterested hand at his brother and soon-to-be sister in law and shifts over to sit next to me. Sarah gives a sour look to the silverware Sean had unrolled next to the plate where he was sitting, and I wonder why he sat across the table from me in the first place.

Did he not expect Sarah and Will to show up?

"Hey, Will," Sean says as the two of them sit down. "You're late, so you missed Gabby's rendition of the soap actress cat fight you all got to witness the other day."

Sarah's mouth falls open in my direction. "You *told* him about that?"

I squirm in my chair. It occurs to me now that Sarah doesn't actually need cause to fire me, since I have to be invited back for every shoot, besides which, I'm pretty sure talking about this off set constitutes actual cause. "I—I thought," I say, "I thought since you guys were family, he'd hear about it from you anyway."

Sarah gives Sean a side glance that tells me she doesn't consider him family, and Will puts his hand over hers on top of the table. I half-wish Sean would take that opportunity to touch mine again like he was doing before.

"It's fine," Will says. "It's not like she went to the tabloids."

Sarah gives him a hard look and then pulls out her phone. "You never know who will talk to the press." She starts typing like she's sending a text message, or maybe writing a memo to herself to tell Courtney not to ask me back again, in case I'm too unimportant to remember.

Will gives me a weary glance, and I shrug at him and give him a little smile, which he's beginning to return when the waiter shows up to take our orders. Sarah continues to text (seriously, if this is a memo about me it's alarmingly detailed) while the rest of us order. She heaves a great sigh when the waiter

147

says he doesn't know if the Vindaloo is gluten free and orders herself a lamb curry.

"So, Gabby," Sean says after the waiter leaves. "What was that you were saying about your brother?"

I look at Sarah across the table, but she's still busy on her phone. Will and Sean seem uninterested in talking to each other, so I suppose that leaves me to keep up the conversation.

Anna-Marie was right to be dubious when I first told her about tonight. This double date is quite possibly the worst idea I've ever had, and that includes the time in high school when Felix and I decided to bleach our hair and used actual chlorine bleach.

"Yeah," I say slowly. "My brother Felix is doing drugs. I really don't know what kind, but he's a cellist, and he sold his instrument to a pawn shop for drug money and then wanted me to buy it back for him."

"God, Gabby," Will says. "I'm sorry."

Sarah gives him a sideways look, then makes an angry huffing noise at her phone.

"What's the matter, Sarah?" Sean asks. "Is *your* brother on drugs?"

Sarah looks confused—clearly not having heard what I said—and narrows her eyes at him. "I'm dealing with work stuff. Excuse me. I have to make a phone call." She scoops up her Burberry and very nearly does hit me on the head with it as she sweeps by and stalks out toward the front of the restaurant.

"Sorry about that," Will says. "She's got a lot on her plate."

She does. I know that, but I'm less inclined to feel any sympathy for her stress after she chewed me out for trying to be nice to her. Sean makes a skeptical noise, and I wonder if he's made the same mistake in the past. I find myself wishing he and I were here by ourselves. But Will looks so miserable that I want to reach my hand across the table and touch him. I knot my hands up in my napkin instead.

"Does she always have to text for work this late?" I ask.

"Yeah," Will says. "A lot, anyway. Since they film every day, there's a lot of details to get worked out, sometimes pretty late at night. Last week she had to drive out to Santa Ana for a pair of slippers after one of the foley people decided to light aerosol hair spray on fire and accidentally set Bridget's up in flames."

I smile and start to make a comment about how much June probably loved that, when I become self-conscious that Will and I are talking about the set and leaving Sean out of the conversation. I elbow him. "You were telling me something before about an injury at your work, from a peeing boy statue? Someone broke their tooth on it?" I frown. *That* doesn't seem right.

Will is now looking from me to Sean with a sort of confused expression. Instead of answering, Sean pulls out his phone suddenly, and I hear it buzzing in his hand.

"I'm so sorry," Sean say, "but it's my sub-contractor. I have to take this. I'll be right back." He stands up, but before he walks away, he leans in and kisses me full on the lips. I'm cognizant of Will still staring at us, but Sean smells of curry and woodsy cologne, a surprisingly intoxicating combination, and once again I feel his kiss all the way down to my toes, which melt a little in my red kitten heels.

Then he pulls back and walks away from the table, and I'm feeling my heartbeat in my ears and am staring at Will, who is staring back at me, stunned.

And now we're the only ones at the table.

"So," Will says. "You and Sean are getting along."

"Yeah," I say, allowing myself to smile. "Thanks so much for setting us up. I guess you really know how to call 'em."

Will looks back at the way Sean went—toward the kitchens, opposite of Sarah—and sighs. "Yeah," he says. "I guess I do. I have to warn you, though, Sean can be . . ." he trails off, as if digging for something negative to say about his brother. I feel bad for him about Sarah, but he's the one who's going to marry her, and suddenly it occurs to me to wonder what the hell he thinks he's doing lecturing me to be careful about the sorts of people I date.

"If you needed to warn me," I say, "why'd you set me up to begin with?"

Will had been lifting a glass of water to his mouth, and it stops in midair. "What?"

I know I should play this off as a casual question, but I'm dying to know. I didn't ask Will to set me up with his brother, and okay, I did ask him to come tonight, but I didn't ask his fiancée to refuse to so much as acknowledge us beyond being snotty and rude.

"Why did you set me up?" I ask. "Don't get me wrong. I like Sean. I'm just wondering what it was about me and about him that made you put the two of us together. Besides my lack of direction, I mean."

Will winces at that last bit, then shrugs. "I just thought—I thought it might make you happy. To have someone."

My cheeks start to burn. It's not so much what he said as the way he said it, like even he can see that I'm lonely and pathetic and have logged more sessions with my Netflix account in the last month than dates in my entire life.

That's the direction he wanted me to lean in. Toward being less pathetic.

"Well, thanks for looking out for my happiness," I say, but it comes out sarcastic, which is the way I meant it, but not at all the way I meant to say it aloud.

Will's brow creases. "Did I . . . do something to offend you?"

I feel like he did, though I can't put my finger on what it is. "No!" I say. "No, I mean it. Thank you. I really like Sean, and I'm glad you set us up, so *thank you*."

Will finally gets the water to his mouth, and I feel the need to fill the silence with more chatter, though all the while some ineffectual part of my brain is screaming at me to stop. "I'm thinking of asking him back to my apartment tonight. Do you know, is he the kind of guy who likes a take-charge woman, or does he like to take things slow?"

Will chokes on his water, and yet still I feel the need to continue. "Not that I like to move fast. Anna-Marie calls me a prude, but I tell her I'm just selective." I cringe. "I mean, she only calls me that when she's drunk and trying to set me up with random guys whose numbers she's deleting from her phone."

Will has managed not to drown in his water, but he's staring me like I have diarrhea of the mouth, which, to be fair, I basically do. "Not that I think he's the one or anything," I say. "But he's handsome and intelligent—but, you know, not pretentiously so—and he's funny. And . . . yeah." Thankfully, I manage to shut the babbling down before I confess that I'm pretty sure I'm not actually ready to sleep with him tonight, but I did some extensive shaving this afternoon, just in case.

I stare down at my appetizer plate, my face burning so hot that I might have just eaten an entire red chili instead of one of those spicy vegetable patties which no one but me and Sean have yet touched.

"So thanks," I say, and Will nods slightly. And because there is still no sign of Sarah or Sean's return, I follow this with "excuse me," and grab my purse and get up from the table so fast I nearly tip Will's water over into his lap.

I don't know where I'm going as I stalk away from the table, but I quickly decide that the restroom is the most logical place. I can stay away long enough that either Sarah and Sean will have returned, or Will might have left—possibly both, since he is no doubt ready to flee from my crazy presence like a clown from one of those burning circus buildings. The restrooms aren't clearly marked, and so I end up heading the wrong way and hit the kitchen entrance. I start to double back, but then I hear Sean's voice.

"I know, baby, I hate working late like this, too. But I'll make up for it tonight, I promise." His voice is the very essence of silk, seductive. He's facing away from me, partially hidden behind a kitschy carved statue of the Taj Mahal.

I freeze, my eyes wide. Then I force myself to breathe again.

Maybe I'm reading his tone wrong. Maybe he has a daughter and is afraid to tell me about her, afraid I won't want to date a guy with a kid. Maybe that's what Will wanted to warn me about, and I just went off on him like—

"The black lacy one, definitely," he says with a chuckle. "Or, you know, I always enjoy seeing you in nothing at all."

Ice pools in my veins. *Nope. Not a daughter.* I take a step back and almost collide with a waiter carrying out a tray of steaming dishes. If my life was a movie, I would have hit him and sent the tray of food flying. But because this is my life, and I can always manage to make things even worse, I manage to duck away only to run into one of the many arms of a statue of Ganesh, face-first.

Pain lances through the right side of my face, and black spots bubble up in my vision. Before I can even suck in the pained breath to swear, I hear a crash as the statue falls to the ground and cracks apart into a dozen bits of ceramic.

"Gabby!" someone calls, and I realize with horror that it's not Sean, but Will, who is racing from our table, eyes somehow wider than they were when I was lobbing compliments of Sean at him like live grenades.

My hand is clutching at my right eye, and I pull it away, relieved there is no blood or dangling eyeball.

"Are you all right, Miss?" The waiter who I oh-so-deftly avoided hovers at my side. The whole of the restaurant, or at least this section by the kitchen, is staring at me, horrified. Ganesh lays in pieces at my feet, one arm (possibly the one that punched me in the face) pointed up at me accusingly.

"I'm so s-sorry," I stammer. "I didn't mean to break your god, I just—"

"Gabby, what in the—" Sean looks briefly furious, then sheds it so quickly I wonder if I'm seeing things as a result of head trauma. "God, are you okay?"

Will opens his mouth and then closes it, his brows knitted in concern. Behind him I see Sarah approaching, staring at the shattered remains of Ganesh with a put-out expression as if this, too, somehow personally inconveniences her, and she's still holding her damn phone.

I flinch away from Sean. "I'm fine," I mumble and back away, my stomach churning like the appetizer is about to make a reappearance. I dig through my purse, come up with only a five and a new pack of breath mints. I make forlorn eye contact with the tall Indian man I guess is the owner or manager who has just arrived at the scene, my face so hot I must match my kitten heels. "I'll pay for the statue, I just don't have . . . I mean not at this moment, I . . ."

The manager's brows knit together. Not angry, but in something like pity. Because my life is pitiful. Because I am pitiful.

What's even worse, I am pitiful in front of Will, who is watching me like maybe he wants to give me a hug, and god, would I love a hug from Will, except that it would be a pity hug, and Sarah is standing right there and she's glaring at Will and—

"Gabby, what were you doing?" Sean's tone is so caring, so innocent. Like he wasn't just lying about working late to someone he calls "baby" to cover up being on a date with me. Like he isn't a complete and total snake.

Anger flushes through me, even as my face throbs. "No, you know what? I'm not paying for this. *You* can pay for this. Then you can go home to your girlfriend and spend the night pretending not to be a cheating asshole."

He blinks, taken aback, and the manager looks between the two of us and takes a step back, wringing his hands.

"Gabby," both Will and Sean say, but I don't stay around to hear what either of them has to say. I carefully step over pieces of Ganesh and past the staring couples and out to my car.

SIXTEEN

I swear up a storm about life and men in general and Sean in particular the entire ride home. Part of me hopes Sarah *does* fire me, because then I'll never have to face Will again and find out if he knew about Sean all along, if this was all just some nasty prank.

But no, Will wouldn't do that. I know he wouldn't. Still, the thought of facing him now—

It hits me, then, that I care so much more about how I've embarrassed myself in front of Will than about losing Sean. Tears prick at the corners of my eyes. It was never Sean, not really, no matter how good a kisser he is (the bastard).

It was always Will I wanted to be with, and I still do. And knowing that, admitting it to myself when I know it's all so hopeless—it just makes me feel even worse, which I didn't think was possible after a public shaming like that.

My mood doesn't improve any when I arrive home to find HD leaning against the wall next to my apartment door.

"What are you doing here?" My tone is far from pleasant, but Ryan Lansing is one of the last people I want to deal with tonight. "Anna-Marie is out."

"She is? I thought . . . Never mind. Have we met before?"

"Seriously?"

He looks at me blankly, and I groan and pull out my keys. "I'll let her know you stopped by."

"Could I . . . Do you mind if I wait for her?"

I look up from inserting my key in the lock. All I want is to get in my rattiest pajamas and curl up in bed with Anna-Marie's stash of Doritos. And then call Fong's and have them deliver, a service they recently started. Possibly because of me. If my life is any indication, Breakup Tubs are a growth industry.

But the look on HD's face stops my snarky rebuff. Honestly, for a guy who always looks like heaven incarnate, he kind of looks like hell. Not in a strung-out Felix kind of way, but just like Ryan Lansing minus the additional clear coat of perfection. His eyes are a bit droopy, his smile sagging, his shoulders slumped.

He's not acting depressed, I can tell. I've been on set enough to know that HD isn't that good of an actor. He looks like he's been through a night roughly equivalent to mine, minus the Hindu God-Slap. My empathy gets the better of me.

"Fine. Come on in."

He follows me in, and it occurs to me how bizarre my life has become. In the past week I've witnessed a diva fight, killed a CPR dummy, broken a religious icon with my face, and now arguably the hottest man on the planet is following me into my apartment, and all I want is for him to leave so I can gorge on junk food and cry to One Direction songs I don't admit to owning.

"You can chill on the couch until she comes home," I say. "I think there's some soda in the fridge. No kale, though."

He still stares at me blankly. Apparently my attempt at humor has fallen completely flat, and he still doesn't remember me. "Do you need some ice on your face?" he asks.

Crap, my face. The pain in my chest from my utter humiliation has been so sharp it has drowned out the dull throbbing of my cheek. "Yeah, probably."

I go into the kitchen, and he calls out "And do you have any super glue?"

I poke my head back out of the kitchen and glare at him. "Did you just break something?"

"Not here. I was with this girl earlier this week and we were getting a little crazy and . . . Never mind. Forget it."

I roll my eyes. The man probably leaves a trail of broken headboards behind him.

Just then my phone buzzes in my pocket. I pull it out and see a text from Will, apparently the second one he's sent since I left the restaurant, asking if I'm okay.

He saw what happened. He of all people should know I am clearly not okay.

I definitely can't bring myself to text him back, as humiliated as I am. Not tonight. Maybe not ever. I open the freezer and see the ice cube tray sitting inside, empty. I wish I could blame Anna-Marie, but I was the last one to make a smoothie, and she's much better about remembering this sort of thing than I am. I sigh and grab a bag of frozen peas to press to my cheek. I pass the decorative mirror Anna-Marie and I bought at a yard sale to class up the place (and be able to check our makeup and hair right before we leave for a date, though she's used it much more for that function than I have). My cheek sports an angry red mark spreading out at the cheekbone, and is already swelling.

"They have hotlines for that kind of thing," HD says, settling himself in on the couch and shifting around the pillows. "You know, if some guy hit you."

"It was a god. I don't think they have hotlines for that."

He blinks. "Probably not. You look like you had a worse night than I did, and that's saying something." He runs a hand through his slightly-less meticulously styled than usual hair and lets out a dramatic sigh.

It's clearly sympathy bait, but I admit, I am intrigued by what HD would consider a terrible night. Someone not recognizing him? His favorite hair gel being discontinued?

I consider just retreating to my room and shutting the door, but the stupid part of me that is tied to social niceties triumphs. I sit down on the other end of the couch from him. At the very edge, so it's clear I can bolt at any time. "So what happened on your rough night?"

"The woman I love has *utterly* rejected me." The way he emphasizes the word "utterly" sounds so much like a soap opera line that the only thing keeping me from rolling my eyes is total surprise.

"Anna-Marie?"

He gives me a look that casts doubt on my intelligence, which I totally deserve for that one.

"What I mean is, you came to talk to Anna-Marie about it? The girl you're sleeping with?"

He shrugs. "Anna-Marie and I have an understanding. And she's great to talk with, especially after we—"

"Gah, stop, I don't need to hear any details."

"—run lines."

Is that what the kids are calling it these days? Still, he's got a point. Anna-Marie is a great one to go to for dating advice. It makes sense she would be good for that even with her sex buddy.

"So you actually, uh, love someone?" *Other than yourself,* I want to follow up with, but I manage to filter that last part out.

"I wish I didn't. It sucks if they don't love you back."

Well, I can sympathize with that. *Not that I'm in love with anyone,* I tell myself quickly. Feelings, definitely. *Strong* feelings, maybe. Really inappropriate daydreams—

"I know," he continues, thankfully cutting into my runaway thoughts. "Hard to imagine me getting rejected, right?"

My sympathy dries up faster than the last remaining Danish at catering. Even though it's true. I stand and start to head out of the room.

"Wait, wait, come back," he calls. "I'm sorry. This woman, she tells me I'm too full of myself, that it drives people away. I'm trying to work on it. Maybe that's why she doesn't love me back."

"Or maybe, just maybe, not everyone is going to love you. Maybe you can be a good person and witty and say all the right things and she still won't love you. That happens sometimes, you know."

Even I am taken back by how bitter my tone is. HD's face drops even further, and he slumps back into the couch.

I pause, then with a sigh of my own, go and sit back down. "Sorry. I didn't mean that. Or I didn't mean to say it like that, anyway. Rough night here, too." I pull the bag of peas away from my cheek to get the point across.

"Yeah, it's okay. You have anything stronger than soda in the fridge? I think we need it."

"Probably."

He gets up and returns with a couple of beers, the fancy kind Anna-Marie likes, or at least pretends to like when we have company. He hands me one and we clink the bottom of the bottles together. I take a sip. It's definitely no Breakup Tub, but it'll do for now.

"So tell me about this girl," I say after we sit in silence a few moments.

He blows the air out of his cheeks before talking. "She's amazing. She's smart and beautiful and strong. She's . . . different from all the others."

"They always are."

He looks confused, so I wave my hand for him to continue.

"She's been sending me signals for a while, but lately she's been cold. Acting like she wants nothing do with me, but I know that's not the case."

"Do you think maybe she's intimidated by your reputation?"

He frowns. "We've slept together, so she already knows I have a huge—"

"No! Um, what I meant is that you get around quite a bit. I mean, you're supposedly in love with this woman, but you're screwing Anna-Marie and probably half the extras."

He doesn't deny this, just takes another sip of beer.

"Most women," I continue, "even women who are *different from all the others*, want someone who isn't sleeping with a dozen other women at the same time. Maybe she thinks you're not capable of that."

HD nods slowly. "I wouldn't think I was either. But for her . . . I think she'd be all I needed. I mean, I know she would be."

Despite everything I know about Ryan Lansing, the pure feeling in this appallingly qualified statement thaws my heart, currently encased in a cold anti-men shell. Just a little, though.

"Then you should probably tell her that. Do more than that, show her. Be there for her and ditch all the others." *Sorry, Anna-Marie*, I mentally apologize. But I'm pretty sure she would have ended it herself at the next post-coital mention of his Charlie Sheen play.

"You think that will be enough?"

"I don't know. But it's a start. Make sure she knows why you love her, why you think she's special enough to give up all the others for." I'm warming to the idea, maybe because my own love life is such a nightmare. Someone else should have a win, even if it is someone who wins in every other area of life on a daily basis.

He smiles, and it's the Trevor Everlake trademark smile that makes panties drop across America. "Thanks. That seems like good advice." The moment is spoiled, though, when he asks a few seconds later, "So what was your name?"

"Gabby. And for the record, I've told you this before. We've met, like, four times already."

"Really? Huh." He appears deep in thought, an interesting expression on HD and one I doubt he has very often. Then he shakes his head and looks back at me. "So you want to fool around?"

"What? I'm Anna-Marie's best friend! And you *just* finished telling me about how you were ready to commit to this other woman!"

"Well, I haven't committed to her *yet*."

I see a twinkle of humor in his eyes, and in that moment I realize he's not quite as clueless as he seems. I smack him on the shoulder, though I can't help but smile. "Good luck, HD."

"My name's Ryan."

"I know." I head back into my bedroom and close the door behind me.

SEVENTEEN

When my mom texts me the next morning to say we're having a family meeting, I'm tempted to think it's because I'm being legally charged for vandalizing a god with my face, thus insulting an entire culture, and the papers got served to her house instead of my apartment.

She follows it up immediately with a second text. *About Felix*, it says.

I sigh. At least she's being upfront about it this time. I'm about to respond when my mother sends a quick third message.

We need you to be there, Gabriella, it says. *Your brother needs your support.*

I'm pretty sure supporting Felix was what I was doing when I refused to help him get his cello back to pawn another day—not that I haven't second guessed that decision about a thousand times since.

I'll be there, I text.

I wonder if Felix will be, or if we're all going to sit down and discuss his clearly out-of-control drug addiction behind his back. It makes me feel like a complete traitor, but if he won't get help, that doesn't sound like a terrible idea. It's also possible that Mom is using Felix as bait to sit us down to talk about the divorce, but I don't think even my mother has sunk that low.

Just after I've gotten showered and dressed and am standing in front of our admittedly sparse breakfast cereal options, my phone rings. I half-expect it to be my mother telling me Felix got wind of her plans to corner him and has stolen a car and a passport and hightailed it to Mexico, but instead my caller ID says it's Sean.

Sean, whose number I definitely should have deleted from my phone.

I think through a large number of reasons I shouldn't answer, but just as it's about to go to voice mail, I give in.

"Hello?" I say.

"Hey, Gabby," Sean says, erasing any hopes I might have that I'd forgotten about some *other* Sean whose number I have tucked away in my phone. "How are you?"

It takes me a second to respond, because I'm trying to discern if he actually cares how I am or if he's merely inquiring about the state of my face. In the end, I answer halfway in between. "Bruised," I say. "You?"

"Oh, god, Gabby. I'm so sorry. I was a dick last night, but let me explain, okay?"

I roll my eyes. "I think the person you need to explain to is your girlfriend, don't you?"

"That's fair," Sean says. "And I did. A lot. But I want you to know, we were broken up until two days ago. When I agreed to go out with you, and when we went out the first time, I thought she and I were over."

I'm not sure whether I should believe this, but ultimately, I suppose it doesn't matter. "But when we texted about meeting at the Indian place, and when you showed up and acted like you were on a date with me, and when you kissed me in front of your brother—"

"I know," Sean says. "I know what it looks like, but let me explain."

I'm pretty sure it *is* what it looks like, and I'm pretty sure any girl with self-respect would have hung up on him by now. But instead I sigh. "Go on."

162

"Look, I told you Will and I don't talk much anymore, right? Well, my girlfriend is the reason. My girlfriend and *his* girlfriend, I guess."

"Because you don't like Sarah. And he doesn't like . . . What was her name?"

"Audra," he says. "Yeah, Will's not a fan of hers. So when he heard we broke up, he wanted to set me up with you—I guess to get Sarah off his back."

My face goes red. "To get Sarah off his back about *what*?"

Sean hesitates. "I probably shouldn't have said anything, but I guess Sarah got it into her head that Will was into you or something." He scoffs. "I mean, really. Anyone can see a mile away that you're not his type."

My heart is pounding in my ears, drowning out the sound of Sean's voice, though I'm pretty sure he does not elaborate. All that makes it out of my mouth is a choked sputtering sound.

"I know, I know," Sean says. "It doesn't excuse me not telling you about my girlfriend. But I knew if I did, you were going to tell Will, and he was going to be all over my ass for making up with Audra, just when we were starting to be able to say two words in a row to each other again and then—"

But all I can hear are endless echoes in my ears. *Not his type. Not his type.*

Somewhere in the middle of this, I find my voice. "So you decided to use me," I say.

Sean hesitates. "I wouldn't say that. More like—"

"I would. I would say exactly that. You decided to use me to get Will off your back, just like he decided to use me to get Sarah off *his* back."

Now it's Sean who makes a sputtering noise. "Gabby, listen," he says.

But I don't listen. I do the thing I clearly should have done the moment I made the grave mistake of answering his call in the first place.

I hang up.

I arrive home fifteen minutes early—this isn't a dinner and therefore shouldn't involve as much prep—but of course Dana's Lexus is already in the driveway. My sister is obsessively punctual, and I wonder if she and my parents have started complaining about (at?) Felix without me. I hurry to the door and find Dana pacing in the entryway. She looks up at me with obvious relief when I open the door.

"Good," she says. "You're here."

Dana is hugging her arms around her shoulders and her eyes are red-rimmed. If I didn't know better, I'd think she'd been crying, but I haven't seen my sister cry since Ephraim was a newborn and the grocery store ran out of Similac Pro-Advance non-GMO baby formula, and she had to make do with a can of regular Advance.

"Oh, god," I say, suddenly gripped with fear that Felix is dead in some crack house somewhere. "Is Felix—"

"I'm here," Felix says, and steps out of the hall. He's also got his arms wrapped around himself and is scratching his forearms through his long, ratty sleeves. He and I meet eyes, and then he looks rapidly away, only to glance back a second later. I'm somewhat relieved to see that he seems sheepish about our last meeting, but I'm way more relieved that he's still alive.

Then I notice Dana staring at me in horror. "What happened to your face?"

I put a hand to the welt on my cheek. When I was a kid, my dad used to make us green eggs and ham. He'd help me count out the drops of green dye and then stir them into the beaten yellow egg. Last I checked, my bruise was reaching a color somewhere between the two.

One corner of Felix's mouth quirks up. "Do you owe money to the wrong people?"

Dana looks confused, but I smile and Felix smiles and for the first time since he's been home, I feel like I see a tiny flicker of my real brother.

Maybe this family meeting is going to be a good thing, after all. I have a brief glimmer of hope that we're all going to sit down, and Felix is going to start at the beginning and tell us why on earth he started doing drugs in the first place, and we can all outline a plan to support him while he gets more treatment.

My hope dims somewhat when my mother appears and ushers us into the parlor. The room is much sparser on decor than the last time I was in here, which might well have been years ago because we only use it when company comes by—something that stopped happening around the time my mother stopped having a new piece of art or furniture or renovation to show off every other month. Felix comes willingly, but he sits in a chair in the corner, draws his arms tight across his chest, and refuses to look at any of us.

My parents stare at each other from their matching love seats on opposite sides of the room, leaving Dana and me the Haute House settee. What I want to do is throw my arms around my brother and tell him how scared I am of losing him, how awful it was to see him like that, how much I want to understand what's happening to him and help him figure out how to get back where he wants to be again. But I dutifully sit and watch Felix while he stares at the bare space on the floor that used to be my mother's Italian rug.

An awful silence settles between us. For once, even Dana doesn't seem to know what to say.

Felix speaks first. "So are we all going to talk about our *feelings?*"

We damn well should do just that, and I open my mouth to say so, but my parents shift uncomfortably, and I remember that we are the Mays family, and the only person who ever talks about her feelings is Dana. Loudly.

"We're here," Dad says, "so that you girls can tell your brother you want him to go back to rehab."

Dana rolls her eyes. "I want him to stop being an idiot and go back to Juilliard."

"Of course, dear," my mom cuts in. "But it'll be a bit of a

process. First, he'll need to go back to inpatient, then outpatient treatment, and hopefully by the time he's stable on the medically assisted—"

"*Medically assisted?*" Dana says. "What the hell kind of drugs are you on, anyway?"

Felix shifts uncomfortably, but he keeps staring at the floor.

I want to defend him, but I'm not sure what I can say. "How long were you in rehab before?" I ask.

Felix looks up at me like this startles him, and his lips twist.

"Tell her, Felix," my dad says.

Felix runs his hands over his face and through his hair, then rests his elbows on his knees. "Ten days."

"Okay," I say. "Is that normal?"

"It is when you walk out and quit," Dad says.

Felix shakes his head. "I didn't quit. I just transferred to outpatient. That's it."

"Yes," Dad says. "And that's going *so* well for you. Where is your cello again?"

Dana's eyes widen. "Where is Felix's cello?"

Felix is drawing in on himself, and I want to swear. Apparently no one told Dana, and she's just going to keep yelling until someone does. "He pawned it for drug money," I say quietly.

"He *what?*" Dana shrieks.

Felix looks nervously at me for a fraction of a second, then shrugs. His shoulders don't rebound, and his whole body hunches. "I owed some people money."

I heroically don't jab a finger at him and tell him I knew it, even though I clearly did. But then, the nervous look in Felix's eyes makes me wonder if he's lying, and he just got robbed while carrying around ten grand and trying to buy drugs.

"Well, aren't we going to get it back?" Dana asks. "Who knows how they're storing it at a—" she shudders, as if the words *pawn shop* are too filthy to pass through her lips.

"With what money?" my dad asks. "What was left has already been funneled into medical bills. We didn't get a full

166

refund when you quit, you know, and another round is going to cost—"

"This isn't about money," my mother says, but before she even finishes the phrase, my dad talks over her.

"I don't see why not," Dad says. "Nearly every word you say to me is about money."

I purse my lips, watching Felix, who is back to staring at the floor.

"What's happening?" I ask him. "God, Felix. What *happened* to you?"

His face turns to stone, and he refuses to look at me. That's when the truth settles in my gut like a boulder. We're not going to talk about this. I may never know the answer to that question.

"Do you want to get clean?" I ask.

A flicker of pain crosses his face, and then his expression goes blank again. In that moment, I hate myself for how long it's been since he and I had a real conversation. When I moved out we didn't see each other as often, but Felix would still text me—mostly to make fun of Mom and Dad or to invite me to his performances. Toward the end of high school, he was always auditioning for and playing with someone: the Los Angeles Chamber Orchestra, the LA Opera, the Junior Philharmonic. When he'd gone away to Juilliard, we'd talked and texted less and less, then finally hardly at all. I'd been sad about that, of course, but I'd assumed it was because my little brother had finally made it to the place he'd always wanted to be and was having too fabulous a time to spare a thought for his boring older sister.

"It doesn't matter if he wants to," Dana says. "What alternative does he have? Be a junkie? Get arrested?"

Mom and Dad look at each other.

"What?" Dana asks. "He's been *arrested*? God, can he even get back into school with a record?"

"I don't have a record," Felix says. "And I'm not going back to Juilliard."

A heavy silence fills the room, and even Dana is speechless. Now Mom and Dad are staring at the floor, and I realize this isn't news to them. They've heard it before.

I cut in before Dana finds her tongue. "What are you going to do?" I ask.

"He's going back to *rehab*," my dad says again, glaring at Dana and me, no doubt for our failure to lecture him on this reality.

"They say you can't force him," Mom says. "Felix is an adult."

"Right," Dana says. "Because adults drop out of college to do drugs and throw away everything they've worked for their whole lives. God, can't you get some kind of power of attorney? He's clearly not in his right mind."

I want to point out that this is, sadly, a thing adults do all the time, but I know that won't help. "Felix," I try again, even though I'm pretty sure it's hopeless. "Won't you at least *talk* to us about it?"

He looks up at me again, this time with the same expression as when I told him I wouldn't buy back his cello. "What are you even doing here, Gabby? I thought I told you to stay away from me."

"Unfortunately," Dad says, appearing to not have heard either my question or Felix's snide dodge, or maybe just not caring about either, "doing drugs isn't grounds to get power of attorney."

Felix shoots Dad a brief death glare—it's clear from Dad's tone that he's fully investigated this possibility—and then goes back to staring at me.

"Then what are we going to do?" Dana says shrilly. "You can't be expected to just let him keep doing this."

"I spoke to some experts," Mom says. "And they say the only thing we can do is to kick him out of the house and stop helping him as long as he's on drugs."

Felix shrinks a bit, but he doesn't say anything.

"We talked about that," Dad says. "We can't just throw him out."

Even Dana looks appalled at this suggestion, and somewhat torn between her usual instinct to side with Mom and the idea of kicking her druggie brother out onto the street.

Felix is folding in on himself again, and despite his usual slumped posture, I realize I don't recognize this Felix any more than the one who called me a screw-up and vomited into the garbage can. I still have no idea what happened in New York, but I know this—he's been through something bad, and whether that was caused by the drugs or caused him to get into them, it doesn't really matter now. Mom and Dad and Dana continue to yell over each other about what should be done to fix Felix, but I get up and sit on the floor next to his chair, down by his eyeline. He looks at me, surprised.

"I'm here because I miss my brother," I say quietly. "And I'm scared that if I leave, I'll never see him again."

I expect him to sneer, but instead he stares at me, and I swear I see his eyes start to shine. He looks away and sniffs and shuts his eyes tight, and I'm even more sure that he's trying not to cry.

"I love you," I say, and even over the yelling, I'm sure he hears me.

We're silent for a minute as the fight goes on, and I'm trying to figure out what else I could possibly say that might help.

"Fine," Felix says quietly, then loudly, over the top of everyone else's arguments. "Fine! I'll go."

My parents and Dana fall silent and stare at him.

"I'll go back to rehab," Felix says. "I'll do inpatient, okay? I'll finish this time."

I want to throw my arms around my brother, but he's hugging his own arms again, and I'm pretty sure he'll just shrug me off.

"Okay, then," Dad says. "Good."

And blessedly, for that moment at least, no one says a word about the money.

EIGHTEEN

Though my romantic life is in a nosedive spectacular even for me, and my family life is a mess in which my brother being back in rehab is considered an improvement over last week, at least my job as an extra continues to go on—which I suppose means that Sarah decided not to fire me. Or, more likely, decided I wasn't worth even the minimal effort that would take after seeing the disaster that is my life at the restaurant Friday night. Fortunately, by the time I am back on set on Monday, the bruise on my cheek has shrunken to a level I hope can be covered with some extra-power film set concealer.

Unfortunately, going to work and getting a paycheck also means I will likely run into Will, and I'm not sure I'm ready for that. Not after that humiliation. Not after realizing how much I'm still hopelessly into him.

I hear Sean's voice echo in my head again: *Not his type.*

"You going to be okay?" Anna-Marie asks as we park the Hyundai in our now-usual spot.

"Yeah, I think so. I mean, I don't have to see Sean here." I haven't told Anna-Marie what really upset me about that night. It's easier to let her think I'm mourning the loss of a potential relationship with Sean.

And really, I could stand to never see that jerk again.

"But Will—" she starts.

Watched me get punched out by Ganesh after listening to me rant at him about how much I like his brother.

"Looks a little like him." I shrug it off as if their resemblance is limited to them both being blond. Or male. "It's no big deal. Chances are I won't even talk with him. He's usually down in the writer's dungeon."

"For a writer, he spends an awful lot of time hanging around the craft services table."

"Writers have to eat sometime, too."

"Yes, and they usually have it brought in to them. He likes to be on the set. To talk to you."

"He did," I say. "Because we're friends. And because his gorgeous fiancée is out on the set." I'm hoping he's going to take the same philosophy that I have towards that night at the restaurant and do his best to block out all memory of it.

She looks unconvinced. "Whatever you say."

I skip the food that morning anyway, and spend the next hour or so out in my car, ostensibly reading a book about some rich white girl who climbs Mount Everest and in doing so "finds herself" (along with finding that mountain climbing is hell on one's French manicure). Really, I am mentally going over the double date for the millionth time. And the last phone conversation I had with my mom, who said that Felix was all checked into rehab and that Dad had moved out and was living in an apartment in Burbank.

When I can't take sitting alone with my thoughts anymore, I head inside.

I pass the live set of a room in the hospital, where Anna-Marie and HD are being filmed. She's pressed back against the wall, covering up a poster of the digestive tract, and he's holding her face in his hands, and they're both breathing like they've either just emerged from a heavy makeout session or are about to start one.

"The truth is, Helena," Trevor says, staring into her eyes.

"I'm in love with you."

Helena draws in a sharp breath. "But your girlfriend—"

"She was never the one. None of them were. But you . . ." Trevor runs a hand through Helena's hair, his finger caressing the silky softness of whatever conditioner they use on set. "You have always been different from all the others."

That's not the first time I've heard those words from HD's mouth. Though in Helena's case, he might have a point, given that she's moved on from framing her previous lover, Diego, for murder and is currently in the process of setting up Trevor for Lucy St. James's mugging.

I wonder if there's a medical diagnosis for an addiction to framing people, and if it's more or less treatable than selective amnesia.

I head to the extras pen to report to Clint, a half hour early. I hand him a pomegranate apricot VitaminWater as I do so, and he tips his cowboy hat to me.

I don't see Karen yet, though I assume she's coming. Ever since her comment to Clint about us being the best receptionists this soap has ever seen, he's seemed happy to keep us together in that role.

Sarah Paltrow steps into the extras area, heading toward Clint with a script in her hand. She sees me and hesitates, an emotion I can't quite pinpoint flickering across her face. Then she opens the script and indicates something on the page, speaking to him in a low voice. He looks back at me, raises an eyebrow and shrugs.

I suddenly have a very, very bad feeling.

This feeling is compounded when Sarah walks my way, in the brisk manner she walks everywhere. "You'd better hope the makeup artist can cover that up," she says, her eyes trailing over my fading bruise and giving no indication she even remembers where I got it. "Especially since you have a line today."

"A what?"

"A line. Of dialogue. Congratulations, you've become a

bit part."

"I-I . . ." Panic twists my guts into dozens of little knots. I am not an actress. I am background. I think of Peter Dryden's brutal indictment of every attempt I made at doing any more. "Why?"

"Will asked if you could have one. I didn't see any reason to say no. Do you?"

Yes! I want to cry out. *I can think of a dozen reasons!*

"What is it I'm supposed to say?"

She flips open the script to the page she already has her thumb bookmarking. I notice a slim silver band on her thumb and realize I've never actually seen her wear an engagement ring.

"Dr. Katarina Gunn is inspecting Lucy St. James for any signs of brain injury. Immediately after Dr. Gunn says 'Don't you think you should tell him?'" you walk in and say, 'I'm sorry, Dr. Gunn, but there's an important call for you on line two.' She says, 'Thank you, Rhonda,' and you walk out. That's it."

I have a name? Granted, the name is Rhonda, but still . . . my character has a name! The panic hasn't lessened, but the same kind of starstruck excitement that filled me the first time I saw Bridget Messler in person is right there along with it. I'm pretty sure bit parts get paid more, too, which I could definitely use.

Then again, they have a far greater chance of failing spectacularly. And if anyone is practically guaranteed to do that, it's me.

"Wow, I, uh—"

"I'm late for my daily attempt to talk Bridget Messler into doing her damn job, which she's refusing until June Blair admits to stealing her fake Emmy. So I have neither the time nor the patience to hear an extra debate whether she can say one line of dialogue. Can you do this?"

I swallow hard. "Yes. I, uh . . . yes."

She snaps the script shut and turns.

"Is Will here today?" I can't help but asking. I was hoping he would avoid the areas where the extras are wrangled, but my mind is reeling about what on earth I said the other night that made me seem capable of putting together a sentence, let alone delivering one in front of a camera. Sarah looks back at me over her shoulder, her blue eyes narrowed, and I remember what Sean said about Sarah thinking Will was into me. Is it really possible she could be jealous of *me*?

"I'd like to thank him," I add hastily. "And you too, of course. Thank you."

"He's in the dungeon. Get back by call time." She stalks off.

I glance at my watch to check the time. I have a little over ten minutes. I was dreading talking to Will after the date—and still never texted him back—but I have to know why he's doing this. I head down the hallway behind the sets until I reach the room called the Writer's Dungeon. I would have expected it to be at least a level down with a name like that, but it's just one of a dozen or so little office-type rooms. This one is easily identifiable by the picture taped to the door: dozens of monkeys at typewriters, ostensibly trying to write Hamlet.

At least the dialogue for *Passion Medical* is a far more realistic goal.

I raise my hand to knock, but the door swings open and a large bearded man stands there, surprised. "Oh. Hey. Are you here with craft services? We placed our order like fifteen minutes ago."

I grit my teeth. Maybe I should wear a placard to work that says "I'm not with craft services."

"Uh, no," I say. "I need to talk with Will Bowen for a minute, if he's here."

"Gabby!" The door swings fully open and Will grins at me from behind the other writer. He cringes a little at my face, but he doesn't otherwise look like he's horrified to see me again. Which makes me doubt his sanity a little, honestly, but I'm grateful for it. The other writer peers out and past me down the hallway, then sighs at the lack of a craft services person bearing their tray of food. He goes and sits down at the table without another word.

Will gestures to the small group sitting at the table, most of

174

whom, I'm surprised to see, are men. They are a wide variety of shapes and ethnicities, but they all project a similar laid-back vibe in their various logo-bearing t-shirts, cans of Diet Coke dotting the table in between laptops and stacks of paper with notes scribbled on them. "Everyone, this is my friend Gabby Mays. She's an extra."

One of the women raises her hand in a half-hearted greeting, but the others barely glance at me before returning to their work.

"Don't mind them, they're just jealous. We don't get many visitors here. So . . . has Sarah talked with you yet?"

"Yeah, I . . ." I look uncomfortably at the writers, who don't appear to be paying attention. There's no way they don't hear, though, considering the room is roughly the size of my apartment's living room.

"Oh, sure," Will says, then guides me out to the hallway, his hand on my back in the same place Sean had put his when walking me out the car. My chest feels tight.

When the door swings closed behind us, I am suddenly unsure of what to say. Will appears less at ease than normal as well, sucking in his cheek and pushing it back out. "Look, Gabby, I'm sorry about Sean. About the whole thing."

Ah. Of course. My insides deaden. I don't know why else I expected he would have done this, but to know it was out of pity . . .

I shrug. "It's okay."

"No, it's not. I never would have set you up with him if I'd known he was still dating that—" He shakes his head. "Never mind. I never liked his girlfriend. She was always really materialistic, and it was obvious she was just into him for his money. I mean, she only started paying him any attention when his business took off. We fought about it constantly, and then a month or so ago he told me he'd broken up with her. Apparently, they got back together."

"Apparently." I debate telling him about Sean's pseudo-apology phone call, but Will places his hand on my arm, and the warmth from his fingers seeps in through my thin cotton t-shirt and pretty much steals all my capability for thought.

"The truth is, he's an idiot and he doesn't deserve you," Will says.

Those words coming from Anna-Marie or another friend might have felt like so much talk, just something you say when a friend is cheated on by some jerk. True, but also a platitude.

When Will says it, though, his intense green eyes fixed on mine, his hand only one thin layer of fabric away from the skin on my arm, I can barely breathe. I can only manage the traitorous thought of *do* you *deserve me? Do you* want *to?*

No. Because he is engaged and happy, and I know deep down he's a better man than his brother.

He clears his throat and pulls his arm away, breaking the eye contact I felt all the way down to my toes. "How are things with your brother?" he asks.

After the whole Ganesh debacle, I'm surprised he remembers.

"Better, actually," I say. "We had an intervention for him— like an actual intervention where we all sat down and talked about our feelings. Well, mostly my parents and my sister Dana yelled about their feelings, but I talked to Felix, and we all convinced him to go back to rehab."

"Really?" Will says. "That's good, yeah?"

"Yeah," I say. "I mean, his cello is still pawned and he still needs to actually *stay* in rehab this time. But it's progress anyway."

Will smiles, like he's actually relieved. Which makes me feel all warm and fuzzy, but is hardly the point. "The line you gave me," I say. "You didn't have to do that."

"I did. I wanted to make it up to you. And obviously my matchmaking skills aren't so great, so I thought I'd do what I could with my writing. Not that the line is a masterpiece or anything." His lips quirk up, and I wonder how I could have ever thought for a moment that Sean had the better-shaped lips of the two.

"Come on, 'I'm sorry, Dr. Gunn, but you have an important

call on line two?' It's got suspense, a call for forgiveness, unnecessary specificity. It's amazing."

That half-smile turns into a full grin.

"I'm just not sure I should do it, though," I continue.

"Why not?"

"You have no idea how terribly I can screw things up." Though considering the microwave fire that cost me my job back when he was my boss and his recent viewing of my destruction of religious iconography, he does have *some* idea. "Even just a line like this, I—"

"Gabby," he says, leaning his head toward me, his face close enough I catch a whiff of fresh, soapy scent, mingled with aftershave. Maybe even a hint of Swedish Fish, though that's possibly just my imagination. "One of these days, you need to change the way you view yourself. You can do this."

Being so near him is dizzying, and having him so earnestly believe in me even more so. I let out a nervous laugh. "Maybe props can get me a top hat and monocle."

He chuckles, then shakes his head. "Your toucan needed that. You don't. You never did." His eyes lock on mine like there's more he wants to say, and my heart pounds a half-time show drumline beat because there's so much more I wish I could hear him say, and just maybe—

Then he blinks and glances down at his watch. "Don't be late to report in to Clint. Even having a line won't save you then." He gives me a quick smile that doesn't quite reach his eyes and steps back into the writer's room. The door closes behind him before I realize I never actually thanked him.

And also, I am letting my hopes where he is concerned get way too high, reading things into his words, into his *friendship*, that aren't there and will never be there. Because he's in love with someone else.

I take a deep breath and head back to the extras area, where Karen attacks me in a bear hug.

"You have a line!" she squeals. "Go Team Reception!"

I return her high-five and force a smile, but now that Clint is directing us where to stand and what to do, the fact that I have to actually say this line, in front of Sarah and Bernard and actors and cameras, makes me want to hyperventilate.

We have two scenes in the reception area before my big acting break. I wish I could talk with Anna-Marie beforehand, but the scenes are stacked back-to-back, and she's not in any of these.

HD, however, is in the first one, being approached by the police for his supposed involvement in the mugging. After the scene is over—with Trevor being handcuffed and holding a long, shocked expression for the camera—he notices me at the reception desk and gives me a little wave, which turns Karen into the one nearly hyperventilating.

I'm not convinced he'd remember my name, but at least after our late night talk about his love life, I've moved up from kale.

As the next scene films, I type my line over and over and over again, trying to ingrain it so deeply into my brain I'll be apologizing to Dr. Gunn in my sleep for the next week.

"You got this," Karen says as we finish up with our waiting room scenes, and June Blair ascends the stage for her hospital room scene. "Breathe, honey. Just breathe and say the line."

I nod. Her reminder to breathe is actually necessary, because I think I'm starting to turn blue. We hug and she leaves the set. My palms are clammy, my legs trembling, as I position myself behind the set door to the hospital room.

I catch a flash of movement from the darkness beyond the set. Squinting, I can see Will there, standing next to Sarah, who is in turn next to the seated Bernard. Will actually came out here to see me do this. I focus on not vomiting on my nursing clogs.

Change my view. I need to change my view of myself, just like Will said.

I can do this. I can say a line of dialogue.

Inside I hear the words "Don't you think you should tell him?"

178

I twist the door handle, step in, and open my mouth.

"What is she still doing here?" another voice cries. "She should be in lock-up with the other criminals!"

My mouth snaps shut as all heads swivel to Bridget Messler, standing with her hands on her hips in front of the set.

"Good god, not this again," June says with a dramatic eye-roll and a bored tone, though she jumps up from the hospital bed. Her paper gown crinkles as she not-so-subtly tries to position herself behind the actress playing Dr. Gunn.

"I thought you took care of this," Bernard snaps at Sarah, who jumps into motion.

"Bridget, we discussed this already. There is no indication that June had anything to do with your missing Emmy—"

"Missing fake Emmy," June grouses.

"—and we've filed a report with the police already."

"For all the good that will do. She's probably already slept with the lot of them." Bridget pushes Sarah's hand away from steering her out.

"This is harassment! I refuse to work in this kind of environment!" June yells at Bernard. "Either that crazy woman goes or I do!" She draws the paper robe around her with as much dignity as she can manage, and storms off the set.

"Fabulous news," Bridget says icily, smoothing back her already perfectly coiffed silver hair. "I suppose we'll all be seeing you on the infomercials." Then, with a satisfied smirk, she takes off to her dressing room in the other direction.

Bernard throws the script to the ground and then his coffee mug soon after, which shatters against the cement. Both Dr. Gunn and I jump.

"Fix this or you're done," he growls at Sarah. Even though she's standing in the dark beyond the set, I imagine I can see her pale. Maybe I'm just feeling pale on her behalf.

Will puts his hand on her shoulder, but she shakes him off and takes off after June.

I grip the door handle and meet eyes with the actress who

plays Dr. Gunn. Her brown eyes are wide, though she attempts a comforting smile. I realize I've never learned her name, which I'll have to rectify. She seems like a nice person. Or maybe I'm just grasping for humanity in a den of vipers.

Bernard screams at a crew member for his drink, then drops heavily back into his director's chair and stares onto the set. I know the moment his gaze settles on me. I feel it like a stone in my stomach.

"Who are you?"

My mouth doesn't work briefly, and finally it does. "G-Gabby Mays, sir. I'm an extra." I don't bother telling him that I've been an extra, sitting in the background of scenes he's been watching for several weeks now.

Will says something to him that I can't quite hear, pointing at the script.

"This girl has a line?" Bernard's disgust is evident. "Who is responsible for this? This is *my* show. Ugly girls don't get lines on *my show!*"

Dr. Gunn sucks her breath in sharply, and her comforting smile drops into horrified pity. A heavy silence settles, and I see Will staring at me, his lips working soundlessly.

My hand drops from the sweat-slick handle. I know I should feel pain, nausea, anger that he would say something like that in front of everyone. Instead I am only numb.

"Clint!" Bernard barks. Clint jogs up to him, VitaminWater slopping out of the top of the bottle as he runs. Bernard points at me. "Get her off my set, and vet the extras better. I'm not running a charity here."

Clint turns to me and starts walking, slowly, his wide shoulders set rigid like he's trying to keep them from slumping.

I don't let him reach the set. I start walking myself, my feet moving of their own accord because my numbed mind can't string enough thoughts together to direct them. I pass Karen, who reaches out for me, but draws back at seeing my face. I pass Clint and crew members and Will.

Will. The pity on his face is a thousand times worse than all the others combined.

I keep walking. I don't change out of my scrubs. I don't get my purse or clothes from my locker. I just walk off the set, and I don't look back.

NINETEEN

I hear Will's voice calling my name when I reach my car. I lean against the front door, my arms still hanging limply at my sides. I don't even have my keys, so I can't get in and drive away. I do have my cell phone in my scrubs pocket, so I could call Anna-Marie and ask her to get my stuff. She can bring the scrubs back with her in the morning. I don't want to mess up her scene, though. Maybe I could just spend a few hours walking around West Hollywood in my scrubs and see if doctors get any perks like free coffee or noticeable respect.

A very, very strange part of me wants to call my mom and have her come get me. That part of me wants to crawl into my childhood bed and have Mom bribe me with candy to smile again.

Except I doubt there's any candy in the house now. And my childhood bed has probably been sold long ago to pay the pool cleaner.

"Gabby!" Will's a bit winded, though it isn't a long run. He may look fit, but I'm guessing his career doesn't require a lot of exercise.

I don't say anything. I can't think of anything to say after what just happened.

"Gabby, I'm sorry. I—that was awful. Bernard's an asshole, but even for him, that was the worst. June's right, the atmosphere

here is toxic. I'm thinking of quitting myself, and—"

"How pathetic do you think I am?" The words have left my mouth before I've even formed them in my mind.

Will blinks, taken aback. "What? I don't think you're pathetic. At all."

"You do. You must. You keep trying to fix my life for me." And then I realize that I am no longer numb.

I am angry. I am mad at myself, mad at Bernard, mad at Bridget Messler and June Blair.

I am mad at Will.

"I'm not trying to fix you, I just—"

"You barely even know me, and you're trying to manage my love life. To improve it. To find me a *direction*. To warn me away from guys like Ryan Lansing and toward guys like your brother, who, for what it's worth, are pretty much one and the same."

"I told you I'm sorry about Sean, I had no idea—"

"And then you decide my work life must not be fulfilling enough, so you give me a line!" My hands clench into fists, my ragged fingernails digging into my palms. "You know I'm not an actress, that I have absolutely no desire to be an actress, that I barely have the talent or looks to be background noise, and yet you think I need this! To draw more attention to myself, to *believe* in myself!"

His mouth sags open slightly, but no words come out.

"I knew something like this would happen! Hell, *you* should have known this! You even fired me once yourself, remember?"

Will's eyes widen. "Gabby, that was—"

"I know, it was more than two years ago. And yes, I almost burned down the break room. So I get it. But this—you made me think for one second that I could do this. That I wouldn't lose the best job I've ever had! But I did, like everyone knew I would, and now you want to quit your job? For what, my honor?"

His mouth closes. He wets his lips and looks down at his shoes.

"What about your fiancée? Sarah got yelled at, too. Why aren't you chasing after her? Is it because she's strong and I'm not?"

He looks up again, sharply. I see his Adam's apple bob up and down as he swallows. His expression is one of guilt, likely because I am right, even if he never saw it that way before.

People crossing the parking lot are looking our direction. But it feels good to yell, good to let it all out, good to take it all out on Will, who I know, even in my fury, did everything with the best of intentions.

"Is it because you think I need saving? Well, maybe you're right. Maybe my life is a complete mess. Maybe I need to not have feelings for a guy who is *engaged*!"

Uh-oh. I definitely hadn't meant to blurt out *that*.

The look of stunned shock on his face that undoubtedly mirrors mine might have been funny had I not just inadvertently confessed my feelings about Will to him in a loud tirade in a studio parking lot.

I swallow, my mind desperate to pretend that last part never happened. To regain some tiny amount of emotional footing in this conversation. "Maybe I do need saving," I say, as flatly as I can manage. "Probably. But you're clearly not the one to do it. So stop trying and leave me the hell alone."

He flinches and steps back. I might as well have slapped him, judging by the hurt look in his eyes. He runs a hand through his honey-blond curls. "Yeah, okay."

I want to take it back, all of it. And yet part of me wants to follow up with a confession, to tell him that even when I was kissing Sean, I was thinking of him. I want to ask him if I'm wrong about any of this, if there's even a remote possibility that he's done any of this because he actually has feelings for me that go beyond friendship.

But I've humiliated myself and suffered enough rejection for the day. I fold my arms and stare in the other direction as he walks away. I keep looking, watching the breeze tremble through the palm tree leaves at the end of the parking lot, long after I can no longer hear the scuff of his sneakers against the pavement. Long after I feel the tears trailing their way down my cheeks.

Anna-Marie brings out my purse and clothes eventually, without me needing to call her. I don't know if Will spoke to her or if she just heard about the incident and how I walked off the set in stolen scrubs.

She doesn't say anything, just sets my stuff on the hood and leans back against the car with me. It takes me a few minutes before I realize she's back in her own clothes, despite her hair and makeup done up like she's going to prom.

"Don't you still have a few hours?" I ask.

"Nah. My only scenes were with Bridget, and she's locked herself in her room. Sarah told the rest of us to go home."

"I guess we both have a free day, then."

Anna-Marie gives me a side glance. "You would've been great, you know. At saying the line."

"Maybe. Probably not. But who knows. It's Schroedinger's line of dialogue now."

Anna-Marie nods. "So you talked with Will? He looked pretty upset."

"Talked is one way of saying it. Yelled at is another."

She turns and studies me. She can appear vapid at times, but it's all an act. Anna-Marie can see through people like she's got a PhD in psychology. And x-ray vision.

I can guess the kind of questions she's going to ask, and I don't want to answer any of them, even in my own mind. Especially in my own mind. "Let's not talk about it right now, okay? I just want to go home."

"Okay. There's just one place I need to stop at first."

Without even saying the words, I know that she's going to drive—despite her usual refusal to so much as touch a gas pedal in LA—and I'm going to sit silently in the passenger seat and turn up the radio to drown out my thoughts.

But my thoughts aren't so easily drowned out. They are a swirling collage of Will and Sarah and Felix and Sean and Bernard and Mom and Bridget Messler and Peter Dryden and the CPR instructor, each resisting my attempts to push them down, back into the dark corners of my subconscious where they belong.

I am distracted enough that I don't notice where we are until the car has already stopped and Anna-Marie says, "Come on, we're doing this."

I blink out of my daze and see that we are parked (illegally) in front of Fong's All-American. Anna-Marie gets out and I follow, the numbness back.

We walk into Fong's, and Su-Lin's smile drops the second she sees my face. "Uh-oh," she says, setting down the hot pink marker she was using to draw geometric shapes on the back of her hand. "I'll go get it."

I slide into my usual booth, and Anna-Marie sits across from me as if she does this all the time instead of only having been here with me once, most of which she spent tallying up the calories of four bites of Breakup Tub on a fitness app.

"Are you sure you're up for this?" I ask.

She cocks a saucy eyebrow at me. "I was the Blueberry Pie Eating Champion of Everett, Wyoming, two years straight. Trust me, I can handle this."

I should be even more bitter that, in addition to everything else, it turns out Anna-Marie is better at eating obscene amounts of sugar than I am. But really, I'm just grateful she's here. And grateful that she doesn't push me to talk about anything.

Su-Lin brings out the Breakup Tub and two spoons. We finish it all, though I barely even taste it.

TWENTY

I have lost my job, been publicly shamed, and, possibly worse, I have blurted out my feelings to Will. Who is engaged. Who will probably now be uncomfortable even being friends with me. And if there's anything that is not bound to make me feel better about my life situation, it's spending more time with my family. But two days after I walk off the set of *Passion Medical* in utter dejection, I get a text from my mom. She needs help figuring out how to downsize. That's what she called it: downsizing. Really it means giving in, though in my opinion without any of the negative connotation usually associated with that phrase.

She's giving in to the fact that they are no longer rich, that keeping up a mansion in one of the most expensive areas of California is no longer feasible. That keeping up the lifestyle that home represented might have cost them their marriage. I don't know if this is an effort to salvage things with Dad or just an effort to come to terms with reality.

Either way, I owe it her to support her. I guess Dana feels that way, too, because Dana's Lexus is sitting in the driveway when I pull up to my parents' house. I almost turn around and drive away.

Mom is bad enough. Dana is worse. And yet, I need

something else to think about beyond Will's shocked, hurt expression as I yelled at him. Beyond the emptiness of sitting at home eating my way through my feelings and wondering what the hell I'm going to do next with my life. And so I trudge up the steps and go inside.

Dana's husband Paul isn't here this time, nor Dad, nor Felix, but little Ephraim comes charging at me full-speed when I walk in, his dark curls bouncing.

"Aunt Gab-Gab!"

I throw my arms around him and squeeze so tight he giggles. The sound of it lightens my heart more than any amount of ice cream and evenings spent watching classic romantic comedies with Anna-Marie. I'm nowhere near ready, either relationship-wise or in life in general, to have children of my own, but my nephew is adorable enough to make the notion appealing. Some day. A long, long time from now.

I hate myself that the idea of my future children makes me think of Will. And hate myself even more for the guilt that floods in. Will didn't deserve to be the recipient of my volcano of pent-up rage and humiliation. He'd only ever tried to help me.

But I don't even know how to apologize without completely breaking down in front of him—and after having started down that path already, I know *that* is a humiliation I can't see myself coming back from. It doesn't stop me from missing him, though. From wishing I could go back to us joking at the craft services table.

Ephraim leads me into the kitchen, where Mom and Dana have made various piles of kitchen appliances and utensils. He drops my hand and grabs a large plastic bowl to put on his head, smiling at me from under the rim.

It's good to know that even genius toddlers can still appreciate the classics.

"I don't think I should get rid of that," Mom is saying. "That melon baller was personally recommended to me by Emeril himself."

"Have you ever used it?" Dana asks pointedly.

"No, not yet, but—"

Dana places the melon baller in a pile of what I'm guessing are discards and sees me. "Excellent! Gabby's here to talk some sense into you, Mom."

Mom turns to me and offers a tremulous smile. Her face is pinched, and she has the circles under her eyes of many sleepless nights. "Thank you for coming, honey."

"Of course." For a moment, I'm tempted to give her a hug. She looks so lost standing among piles of her life being taken away from her. But Mom never was a hugger.

"She wants to keep the Lladros. *All* of them." Dana points to the ornately carved cherrywood china hutch in the dining room, filled with the lovely statues I used to stare at as a child and wish I could play with. Wish I could *become*, really—all grace and smooth lines and delicate perfection. One in particular, a statue of a ballerina, always reminds me of my childhood—but in a good way. Some of my earliest memories are of that statue, drawing pictures of her and posing myself in the same pirouette (or the five-year-old Gabby approximation of that same pirouette). There's not much in this house I'll be sad to lose, personally, but that statue would be one of them.

Mom's chin drops to her chest, as if she's already mourning their loss like I am. She picks at a fleck of some kind of dried crust stuck to the countertop. Apparently, she hasn't had the maid here recently.

"Let her keep them," I say. "They don't take up much space."

Mom looks back at me, surprised, and I think I see genuine gratitude in her deep blue eyes. Dana, for all her brilliance, apparently hasn't made the connection that Mom can't get rid of the Lladros because Dad gave them to her, one each year on their anniversary. Or maybe Dana does see it, and just doesn't understand.

Dana rolls her eyes and gets back to picking through the stacks of orange peelers and melon ballers and miscellaneous utensils that in some cases look more like medieval torture devices than anything that could be used to prepare food. Once again, I notice that Dana looks more tired than I'm used to seeing her, and her tone is even more on edge.

"I saw you on TV," Mom says, still picking at the crusty spot. "On *Passion Medical*. You told us Anna-Marie was on the show, but you didn't mention that you were, too."

Because the moment I tried, I got cut off and Dad announced that Felix had been in rehab, and no one wanted to hear about my work as an extra/fake receptionist at that point, is what I want to say. But no one wants to move on from that night more than I do.

"I'm just an extra. Anna-Marie's the actual star."

"Well, someone needs to tell your roommate's hairdresser to hold back on the hair spray. That scene where she was sleeping with Diego on the cafeteria table after hours? I thought that ketchup bottle was going to get stuck in her hair and never come out."

I wrinkle my nose at the image of Anna-Marie sexing it up on a dirty cafeteria table (a scene I wasn't aware of), as well as any implications of what might happen with a ketchup bottle.

"I'll let Anna-Marie know. I'm not working there anymore."

Mom stops furiously picking at the counter top, and Dana looks up from the piles of utensils to share a significant glance with Mom.

"What?" Dana asks, her brows drawing together. "You lost another job? Are you actually trying to fail?"

"Dana," Mom says, but as usual, Dana just keeps going.

"Are you actually ever going to *do* something with your life, Gabby? Because it doesn't seem like—"

"Dana!" Mom's shout surprises Dana as much as it does me. My sister closes her mouth, and mine gapes in amazement. I'm not used to my mom defending me, especially against Dana.

Mom doesn't look at me, though. She just clears her throat and picks up a whisk, frowning at it in disappointment. In reality, she probably considers the whisk a more valuable addition to the household than I ever was.

"It wasn't my fault," I say quietly. "Losing this job. I was good at it, you know."

Dana cocks an eyebrow at me, but I stare her down until she looks away. I'm not sure why I want them to believe me, but I *was* good at it. At being a nobody, a faceless body in the background, a bit of decoration meant not to draw attention.

"Of course, dear," Mom says, and she squeezes my arm. Her smile is strained, falsely chipper. She holds up a metal utensil that looks more like it belongs at the end of Captain Hook's arm stub than in a kitchen drawer. "Butter curler. Keep? I've found it quite useful."

Dana groans and snags it from Mom's hand to toss in the discard pile.

We work for another hour in the kitchen, and thankfully neither of them asks any more about my job or my love life. It's a good thing, too, because in my current state I might very well burst out crying or see if Emeril's personal melon baller guarantee extends to using it as projectile weapon. Either option is not likely to improve matters.

Likewise, neither Dana nor I ask Mom about Dad or about where she's going to live. That will all need to come up eventually, but instead we move into the bedroom and buckle down to business there, sorting through designer clothes and purses and shoes, through artwork and a surprising number of rare signed vintage records I had no idea my mom collected. We look up prices on eBay and make piles of things that will be worth selling, things to donate, and things Mom's too attached to get rid of. And though I'm not sure why she'd want to bring a ten-foot tall porcelain giraffe statue into what will most likely be an apartment or condo, I don't fight her on what she isn't ready to give up. After a few attempts to convince her otherwise, Dana gives up as well. Sooner than I'd expect from the sister who generally seems to regret that she has but one life to give for her ironclad opinions.

Keeping busy is good for all of us, it appears. Certainly better than speaking to each other has been lately. Or maybe ever.

Eventually Ephraim gets whiny, and Dana leaves to set him up in the family room with some science DVD for genius kids. ("Ephy can't get enough of Neil Degrasse Tyson," Dana proudly announces.)

When she leaves, I look over at Mom. "What's up with her? She seems . . . I don't know. More *Dana* than usual." By this I mean self-righteous and irritating, which is certainly true, but in some ways, she's actually seeming less Dana than usual as well. Distracted. Exhausted.

Mom just shakes her head, her lips pursed tight. "It's been a long few weeks for all of us."

Well, I can sympathize there, I suppose. Except that other than having to be here prying scarves and whisks from Mom's tight grip rather than spending the day shining her trophies or whatever Dana normally does, I can't imagine what my sister could be so miserable about.

Then again, I hadn't had the faintest clue what was going on with Felix, either, and he's the one in the family I was supposed to be closest to.

"So how's Felix doing?" I ask finally. "Does he get to call you?"

Mom runs her finger over the soft leather of a handbag in the "to sell" pile. "He's called once since he went back. He sounds good."

"*Good* good? Or, like, alive good?"

She flicks her gaze at me. "Good good."

"Good. I mean, great. That's great."

Except my brother is still in rehab, and if it didn't work for him before, it very well might not again. And even if it does, who knows what he'll do next, what with his scholarship gone and, worst of all, his cello.

I think of the look he gave me when I asked if he wanted to stop using the drugs, the flash of pain that had crossed his face, as if I was reminding him of some deep-buried trauma. I glance back at the boxes holding all the material memories of Mom's life—which for her were the average mom's equivalent of photo albums and that curl of hair from their baby's first haircut. I think of Dad in his library, desperately calculating any way to keep both his Mercedes and his dignity. I think of Bernard calling me ugly and Will's face when I yelled at him, and I wonder if anything will be great again.

A toddler whine sounds from the living room, and Dana pokes her head back in. "Mom, he's missing his blue sock. Have you seen it?"

"A two-year old's sock?" I ask. "You think she's seen anything that small in all this chaos?"

"I put it back in his room, in his sock drawer," Mom says. "It's getting full, you know. And here you want me to get rid of my belt collection. That child has more socks than—"

She cuts off at seeing Dana's face, and it takes me a moment to make the connection of Dana's now bloodless cheeks and wide eyes with what Mom said. And then it hits me like a slap by Bridget Messler.

"*His* room? Here?" I look back and forth between them. "Why does he have a room here?" Even though I can guess already by the way Dana's eyes narrow in a glare at Mom, and the way Mom looks around like she wishes she had a whisk to frown at.

"Is Ephraim living here with Mom?" I blink at them, and then my jaw drops. "Wait, Dana, are *you* living here with Mom?"

Dana folds her arms across her chest and lifts her chin, giving her that extra half-inch of haughtiness. "It's just been the last couple weeks, but yes. Until we find our own place."

Mom shakes her head, her eyes locked on some place above my head, and for once I see the typical motherly disappointment directed (passive-aggressively, of course) at someone other than me. Or more recently, my father.

But I can barely take my eyes off of Dana. "Are you and Paul getting a divorce, too? What the hell is going *on* with all of you?"

"Really, Gabby, that's not called for," Mom says, though I get the feeling that her admonishment is more directed at me for grouping her problems with Dana's than at actually bringing up her divorce.

"We're separated," Dana says with a sniff. "Paul and I have discussed it, and we don't believe in divorce. Not until Ephraim is much older. The studies clearly have shown—"

"Why?" I couldn't care less about studies. "Just this past Christmas, Paul surprised you with that big Greek Isles cruise for the two of you."

She stiffens even more, if that's possible. "That was what started it, actually. Paul had been accusing me of working too much, and we started fighting about it all the time. That was his none-too-subtle dig at how I needed to take time off."

I blink, waiting for more. Waiting, perhaps, for the shocking reveal that the travel agent he'd used to book the trip was also his mistress. Or that there's a secret bank account she'd traced the cruise tickets back to. But she doesn't say anything more, just stares at me as if daring me to speak.

I take that dare. "And?"

"And!" She flings her arm out, looking at Mom for support against her obviously maritally challenged little sister, but Mom busies herself with putting her designer heels into a box. Dana returns her glare to me. "*And* he obviously has no respect for my career! He wants to be the big man in the industry, doesn't want to get edged out by his wife. *I'm*, of course, the one that needs to take time off, to spend more time with Ephraim."

I refrain from pointing out the cruise would have actually forced Paul to take time off as well, unless he was planning on sending a body double for two weeks of olive tasting and couples' Swedish massages. Once started on her anti-husband tirade, she appears to have no desire to stop.

"Why do you think he wants to go into business with Dad? So we can make enough money that I have to stay home. He claims that's not his intention, but has he offered to scale back on work himself? Has he—"

"Was anyone going to tell me?" I cut in. "Ever? Or are we waiting for the next fun-filled family dinner?"

Mom and Dana meet eyes again, doing that unspoken mother-daughter conversation thing I apparently missed the training session on. Finally, Mom clears her throat. "Things have been so . . . up in the air for you lately, Gabby, we didn't want to burden you."

"Up in the air," I say numbly. "You mean, because you think my life is a mess."

Felix's words echo in my head: *You mess up all the time. No one gives a shit.*

Mom grips a pair of silver Louboutins and doesn't answer. It feels like my conversation with Will all over again, only worse. Because my whole life, all I've wanted was to fit into my over-achieving family. All I've really wanted was to be part of them, rather than the background to their perfection.

But they aren't perfect, are they? No longer are their lives spotlights that only serve to cast mine in shadows. In fact, something has suddenly become very, very clear to me.

They never had been.

"Why don't I get started on dinner," Mom says, as if I hadn't just had a life-altering revelation.

A life-altering revelation I am not about to keep to myself.

I jump to my feet. "No way. You don't get to call my life a mess and run. You stay right there."

I must have been picking up a few lessons from Sarah ordering around her prop minions, because Mom actually does so, her eyes wide.

She starts to look over at Dana, but I cut that off, too. "And none of that, either, that weird telepathic thing you guys have when it comes to judging me."

Mom has the decency to look slightly shamed, but Dana just purses her lips. The judgment isn't going anywhere any time soon.

But I know one thing—I have their attention now, in a way I haven't before, maybe ever.

"Look, maybe I have screwed up a lot," I say. "I dropped out of college, I don't have a boyfriend with an Ivy League degree or a large investment portfolio, or even a boyfriend who, you know, exists. I can't even keep a job as glorified set dressing for a soap opera. I can't . . ." I trail off. I should probably get on with my point, rather than confirming theirs.

"I've always known I wasn't like you guys. I wasn't like you, Mom, with your perfect marriage and successful career, or you, Dana, with your drive and your brains and seriously, how did you end up both the smart *and* pretty one? It sucks! Or Felix, who is so gifted and creative . . ." My stomach clenches at the mention of Felix, at hearing his voice in my head, begging me for help and raging at me in fury when I wouldn't.

The voice of someone not my brother at all.

I let the ache continue to fuel my anger.

"But you know what? You don't get to call my life a mess anymore! None of you! You left your husband because he bought you a *cruise*? And Mom, you and Dad are getting divorced because it's 'just time'? And Felix is in rehab and no one tells each other *anything*."

I feel like tears should be springing up in my eyes like they were with Will, but this feels too right to be sad about, too long overdue. Mom opens her mouth to speak, then closes it, while Dana just folds her arms and stares at the floor.

"I love you guys, I do, but I'm done. I'm done thinking that I'm somehow not worthy of being in this family, that I'm some weird genetic accident. And I'm done being treated like the one you all have to pity. I'll figure out my life, okay? I will."

I swallow, and it hits me that I actually mean it. I've tried to tell myself this so many times, and it's generally as meaningless as telling myself I'll try Bikram yoga someday, but this time I feel deep down that it's true.

196

"I can *do* this. I can make something of myself," I continue, buoyed by this understanding. "And if I were you, I'd worry more about figuring out—"

My phone rings from my pocket, cutting off the dramatic end to my tirade with Marvin Gaye crooning out "Sexual Healing." I flush, inwardly cursing Anna-Marie and her constantly changing my ring tone when I'm in the shower.

"Your own lives," I finish, with much less indignant flourish than I had intended, fishing my phone out of my pocket. Even during the personal awakening of the backbone I was starting to think I'd been born without, I can't turn away the sharp stab of hope that maybe Will is on the other end. Apologizing. Declaring his love to me. Even just accidentally butt-dialing me.

It's not Will, but Anna-Marie.

I debate just declining the call, but Anna-Marie should be at work still, and she never calls me from work unless she needs a ride.

Mom raises her eyebrow. Answering the phone during conversations is a big no-no on her social etiquette list, along with having a ringtone about sex, I'm guessing.

"I've got to, uh—I'm going to take this," I say, trying to keep the forceful, 'I don't give a shit about your opinion' vibe I'd been doing so well with. Dana rolls her eyes and turns to head up the stairs. Mom gives me a long look I can't read, then stands up and leaves the room.

Apparently, my allotted rant time is up.

I answer the phone. Anna-Marie is sobbing on the other end.

"Anna! What's wrong?"

"They fired me," she says, her words choked between fresh sobs. "Sarah j-just called. They're going to get a new Helena."

"What? How—"

"She said she found Bridget's fake Emmy hidden in my work locker! I swore I didn't take it, but she wouldn't believe me. I'm not allowed to go back to the set, and Bridget's even thinking of pressing criminal charges! It's all over, I'm done in the industry!"

"Oh, Anna," is all I can say, and my heart breaks at hearing my best friend break down over the phone. I listen to her relate the conversation in painstaking detail, as I leave the house without even saying goodbye to anyone and get into my car. My newfound determination to fix my own life surges in me past all rational thought, and apparently this determination includes fixing my best friend's life too.

It's the only way I can explain my next words:

"I'm on my way home. And we're going to fix this."

TWENTY-ONE

Determination to fix things can only take one so far, especially when the one who needs the help is in straight-up wallow mode. And Anna-Marie is riding that wallow train right into self-pity junction. I know this train well, having taken it so many times (and so recently) myself.

We don't eat ice cream together to bring Anna-Marie out of her funk. That's my coping mechanism, not hers. We do drink copious amounts of wine and spend the evening bad-mouthing everyone involved with *Passion Medical*—some deservedly, some not—and every stupid, overly contrived storyline, all deservedly (sorry, Will). We watch *Buffy the Vampire Slayer* and cry at the end of season two. We drunkenly dance to songs from boy bands that haven't existed since we were in high school. We fall asleep somewhere around four AM and wake up to vomit around seven.

All in all, a respectable, if somewhat clichéd, way to dull pain for an evening.

But it doesn't make things any better the next day. Anna-Marie doesn't drag herself out of bed until well into the afternoon, and even then it's only to flop onto the couch listlessly.

Old Gabby would have just let her. After all, Old Gabby has done plenty of listless couch-flopping herself. New Gabby, the one determined to take control of her life and apparently now Anna-Marie's, is going to help her friend make this right. Somehow.

Okay, so New Gabby doesn't exactly have a plan. She's New, after all.

I flop next to Anna-Marie and put my arm around her, even though she still smells faintly of vomit. "All right. We've drunk and Whedoned. Now what can I do to help you fix this?"

"My life's over. There's nothing anyone can do for me."

"Your life isn't over. You're Anna-Marie Freaking Halsey!"

She mumbles something into a couch cushion. I can't totally make it out, but it had the word "criminal" in it.

"You didn't steal that stupid statue, and everyone knows it. I bet even Sarah knows it but just wanted the whole thing done with so badly, she didn't care what you lost in the process." Any pity I had on Sarah for having to constantly scurry around making things perfect for Bernard is long gone. "You'd never do something like that. You have no reason to. June, on the other hand—"

"You think June framed me?" Anna-Marie lifts her head off the cushion enough to drag an already snotty sleeve back under her nose.

I frown. Last night had been about emotional triage, and lots and lots of wine, so we hadn't really gotten into the details of it all. But the truth is, someone put that statue into Anna-Marie's locker. The irony of Anna-Marie being framed after her character has tried to put half of Hartsburg in jail for crimes they didn't commit isn't lost on me, but I don't think now is the best time to bring that up.

"I don't know," I say. "I mean, she really is the one most likely to have taken the statue, right? No one else hates Bridget as much, and with their history, June definitely seems to know how to push Bridget's buttons."

"But what does that horrible shrew have against *me*? I haven't done anything to her."

Except maybe call her a horrible shrew, bat-shit crazy, and a handful of other names over the past several weeks. Though it's nothing that isn't being said by the better part of the *Passion Medical* crew and probably a large portion of the soap-viewing public.

"You can't think of anything she might have against you?" I ask. Anna-Marie's eyes dart away too quickly, and I sigh. "Okay, spill it."

Anna-Marie lets out a little huff. "She may have caught me doing an impression of her latest rant for some of the sound crew. Complete with pantyhose."

I wince. June would not have taken that well.

She tugs her lower lip between her teeth, cringing, and I have a terrible feeling that there's more. She confirms this by continuing with, "And I *may* have used a couple prop mustaches to give myself these massive bushy eyebrows, you know, because June has some serious eyebrows and—"

"Anna-Marie Halsey!"

She looks chagrined. "I know! I just got carried away, and Max the cute boom mic guy thought it was super funny and . . . I shouldn't have done it, I know." She picks at the edge of an old wine stain on the couch.

Really, her impression *was* probably hilarious, and part of me wants her to re-enact it right now. But maybe that, too, should be saved for whenever I bring up the whole irony thing.

"But for her to *frame* me, to get me *fired* . . ." Anna-Marie continues, her eyes narrowed. I can see her listless wallowing turning into a desire to track down June Blair and beat her with a giant party sub.

"We don't actually know it was June," I say quickly. "Lots of people could have taken the statue. Bridget's dressing room isn't exactly Fort Knox. And neither is your locker. Is there anyone else you can think of who might . . . I don't know, have wanted you to take the fall for it?"

Anna-Marie sits sullenly for a few minutes, but I can tell she's thinking it through. "I congratulated one of the makeup artists on her pregnancy," she says.

"Let me guess, she'd just had a big lunch or something?"

"Oh no, she's pregnant. I thought everyone knew. Problem is, her boyfriend was right there, and he definitely didn't." Anna-Marie grimaces. "Turns out it isn't his."

"Yikes."

"She's better off. Their very public breakup fight had a lot about him being obsessed with Nickelback and frisbee golf." She shudders. "But I doubt she would have taken the statue to begin with. She's Team Bridget, all the way." Anna-Marie's brow is furrowed.

"Okay," I say, chewing on my lip. "Is there anyone else you might have—"

Anna-Marie's glower turns on me. "How many people exactly do you think I've managed to piss off enough to *frame me?*"

"That's not what I—" Okay, it sort of is what I meant, but the truth is that while Anna-Marie can be a bit over-dramatic at times and has a tendency towards bluntness, she actually gets along pretty well with most people. "Look, for all we know, whoever stole the statue didn't actually have a grudge against you. Maybe they just needed *someone* to take the fall for it, and your locker just happened to get picked."

"Lucky me," she mutters, hunching back into the couch cushions.

"If we could just figure out why someone would take the statue in the first place, like who would benefit from that . . ." I run through names in my mind, but nothing seems to make sense. If it wasn't June who did it, whoever stole the statue would have to know Bridget would blame June for it. And Bridget and June's feud continuing seems to only create problems for most of the cast and crew. Sarah and Bernard are both more miserable and on edge with everything falling apart, the writers are scrambling to churn out new scenes at the last minute, and I hadn't noticed any of the other actors in particular getting more screen time or attention. "Maybe one of the crew stole it to pawn or something, and hoped that Bridget wouldn't notice, but she did, and—"

Anna-Marie groans and slumps back onto the arm rest. "It doesn't matter. I'm the one who got fired for it. And maybe not everyone will believe I did it, but Bridget does. One of the great acting legends, and she thinks I stole her Emmy!" Tears swim in her blue eyes.

"Fake Emmy. And acting legend may be overstating it." But my heart is breaking for her. Bridget is one of her idols, the whole reason she wanted to give this soap opera thing a real shot. To have someone you admire so much think of you that way . . .

"If I could just *talk* to her, maybe she'd believe me," Anna-Marie says with a sniffle. "But Sarah made it very clear I'm not allowed back on set. That they'd call security if I tried. They're mailing me my things! Like after some awful breakup!"

This is taking a far worse toll on Anna-Marie than any breakup she's ever had, awful or not. I desperately wish there was something I could do.

And then I think of something.

I pat her greasy head. "I'll get some more DVDs to watch." But instead when I go into my room and close the door behind me, I pull out my phone and scroll through my contact list until I find Will.

My finger hesitates above the button. After our last conversation—a word I use loosely—there's a good chance he won't want to talk to me, let alone feel like he owes me anything. There's a good chance I shouldn't be so keen on talking to him or calling in favors.

But this is my chance to do something real to help Anna-Marie. And, well, talk to Will again. No matter how much that scares me.

I press the button, finally understanding the phrase "having your heart in your throat."

He answers on the second ring. "Gabby, hey." I can't quite

read his tone. Not angry. Not excited. Maybe . . . cautious?

"Hey," I respond, my mind suddenly frozen up.

He saves me from my sudden inability to perform basic societal functions like talking on the phone. "I'm really glad you called. The other day . . . I just really want you to know I'm sorry. And now, with Anna-Marie . . ."

Her name gets the gears chugging along again in my brain. "Anna-Marie. Yeah. She's pretty upset. Sarah accused her of stealing Bridget's Emmy. You know she didn't do it."

There is a pause and then a sigh. "It was found in the dressing room, Gabby. In her personal locker."

My mouth flaps open so suddenly I am truly glad we are having this conversation over the phone and not in person. "You actually think she stole that stupid Bubble-Time award!"

"No, no," he says hastily. "I don't, really. It's just, the evidence is all there, right? Sarah was in a tough spot. Bernard's been threatening—"

"I don't care about Sarah or Bernard. I care about my friend, who is totally innocent and lost a job she loved."

"I get that. I do. But I don't think anyone will listen to me. Bridget and June are back to barely tolerating each other, and even though it's totally unfair, they're the ones Bernard cares about."

The ones Sarah cares about, too, I want to add, but I don't. I don't want to beg him to talk to her on Anna-Marie's behalf, don't want to think about them having late-night conversations in a bed covered in scripts and all the evidence of their shared life, both personally and professionally.

"I know. I don't need you to talk to anyone. But I am going to ask for a favor."

A longer pause this time. Then: "Because of how truly bad I feel for all that I've cost you, I'm tempted to say 'anything.' But I can't promise that. I'm just a lowly writer."

"I don't need a miracle. Anna-Marie just wants to have a few minutes with Bridget. To make sure Bridget knows she didn't do it."

He groans. "Not a miracle? You might as well ask for me to get her job back. Which," he adds quickly, "I have absolutely no way to do."

"A couple minutes, that's all."

"And what if she does convince Bridget? Then Bridget and June are back to hating each other and refusing to work together."

"Maybe," I say, trying to keep the frustration out of my voice. "But Anna-Marie deserves a chance to speak for herself, don't you think? This isn't a soap opera. This is her life."

Then I say the word I had promised myself I wouldn't, because it would be too pathetic, too needy. But I *am* needy, on my friend's behalf anyway. "Please."

I can practically hear him thinking. "I'll see what I can do," he says, finally. "If I can arrange this, I expect a dozen cronuts in payment."

I didn't expect to smile at any point during this conversation, but it happens. "A dozen? Try one. I don't have a job anymore, remember?"

"Ouch. Yes. One it is. With chocolate filling."

"Done."

TWENTY-TWO

"This is probably a bad idea," Anna-Marie says as we sit in my car, parked closer to the other studios on Sudser Lane than the *Passion Medical* one so no one will recognize my cheap Hyundai.

She is very likely right. Will certainly thinks so. But he also feels like he owes me, and this is what I asked of him in the heat of my hungover indignation.

Plus, it feels good to actually be *doing* something. Old Gabby let things happen to her. New Gabby goes out and bribes her crushes with donuts to help her engage in dubiously legal activities.

It feels like an improvement.

"It'll be good. You'll have your say with Bridget and a chance to declare your innocence."

"Which will be good for what, exactly, when she yells for security and they put me in prison?" She wrings the seatbelt strap across her chest in her hands.

"Hartsburg city jail? That thing only has three walls."

She does not appreciate my attempt at humor. "Real prison."

"You're not breaking any laws. The worst thing they can do is escort you out."

The look on her face indicates she thinks that to be a worse fate. After all, every starlet needs at least one good mug shot, but no one wants to be the crazy person escorted off a set.

"We don't have to do this," I say. Part of me really hopes she'll take me up on this. The other part of me—the traitorous part—really wants to see Will, and knows I won't have any reason to after this.

She purses her lips, then unclicks her seat belt. "No, I can't have Bridget Messler think I'm a thief. I can't have it."

"Thata girl."

I'm sounding much more confident than I actually feel, though my nervousness selfishly is more about seeing Will again. I take a deep breath and text Will as we walk toward the set, so he can be prepared for our arrival. We are dressed in crew member black and oversized sunglasses, and Anna-Marie has her hair pulled back under a baseball cap. I can't tell if we look more like we're ready to move props or rob a convenience store, but we should blend in nicely once inside.

Will meets us out in the parking lot. He looks uncomfortable, trying too hard to be casual, leaning against the side of the building at too steep an angle. I am reminded that he is no actor.

He smiles when he sees us, but his fingers fidget with a pen, which he drops and has to pick up again before we reach him. Twice. Something about him seeming so nervous makes me slightly less so.

God, he's adorable. And I am awful for making him do this. I really hope we don't end up getting him fired, too, given that it wouldn't take Sherlock-level detective skills to find out he was the one who messengered us the guest passes that let us on the lot.

"Are you really okay with this?" I ask when we get close enough.

His eyebrow raises. "Do you have my cronut?"

I pull it out of my purse. "I had them put extra sprinkles on it."

The dimple appears in his cheek. "Then I'm okay with this.

Hey, Anna-Marie," he says, as if he just noticed her for the first time.

I don't think that's ever happened when Anna-Marie and I are standing near one another, but she doesn't seem to mind. "Hey, Will. Thanks so much. I didn't steal it, you know. I would never do something like that."

"I know. And I'm sorry. I'm sorry on Sarah's behalf, too."

I'm not entirely sure what this means, but apparently enough that he's willing to arrange a meeting with Bridget for us. For Anna-Marie, at least. I'm just there for moral support. And maybe one last round at the craft services table.

We keep our heads down as we walk in, and Will stops us just before we turn the corner to walk past the bustling set. The scene in progress is Trevor Everlake with the actress playing his current girlfriend, Laura, the Black girl he'd been passionately kissing back when he was supposed to be operating on Oliver Hart.

They aren't kissing now. Laura is swiping tears from her eyes. "How could you cheat on me, Trevor? And with *her*!"

Trevor looks chastened. "I never meant to hurt you. But my heart is Helena's, and—"

Laura gasps. "You love her?"

I miss whatever Trevor is about to respond with, because Will leans in close to me and my heartbeat starts pounding in my ears.

"Gabby, I'm really sorry about what happened. You were right that I was meddling. You were right about everything."

My breath catches. "I was right about—"

Will flinches. "Not about you not being strong. That's not why—I just—I need to—"

I need to not have this conversation, right here, right now, with a guy who is still engaged to the person who got my best friend fired to save her own ass. "Are you sure this is where we should be waiting?" I ask.

Will hesitates. "I think so," he says quietly. "Let me go check Bridget's schedule again, make sure they haven't made any last minute changes."

I nod, while Anna-Marie looks more panicked than ever. Which makes sense, I suppose. She's the one planning on lying in wait for Bridget Messler in her dressing room and praying the old woman doesn't have some kind of secret judo mastery and a low threshold for using it.

Just as Will leaves, I hear Bernard yelling at someone. Apparently the scene is over. We almost get run over by an irritated HD, pulling a pack of cigarettes out of his pocket as he turns the corner to head outside.

"Ladies," he says, with a tight smile and slight tip of his chin, his eyes not really landing on us as he passes us. At least I think they don't, until he stops and does a double take. "Anna-Marie? What are you doing here, you're not supposed to be—"

"I know," she says, and I can tell by the way her left cheek sinks in slightly that she's chewing it, debating how much to tell him. "I just . . . I forgot something in my locker, and . . ."

HD raises an eyebrow. For an actress who excels in improv bank robbery musical theatre, Anna-Marie is a crappy on-the-spot liar.

"Fine," she says, breathing out in a huff. "I didn't steal that statue. And I just wanted a chance to tell that to Bridget myself. That's all. I swear."

HD fiddles with a cigarette between two knuckles and then nods. "I get it. I never thought you were the one who stole that ridiculous thing, anyway." Anna-Marie looks relieved, at least until he continues with, "You have no reason to get that desperate for attention until you're at least thirty."

Then she looks like she might murder him, so I step in.

"We'll just be here for a few minutes and then we're gone. Please don't tell anyone, especially Sarah."

He notices my presence finally (not a big surprise there), and breaks into a dazzling grin (which is a huge surprise, and makes parts of me tingle pleasantly, damn him). "Hey, it's you."

"You noticed," I say.

His smile slips as he tries to process my reply, but then he gives up and launches ahead anyway. "I wanted to thank you. For your advice the other night."

Anna-Marie's eyebrows draw together in confusion, and it occurs to me that I never told her about HD's discussion with me. Between the whole Sean thing, and the Felix thing, and the Will thing (basically between all the men around me making my life miserable), my weird bonding session with HD had totally slipped my mind.

"Uh, no problem. It, um, worked out?"

HD grins again, though not in the usual hot Trevor Everlake way. Kind of in a dopey way. The way of a guy in love. "Totally. I told her everything I loved about her, every little thing I've noticed this past year that makes me wish I could be with her every minute of every day. And she was super into it."

"Who are we talking about exactly?" Anna-Marie asks, her nervousness giving way to curiosity. The girl does love good gossip, even about her lovers, apparently. "I'm not jealous, by the way. Just really, really confused."

HD gives her such a patronizingly sympathetic look that I itch to smack him. "It has nothing to do with you, of course. You were great. You were—"

"I said I'm not jealous!" Her tone doesn't help her case, though I know it's true.

"Great, I'm glad," I say, looking past him for Will. Despite our shared night of airing our various romantic grievances, HD's love/lust life isn't really at the top of my priorities right now, especially since his talking to us for very long could draw undue attention.

"She's dumping that writer's ass tonight. She's wanted to be with me since the first time we hooked up, but she doesn't like hurting people's feelings."

Anna-Marie snorts, but I have the sudden sensation of my guts dropping down to my feet.

It can't be, can it? "A writer? Oh God, it isn't . . . It's Sarah, isn't it? Sarah Paltrow." I sound about as strangled as I suddenly feel.

HD smirks. "Even BB can't resist this."

"God, you're an idiot, Ryan," Anna-Marie mutters. But she's watching me carefully, like she knows everything going on in my head before even I do.

I don't bother to tell him that calling his new love BB when she probably understands perfectly well what that means is not a great idea. Instead I'm a jumble of emotions: panic, guilt . . . excitement? More guilt because of that last one.

"She's engaged," I manage.

HD waves his hand dismissively. "I told you, no longer a problem. Or won't be."

My mouth is dry, my thoughts reeling, then going back to rest on another bomb he'd dropped.

"You hooked up with her? Before today?"

"Of course. I hook up with everyone. No offense intended."

"None taken," Anna-Marie and I both say absently in unison and look at each other.

But all I can think about is Will. My poor Will.

No, I correct myself. Not *my* Will. Never *my* Will. He was always Sarah's Will, even when she wasn't always his.

"Will," Anna-Marie says urgently, looking pointedly over HD's shoulder.

There he is, walking back in a way that looks even more fake than his previous attempt at casual standing.

HD looks back and gives Will a nod.

A nod. As if he isn't sleeping with Will's fiancée and about to be the cause of breaking Will's heart.

I hate HD right now. And even though I really truly had no idea about HD and Sarah, I hate myself for giving him that advice.

"Thanks again," he says with a wink and heads outside before I can strangle him with his stethoscope.

"Shit," Will says, his eyes wide. "Ryan saw you guys?"

Anna-Marie nods. "But it's cool. He's not going to tell anyone."

211

Will looks skeptical at the thought of trusting HD (as well he should be), but then he meets my eyes, and I realize I've been openly staring at him. And probably with horror. "Gabby, are you okay?"

I swallow past the Bubble-Time award-sized lump in my throat. He deserves some kind of warning, right? Some hint, at least?

Anna-Marie is watching me intently, and I can see the pleading in her eyes. I can't say anything now, not when Anna-Marie needs her time with Bridget. And maybe I shouldn't say anything at all, even then.

He's not my Will. Not mine, I repeat over and over in my head.

"Just want to get this over with before anyone else sees us," I say, and he eyes me for a heartbeat longer before nodding and gesturing us to follow him.

Guilt is a solid thing in my chest as we walk behind him past the set, where people are scrambling about to set up the next scene. I keep my face hidden by the brim of my hat, though I probably don't need to do so, because the only people who are likely to recognize me are Karen, Clint, and Sarah. The first two aren't anywhere to be seen, and the last one is busy watching the live set.

The scene about to be filmed is a bigger one, apparently, another gala of sorts where everyone is dressed fancier than normal and carrying around tall flutes of what appears to be champagne but is really just cheap sparkling cider.

Katarina Gunn is up there, and Diego, along with Lucy St. James (June, who I can't help but glare at even as I'm admiring how elegant she looks in that sparkling column sheath) and Dame Sondra Hart, Bridget Messler herself. Bridget's face is pinched and pale, and she's gripping the glass so tightly I think it's going to shatter. I wonder if Sarah or Bernard notice, but Bernard is too busy yelling at the actor playing Diego to have "more fire in his eyes," and Sarah is hastily scribbling notes.

"Bridget has one more scene, and then she's done for lunch,

so you'll have your time then to—" Will starts, but Anna-Marie stops so suddenly I run into her.

"Who is *that*?" she hisses. There's only one actress up there I don't recognize, a gorgeous dark-haired woman in an off-the-shoulder red cocktail dress.

"Um." Will looks at me for help, but I am clearly no help to anyone right now. "That's Helena," he says.

"*No.* They already have a new Helena? Those pieces of sh—" Anna-Marie hisses. I grip her arm so she won't storm the set. Not that I think she really would, but it's better to be safe than sorry.

Anna-Marie shakes off my grip, which isn't hard, since my palms are unreasonably sweaty. "How can they already have a new girl? Wait a minute, were they *planning* on firing me? Was this all—"

"Why don't you go to the dressing room now?" I cut her off before she can work herself up any more. "We know Bridget's not there, and we don't know how much longer this scene will last."

Anna-Marie scowls, but nods. Then she stalks off to the dressing rooms, and I'm hoping no else notices how she looks like she's within an inch of upending the craft services table out of pure spite.

I stand there awkwardly with Will, wishing I didn't know about HD and Sarah. Wishing even more that I hadn't been part of what Sarah is about to do to Will.

Up on the gala set, Lucy St. James clutches something to her chest, her expression one of horror and anger. She stalks up to Sondra Hart, who is chatting with Oliver.

"You," Lucy gasps, and Sondra turns to face her. For a moment, I worry it's actually June about to attack Bridget, rather than just their characters facing off, but everyone else in the scene keeps going, miming silently in the background. "It was you all along!"

"I'm sure I have no idea what you're talking about," Sondra says, drawing herself up stiffly.

"My mugging," Lucy insists. "He was paid with this!" She

thrusts out her hand, and I can see the thing she was clutching earlier is some kind of necklace, the gold glittering under the set lights. "This could only have come from you, you . . . you monster!"

Despite this scene being the climax of the mugging arc, I'm less paying attention to the actors than I am trying *not* to pay attention to the fact that Will is watching me. Like he knows I'm keeping something from him.

"Bridget doesn't look too good," I say, partially because I need something to say. And partially because Bridget really doesn't look too good. As I watch her, she sways, gripping the back of a couch. Possibly an acting choice, but her face is pale even underneath her layers of makeup, and the way she's leaning onto the couch makes it look like she's trying to keep her knees from buckling.

Will follows my gaze. "I heard her complaining about chest pains earlier, but when Sarah tried to call a doctor, Bridget just said something like 'the show waits for no health crisis' and demanded to do her scene." He let out a weary breath, shaking his head. "I swear, that woman lives to make everyone's lives more difficult."

By everyone, he really means Sarah, of course.

Sarah. Who he still loves, who is about to—

"Gabby," Will says, his voice soft, much lower than the voices of the scene being filmed in the background. I can feel my nails against my sweaty palms as I ball my hands into fists. Is this where he's going to bring up the feelings I confessed the other day? Is this where he's going to tell me once and for all that he just wants to be friends, even though deep down he really wishes he'd never have to see me again?

I already told him I don't want to talk about it. "We don't have to—" I start, but he shakes his head.

"No, I need to tell you. I trust you, Gabby, and I need to tell someone . . ." He stares down at the floor. "Sarah and I—things haven't been going well, not for a long time."

My breath catches in my throat. What is he saying? Is he ending things with her?

If he wants my advice, do I tell him what I know? I have to, right? Would that be genuine friendship or just self-serving?

As my mind reels, I glance back at the set, both trying and not trying to see Sarah there. Who I end up really seeing, though, is Bridget. Her eyes are blinking too rapidly, and she struggles to suck in a breath as June continues to rail at her with her character's accusations.

"I just don't know if I should—" he starts again, but I cut him off, a new horror settling in my stomach.

"I don't think she's doing it for attention," I say. "I think she's really—"

And before I can finish, Bridget collapses.

TWENTY-THREE

There is a single frozen moment in which no one does anything, just stares in shock. Thinking, I'm sure, that this is just the old actress's bid for attention. Even seeing how bad she looked before collapsing, the thought runs through my mind.

Then Sarah jumps up on to the set, bulldozing her way through gorgeously-attired actors.

"Bridget!" she yells, pressing her hands against Bridget's face, against her neck. At least I think that's what she's doing, from what I can tell around the press of people blocking my view. I can only partially see her through their feet (thankfully many of the women are wearing shorter cocktail dresses rather than the floor-length ball gowns). "Someone call 911! June, call 911!"

June Blair blanches. "I don't have my phone! You told us not to bring phones on set!"

Sarah swears loudly and creatively.

Will has his phone out and is dialing. "Sarah, I've got it! I'm calling—yes, we have an emergency . . ."

Though I have the urge to duck behind him as Sarah's head swivels in my direction, she clearly either doesn't notice me in all the chaos or doesn't care. "She's not breathing," she calls out. "Does anyone know CPR? Someone here has to know CPR, we're on a bloody hospital show!"

My throat closes up, and for a panicked second I pray that someone will jump in and save the day. Someone other than me. But the actors are all looking at each other in horror, the crew members are standing stock-still. Clint clutches his VitaminWater like a talisman. Over behind the reception desk, Karen is fluttering one of her hands wildly over her chest like a wounded bird. Bernard drops his head in his hands.

With my throat feeling paralyzed, it's a wonder any voice at all comes out of me. But it does, if not loudly. "I do."

It is enough to get Sarah's attention. "You!" Her face pinches tight, and then she waves me forward.

I run to the stage, the panic making my legs rubbery. Will I even remember what I learned in that stupid CPR class? I'm not even certified! The teacher said I killed Steve!

No. That dummy would have lived. I'm sure of it.

I can do this.

Of course, that was what I thought before my big line, and look how that turned out.

I push aside the terror-stricken arguments with myself and kneel beside Bridget. The woman looks so much older close-up, her face pale, her caked-on makeup cracking along her wrinkles, her closed eyelids a sickly purplish hue that I don't think is all eyeshadow.

She is clearly not breathing.

"She's in respiratory failure," I announce, rather unnecessarily. Since Will had already called 911, I know that the ambulance is on its way. I just have to keep her alive until they can make it here. "Do we have a defibrillator anywhere?"

Sarah nods, her own face ashen, and dashes off.

I suck in a shaky breath and try to imagine it's a torso of a dummy I've named Steve in front of me and not the most revered actress in the soap opera world. And an old, fragile one at that.

I begin the chest compressions. It comes back to me quickly, all the notes I dutifully took that day, that cheesy video I watched, the feel of cold rubber under my hands as I fought to save Steve the dummy's life.

It is different, of course, on a real live person, and I can't completely shake the knowledge of who exactly I'm working to save.

But I do it anyway. I settle into the rhythm, chest compressions over and over. Still nothing. I try to ignore the dozens of people watching me, the murmurs, HD asking "What the hell's going on?" as he returns from his smoke break.

I can't do this, I think. *I'm messing it up, like I always do, only this time it's someone's life at stake and—*

"No," I growl. It's meant to be in my head, but it spills out of my lips, and I don't care that everyone hears me. "Do this, Gabby. Do this."

I begin the next round of compressions, gritting my teeth together as if I can will this to work, *will* her to live.

"I've got the defibrillator!" Sarah yells, knocking people aside to drop to her knees beside me.

Panic squeezes my innards. The defibrillator. I'd been drilled into asking for one, and I'd seen the video tutorial, but I'd stomped out of the class before practicing how to use one.

Well, no time like the present.

I finish my round of compressions and reach to grab it when Bridget shudders and gasps, her eyes flying open wildly.

She's not the only one to gasp. I do as well, utterly shocked by my own success.

"Bridget!" Sarah says, attempting to hold one of the woman's bony hands, but Bridget Messler is having none of it, her arms flailing about as she sucks in deep breaths. Several people standing around us cheer and clap. Karen yells, "Team Reception!" Bernard, on the other hand, tosses his script to the ground with a loud curse and a "That's it, I'm done," and stalks off the set.

I'm too stunned to know what to do next. I'm not even sure this was covered in CPR training, at least not the part I was there for. Sarah speaks to her in soothing tones I wouldn't previously have thought the cold Brit capable of. I feel a hand on my shoulder and look up to see Will. He grins at me, and suddenly it hits me: I saved Bridget Messler's life.

The EMTs push through the crowd. I was so involved in my CPR I don't even remember hearing the ambulance siren, and wow, they came quickly. Is there a special hospital for elderly actors right here on the lot? They do their thing, checking her pulse, applying an oxygen mask, lifting her onto one of those collapsible little cart-beds. I stand in a daze, watching it all, barely feeling the comforting pressure of Will's hand on my back until all at once it's gone.

"I'm going to go see her to the ambulance," Will says, and I nod, only belatedly realizing he's actually saying this to Sarah when she nods too.

He heads out with them and Sarah has finished telling one of the EMTs what happened—with a point over to me during, I'm assuming, the part about performing CPR—when she finally focuses on me. Her face is still pale, her expression unreadable.

I swallow, and try to think of an explanation for why I'm here, for why I was standing so very close to Sarah's fiancé just moments before Bridget collapsed. I prepare myself for having guards drag me out, heroic saving or no.

Sarah flings herself at me and wraps me in a tight hug. Even just having saved a woman's life is not more of a shock than this. I don't know what to do with my arms, which are mostly pinned at my side. I awkwardly pat her on the back as much as I can.

"Thank you," she whispers, and when she pulls back I see tears shining in her blue eyes. Then, as if suddenly aware that we're standing in a crowd of actors and crew members, she clears her throat. "But I think you need to leave the set now. You and Anna-Marie."

My gut twists. "I, uh, don't know what—"

"I know everything that happens on my set," Sarah says, giving me a hard look that is somewhat lessened by her previous display.

"Anna-Marie didn't do it," I say. I keep my voice low, but I know several of the actors around me can hear. "Anna-Marie would never steal that statue and you know it, Sarah. You know who did." I glare at June Blair, who crosses her arms in front of her chest, but doesn't otherwise react.

Sarah shifts, her whole frame rigid.

"And I didn't break it, either." Anna-Marie's voice comes suddenly from behind me. I spin around to see her standing just below the set, holding up a golden statue that does, admittedly, look very similar to a Daytime Emmy award, except the figure is holding up a cluster of what looks like soap bubbles rather than a large globe.

"You both have five minutes, and then I'm calling security," Sarah says, the icy demeanor fully back. HD places a hand on her shoulder, and she shrugs it off.

"What do you mean, break it?" June Blair asks, her dark eyes narrowed. "I thought it was just stolen. And *not* by me." This last she says with a withering glare at me.

Anna-Marie steps up onto the set. "I was waiting in Bridget's dressing room to try to talk to her, and I saw this. Look," she says, pointing at a thin crack along the part connecting the figure to the base. "Bridget had showed me her Emmy—"

"Fake Emmy," June mutters darkly.

"—only a few days before it went missing. It's been broken since, and whoever super-glued this thing back together did a shit job of it."

She's right; I can see the bubble of badly applied glue frozen in mid-drip just below the crack. My mind is struggling to latch onto something, but between the CPR and the revelation about HD and Sarah . . .

"That doesn't prove anything," Sarah says. "It was still found in your locker, and you just admitted to having seen it only days before it was stolen."

HD.

Superglue.

Sarah.

Everything clicks horribly into place, even before I see the way HD is staring at the fake hospital floor to avoid meeting anyone's eyes.

He really isn't a very good actor.

"It was you," I say, the words escaping my lips before I can think of the possible repercussions. "You and H—Ryan. You and Ryan were having sex in Bridget's dressing room and you broke the statue."

The actors and crew members around us are looking back and forth between each other, gauging each other's reactions. Katarina Gunn gapes openly; June looks strangely thoughtful. Sarah's face goes bone-white, and then her cheeks start to turn bright pink.

Fury builds up in me, hot and reckless, and as she opens her mouth to defend herself or to call security or whatever she thinks might stop me, I cut her off.

"And then you framed Anna-Marie for it. Was that because she slept with Ryan? You got her fired, and now you need to make this right."

I have never stared someone down so openly, especially someone like Sarah, but New Gabby isn't backing down. This woman has lied and cheated and hurt two of the people I love—

I blink, my heart stuttering at that thought.

I love Anna-Marie, of course. She's my best friend. But Will. Can I use that word for him? Can I *not*?

I know the truth then, that I do love Will, and more than that—I'm *in* love with Will. My breath gets caught somewhere in my throat.

Is he still outside with the EMTs? I start to scan for him, but stop when Sarah grabs the walkie-talkie clipped to her belt.

"This is ridiculous," she says. "Leave now or you will be escorted out, and I will ensure that Bridget presses charges against you both."

I have no idea how I could be involved in any charges Bridget wants to press, unless I broke her sternum saving her life—oh god, I really hope I didn't break her sternum—but I am not leaving until Anna-Marie's name is cleared, even if I have to shout out my case to every extra and actor and lighting technician I pass as I'm being dragged out.

HD, however, saves me from this with a clearing of his throat. "Babe," he says, squeezing Sarah's arm. "Don't do this, okay? Let's just—let's do what she says. Let's make it right."

Perhaps Sarah has looked at HD lovingly at some point in the past, but she now appears to want to jam her walkie-talkie straight through his chest like some kind of finishing move in *Mortal Kombat: Soap Opera*.

HD doesn't seem bothered, he just lowers his hand from her shoulder to take hers. Then he looks at Anna-Marie and gives a little half-hearted shrug. "Hey, I'm sorry, but Bernard was going to fire you anyway. He never liked you. He'd wanted to hire someone with more experience."

"Ryan, I swear if you don't shut the hell up—" Sarah starts, but Anna-Marie cuts in over her, furious and hurt.

"I knew it! The minute I saw that new Helena, I knew that piece of shit director had it out for me!" The actress now playing Helena shrinks back behind Oliver Hart. I make my way over to Anna-Marie, sensing an explosion that may need to be contained. She's right, though. Bernard clearly has anger management issues, but he did especially seem to have it out for Anna-Marie.

HD continues. "So Sarah thought, well, we might as well . . ." He shrugs.

I remember Bernard's conversation with Sarah, her mentioning agents she was talking to, him mentioning a problem needing to be fixed—had that problem been *Anna-Marie*? Anna-Marie, who does her job reliably and professionally and is *great* at it?

I don't hate people often, but he's definitely on the list.

"And you!" Anna-Marie continues, rounding on HD. "How could you do this to me? I sat through the whole first act of your terrible play, which by the way does *not* 'fill an important void

222

in our cultural heritage,' no matter what your college drama professor says—"

I squeeze Anna-Marie's arm, and she wisely stops ranting, folding her arms across her chest with a loud huff. HD looks wounded at Anna-Marie's words—way more torn up about her critique than about, you know, framing her.

Sarah glares at both of us, but judging by the way it intensifies towards Anna-Marie, I have a feeling Anna-Marie's sleeping with HD might have weighed more heavily in Sarah's decision on who to frame than even he knew. "That's it," Sarah says. "I'm calling security."

HD grips Sarah's hand. "No, don't. We owe them. Look, without Gabby, we might never have gotten together. She's the one who convinced me to go for it, to tell you how I really feel."

I cringe, not wanting any part of this. "No, I didn't . . . well, okay. I mean, I may have said—"

HD continues on praising me even as he ignores my presence completely. "It was Gabby's advice that took it from just sex to—"

"To what?"

My heart plummets at that voice, so familiar, and yet never, never this cold.

Will.

He knows. And he knows I had a part in it.

He knows about my feelings for him, too, so he must think I did it on purpose.

"Oh, Lord," I hear Karen gasp from over by the reception desk, echoing my thoughts exactly.

I follow Sarah's wide blue eyes to where Will is standing just past the director's empty chair, next to Clint, who takes a big swig of his VitaminWater.

"To what?" he repeats, his face strangely expressionless. "It was just sex, is that all you were doing with my fiancée? And now it's what? What is it, Sarah?"

"Will," Sarah says. She drops HD's hand and takes a step

towards Will.

He shakes his head, and now I see it, the pain in his eyes as he looks at her, the tremble to his hands. "Never mind. Whatever it is, it has nothing to do with me anymore."

His gaze shifts to me. He doesn't say anything, but I am rooted to the spot by his look of betrayal, like *I'm* the one that threw away a guy like him for a jackass like HD.

I'm not. But I am at least partially to blame for what happened, and entirely to blame for him finding out about it this way, in front of everyone.

And he knows it.

I want to say his name, but no sound comes out.

He turns and walks away, and everyone on the set watches him in silence until he disappears around the corner and out of sight.

"Get out of here," Sarah says to me, in a voice barely above a whisper. Her eyes are red-rimmed, holding back tears. Tears I can't feel any sympathy for, not on her.

Anna-Marie is the one squeezing *my* arm now. "Come on, Gabby. Let's go," she says quietly.

Numbly, I follow her. Past June and Katarina Gunn and Karen, past Clint and his VitaminWater, past the catering table.

We make it outside, the bright sun blinding us. When the glare fades, I look around for Will, but can't see him anywhere.

Which is probably a good thing, since I am totally sure he doesn't want to see me right now.

"She has serious issues," Anna-Marie says, sounding much calmer now. "Like certifiable. Having sex in Bridget's dressing room? Framing me after she broke the statue? And I can't believe Ryan went along with it. What an asshole. I knew I should never have slept with him."

I want to say something to make her feel better—it can't be easy finding out that your sex friend took part in getting you fired—but I can't seem to make my thoughts move beyond that look on Will's face.

"That stuff about Bernard," I finally manage. "I'm so sorry.

You were great as Helena. He's just—"

"A total dick? With a god complex and drinking problem?" She shakes her head, as if clearing it of anything related to that tool of a director. "Whatever. I'll show him when I win my own Bubble-Time award."

"But you didn't even get to talk to Bridget," I say. "What are we going to do now?"

"It doesn't matter! Everyone knows what really happened now. That'll get back to Bridget. Hell, she'll probably read about it on about a dozen gossip sites before she gets out of the hospital." Anna-Marie beams at this, possibly far more than someone should be when referring to another person being in a hospital.

"And you were *brilliant*," she continues, throwing her arm over my shoulder as we walk. Leave it to Anna-Marie to be the one comforting *me* after all that. "Absolutely freaking brilliant. I had no idea you knew CPR!"

I sigh. "I took a class on it recently, but I didn't tell you because I didn't want you to realize I was trying to plan my life using a community education brochure."

Anna-Marie gives me a small, sympathetic smile. "I think I figured that out somewhere around the cake decorating class, actually. At least the CPR turned out to be good for something."

"I never got my certification," I say, digging the keys out of my pocket as we reach my car. "I got kicked out of class."

"Who cares? You saved Bridget Messler's life!" She shakes her head, still having trouble believing it. I do too.

But she's right. I failed at the class itself, but I did it. I saved someone's life.

And it felt amazing.

I try to hold on to the memory of that as we drive home.

TWENTY-FOUR

I have no idea how long one should wait before calling the person whose engagement you are indirectly responsible for ending. There's a good chance the answer is "just don't." But Will is my friend—after all we've been through, I hope I can at least still call him that—and I'm worried about him.

I'm also desperate to see him again, even if he hates me. Sad, but true.

A few days pass, with Anna-Marie stationed firmly on the couch, during which I sit next to her with my laptop and consider new employment options. Normally, I would be making a half-hearted attempt to pick up applications from random stores at the mall and call it a day, but I can't go back to just floundering around.

I find myself clicking through my college website, through all the degree programs I'd barely bothered to consider before, for one in particular: nursing. Even when I was just taking that CPR class (before, of course, the call from Felix that prompted my dramatic exit) there was something so satisfying about learning a tangible skill that could help someone—that could (and did!) save someone's life. I was always more interested in the fake medical disasters on set than I was in the spotlight. And when it comes to the schooling, I haven't been away so long I couldn't go back, though the thought scares me.

The thought of spending my life jumping from one entry-level retail job to another scares me more.

"A nursing degree, huh?" Anna-Marie says from next to me, squinting over my shoulder. I hadn't even heard her pause her video game. I have a strong urge to close out of the page, as if I've been caught on some anime porn site.

I resist this urge. New Gabby is allowed to dream big dreams. New Gabby is starting to have big dreams at all, which is probably to be encouraged.

"I'm thinking about it," I say casually, as if I haven't been spending the last few days trying to figure out how far I could stretch my savings before I have to take out student loans. And then researching how exactly one goes about taking out student loans.

"I don't know," Anna-Marie says, setting down the controller, her lips pursed in consideration. My stomach drops.

"You don't think it's a good idea?"

"I don't know how Fong's is going to stay in business when you're doing something you'll be so amazing at."

I groan and laugh, settling further back into the cushions. "If their business fails, it'll be because I'll be eating ramen for the next several years."

She smiles at me and then turns back to the game, unpausing it. "Add some maple syrup and it'll feel just like you're eating their Waffles Lo Mein."

I don't know that she's right, that I'd be amazing at this. I know that being a nurse will be a ton of studying and hard work and probably getting thrown up on a lot. And I know that my one lucky instance of heroism in saving Bridget Messler is bound to be outweighed by the many people I can't save, can't even help.

But I also know how good it felt to at least try, with everything I had in me. And that's a feeling I want to repeat.

I wish I could tell this to Will. That I finally have an answer—or at least a possibility of one—for that question he asked me my first day on set: "What is it you want to do with your life, Gabby Mays?"

Right now, what I want to do is talk to him, but I keep remembering the look of betrayal on his face. So soon after he said he trusted me.

A ding on my phone nearly gives me a heart attack, but it turns out to be a text from Karen.

Hey girlie. Missed you this week. Team Reception isn't the same without you. New girl sucks, can't even fake type right.

I smile, though her words open a little wound in my heart. I miss my station at the fake hospital reception desk. I miss laughing with Karen between takes and slipping each other dirty jokes on post-it notes while the cameras are rolling.

Miss you too. I text back. *Give the new girl a chance, though. Fake typing skills don't come naturally to everyone.*

And then, because I can't resist, I ask: *So what happened after we left?*

I chew on my lip while the little bubbles indicate her writing her response. I really hope to hear about Will, but honestly any news from that debacle is welcome.

Well, BB's gone.

My eyes widen. *What?*

June Blair told Bernard all about the statue thing. She said she'd actually heard people having sex in Bridget's dressing room the day the thing was stolen. Said your story checked out, since she never did believe Bridget could possibly be the one doing the bedroom boogaloo, at her age.

I refrain from commenting on the term 'boogaloo.' *Seriously?*

Crazy, right? Dame Sondra Hart will be making freaky love well into her nineties.

No, I mean about Sarah.

Bernard fired her right then.

I have no idea how to feel about this. Partly satisfied at karma's quick work on this one, and partly sad. I really don't like Sarah, and hate what she did to Will and Anna-Marie, but she loved her job.

Karen and I text back and forth a little bit and make a vague plan to go get drinks sometime that I hope will happen, but who knows? Karen, unlike me, has a husband and kids and a life outside of being an extra.

I discuss this latest news with a distracted Anna-Marie, who is alternately listening and yelling at the zombies she's slaughtering on-screen. After replenishing her stock of ammo, she turns to me.

"Enough talk. Call Will. It's been days. He needs a shoulder to cry on, and your shoulders obviously want to volunteer."

She is right, my shoulders are feeling very service-oriented right now. But that doesn't change one fundamental fact. "He hates me."

"Maybe. And maybe he doesn't blame you at all, because it's not actually your fault. Look, Gabby, I've seen you crush on this guy for weeks now, and he's finally available. Go to it, before I pass him a note asking him whether he likes you, check yes or no."

I pretend to consider this. "Actually, I like that plan better."

Anna-Marie shoves into me with her shoulder. "Go. Though when you're up, can you toss me the Doritos from the counter?"

I sigh. I'm all for *Buffy the Vampire Slayer* marathons and foods more full of trans fats than any other ingredients combined, but doing this for days on end isn't Anna-Marie. She's wallowing again, and I'm not sure how to get her back on her feet.

One thing at a time.

After handing her the mostly empty bag of Doritos, I decide to text him. Texting is less scary than calling, especially with a situation like this. I take an agonizingly long time fussing over what to say, and ending with perhaps the dumbest, most bland text ever:

Hey Will. I'm so sorry about what happened. How are you doing?

I hit send and wait.

And wait.

And start to consider making Anna-Marie hold my phone so I won't be able to keep staring at it.

After what feels like hours, but is in reality twenty-two minutes, my phone buzzes.

I've been better. But I'll survive. Thanks for asking.

I'm not sure what to make of this. It's not the friendly banter we normally exchange, but it doesn't feel like an "I hate you, please delete my contact info from your phone" level brush-off, either.

I want to apologize for my part in his pain, but would rather not do so over text. I consider for a moment. And then it hits me: Will needs a Breakup Tub.

Do you mind if I come by your place? I have an idea of something that will make you feel better. ;-)

A minute passes before his reply. A reply which consists of a raised-eyebrow emoji. Then I realize what my last text sounded like I was offering.

I swear, panicking, and start typing. Anything has to be better than what I just sent.

Ice cream! Just ice cream, I swear. A friend bringing a friend ice cream.

A few seconds pass. I am in agony. In the texting equivalent of runaway mouth syndrome, I send a follow-up: *Not sex.*

Still nothing from Will.

Can we just blame this all on autocorrect? I send in desperation. And then another: *Damn you autocorrect!*

He doesn't respond to stop my texting diarrhea, and I groan and slump back against the wall.

"This was a terrible idea," I call out to Anna-Marie.

"Why?" The sounds of video game death filter back along with furious button clicking.

"Because I think I just offered to cheer him up with sex. And then took it back. And then—"

A text appears from him: *Ice cream with a friend sounds great.*

Come on over.

"What?" At least this is enough drama to get Anna-Marie to pause the game. "I leave you alone with your phone for two minutes, and you booty call the guy?" She scurries over to me, grabbing for the phone, and reads his last text.

"Ice cream? Is that code for something?" She looks dubious.

But I can't stop smiling. I'm going over to Will's.

TWENTY-FIVE

Will's apartment is about a thirty-minute drive from mine, which is pretty close in LA terms, but too long for the ice cream in the Breakup Tub to not become soup on the floor mats of my Hyundai. So I buy two bags of crushed ice from the corner store, pack them around the Styrofoam container in my trunk, and call it good.

I shouldn't be so happy to see Will. He's bound to be miserable, after all, and no amount of ice cream will make up for losing his fiancée to a horndog soap opera star. And despite how thrilled I was that he's still willing to see me (even after my awkward texting), I can't fool myself into thinking he'll *really* be excited about it. Especially given the part I played in the whole thing.

But he did ask me to come over.

His apartment building is sleek and gray and modern, a far cry from the 70's-era squat yellow brick building Anna-Marie and I could afford. I wonder if he comes from money or if being a soap opera writer pays more than I would have guessed.

Though I suppose until recently, he was sharing the place with Sarah, who was probably doing somewhat better, at least.

I take the elevator up to the fourth floor, admiring the clean white modular hallway benches and sharp metal wall sconces. All we have in our hallway is the large trashcan the neighbor slowly fills with empty beer cans. As I reach his door, my pulse picks up, like just being in his proximity is enough to get my heart pumping faster.

Maybe it is. Maybe it always has been.

I knock twice at his door, holding the ice-cold container in my hand and wondering if this is actually a very, very bad idea. Do I want to be that girl? The one who brings ice cream and lets the guy bear his soul about the woman he really wants? The one who is good for a stupidly funny text message and maybe a drunk kiss or two, but not for a real relationship?

He opens the door, and the moment I see his drawn expression, I know that no, I don't want to be that girl. Maybe for someone else it wouldn't be so bad, but not for *him*. But it's too late to back out now, at least for tonight. For tonight, I can apologize, and for a while, maybe, I can just be his friend. But ultimately, I know it will hurt me worse than being in the friend zone ever has before.

This isn't about me, and I want to shelve that problem for another day, but just seeing him like this, hair mussed and clothes unkempt, wearing a wrinkled button-down shirt half tucked into a pair of loose jeans with a sauce stain of some kind on the knee . . . He hasn't shaved in a few days, either, though the scruff actually looks pretty good on him. The whole package makes me want to put my arms around him and hold him and tell him that everything's going to be okay.

That would definitely be an invitation to become *that girl*. Plus, he could probably stand to take a shower before doing any significant cuddling—though I'm so desperate I'd be up for it anyway. Dark circles ring his eyes. He could also probably use some sleep.

Um, also not with me.

"Hey, come on in," he says, stepping out of the way so I can enter his apartment and stop awkwardly assessing him on his doorstep. The first thing I notice is that it looks like the place is an art gallery being overtaken by a hobo. Sleek modern furniture, all uncluttered lines and smooth surfaces, are covered with t-shirts and empty coffee cups. Papers are strewn across the glass coffee table, and a stack of marked and color-coated index cards has spilled over onto the floor, creating a neon rainbow against the too-white carpeting.

A laptop with a mostly blank page is open on the counter, and the TV is on, an overly excitable woman hawking specialty hair products that, judging by her tone, will bring about world peace if enough people just spend the low, low price of $19.95 plus shipping and handling.

"Doing some hair-care shopping?" I can't help but ask as he closes the door behind me.

He wrinkles his nose. "Nah, I just like having it on. It's weird, but it's kind of like white noise to me." He looks around his apartment as if noticing the mess for the first time. "I probably should have cleaned before you got here. I've been . . . distracted."

So have I, but mostly by worrying about him. "I didn't come over to judge your housekeeping abilities. I came to bring you happiness in the form of the very pinnacle of humanity's food creations." I hold up the container.

"I'm intrigued." He sounds like he's mostly faking interest, but at least he's trying.

"Behold, the Breakup Tub." I pop open the foam container and let him bask in the glory.

Now he really does look interested. "Are those brownie bites *and* cookie dough in all that chocolate and caramel?"

"I think there's also bits of cheesecake and marshmallows, but it depends on how the chef is feeling today. Once he threw in some gummy bears. That was after I lost the jewelry store job."

"You get this often?" He appears stunned, like he isn't sure a human being could possibly eat all this and survive.

"Not often." Then I feel bad for lying and amend with a "Well, maybe often lately. But it helps. For, you know, when you want to eat away your emotions."

A smile tugs at his lips. "That does sound good right about now."

I followed him into the small kitchen—farther behind than I'd like, because let's face it, I mostly just want to full-body tackle him and make out with him on the floor.

Will digs two spoons out from a drawer. The kitchen table is small and rectangular (also weirdly ultra-modern, in black and chrome), pushed against the wall on one side. It's relatively clean (he's obviously been doing most of his eating in the living room, though the pizza boxes on the counter are piling up), but there are file folders and a *Writer's Digest* magazine cluttering one side. I pull out a chair at the table's head, and he takes the one closest, facing the wall, and there's only this (ugly chrome) table corner separating us. His knee brushes the faintest bit against mine as he sits down, and he doesn't move it away. Does he even notice?

We take the first bites. He swears. "You weren't kidding. This is amazing. I'm trading in my hard whiskey habit for good."

I scan the room, seeing more coffee cups and cans of soda lining the counters, but not even a single beer bottle. "You have a hard whiskey habit?"

"Not really. I mean, the day I found out—when I got home I tried to develop one, but the only thing more emasculating than finding out your fiancée's been cheating on you with Ryan Lansing is finding yourself throwing up after four shots of Jack Daniels."

I wince in sympathy. The mere mention of Sarah, not to mention the clear amount of pain he's in over her, takes away from the taste of my own chocolate and caramel-coated bite. "Is it . . . really over between the two of you? She's with him now?"

"She is. Which, you know, if he's the kind of guy she wants, then it's better." He stares at the spoon in front of him.

"Maybe," I say. I've comforted guy friends through breakups before, but never one I personally had feelings for. It changes the dynamic drastically.

Not to mention the slight issue of my being partially at

fault for this.

I can't take it anymore. "I'm so sorry, Will. I know you heard what H—what Ryan said, about me being to blame, and it's true."

Will eyes me over a spoonful of ice cream, brownie, and what looks like M&Ms. "Yeah, I wondered about that. I'm not sure I get how you fit into it."

I groan. "I'm still not quite sure myself. It happened . . . right after I got punched by Ganesh, actually."

"Ugh, I'm sorry. I clearly deserved this, whatever you did."

I shake my head. "No, it had nothing to do with you. I got back to my apartment and H—Ryan was there."

Will closes his eyes. "If you're about to tell me that you, like all women on set, hooked up with Ryan Lansing, I think I'll pass on the details."

I smother a smile, because god, does Will *care* who I sleep with?

Probably not. I'm just reminding him of Sarah.

"Um, no. I didn't. He was there waiting for Anna-Marie, who he was sleeping with at the time—"

"Of course," Will says.

He has reason to hate Ryan, so I ignore this slight on Anna-Marie. Although, she did in fact sleep with Ryan Lansing, so I'm not sure exactly what I would say in her defense. "And he looked like a total wreck, so I asked him what was wrong. He was telling me about this woman he was in love with, and I advised him to stop sleeping around and just be with her. I had no idea he was talking about Sarah, I swear. If I had known . . ." I trail off, because suddenly I'm not actually certain what I would have done had I known back then.

Certainly not outed them in front of not only Will, but the entire cast and crew of *Passion Medical*.

"Ryan Lansing in love," he says, shaking his head. Then he looks up at me with a sad smile. "It's not your fault, Gabby. At all. Sarah and I weren't working, I'd already told you that. I've known it for a while. We both have. I mean, look at this place. It's in my name, but the only thing that's actually mine here is

236

my computer."

And the assorted dirty laundry spread over the low back of the uncomfortable looking armchair, I'd guess. "I did think this place doesn't really strike me as . . . you."

He nods, taking another bite. "I convinced myself I liked it, but god, I hate that couch. And the stupid minimalist artwork. Sean was right. She tried to make me into something I wasn't."

"Yeah," I say, around my own bite. "Sean didn't seem too fond of her."

He looks up and frowns. "I'm sorry. I shouldn't have mentioned him. Just because he might have been right in this instance doesn't make him not a total dick."

"Well, even total dicks have their moments."

"Like Ryan Lansing?" He mutters this into a spoonful of whipped cream.

I remember the sympathy I'd felt for HD when he was confessing his hopeless love.

"Whatever," Will answers himself. "It doesn't matter. I don't think she even really wants him. I think she just . . . doesn't want me."

His pain cuts me even more deeply than I'd imagined. One of his hands, the one closest to me, is resting on the table, and I grab it without thinking. It's warm and just rough enough. The hairs on my arm stand on end, and his eyes lock onto mine, and they are so, so green and deep.

I clear my throat, turning the awkward hand grab into an undoubtedly even more awkward grandmotherly hand pat. "I'm sorry she hurt you," I say.

He shakes his head. "Yeah, it sucks that she did that," Will says. "But that's not what bothers me."

"Really?" I ask. "What is it, then?"

Will looks me in the eye, as if he's deciding how much he wants to share. I look away. "You don't have to—" I say, at the same time he says, "I'm actually not—"

We both stop and stare down at the ice cream.

"I'm actually not sad that it's over," Will says.

This surprises me, and I hold my spoon awkwardly over the ice cream. "Because it wasn't working?"

"Because she wasn't the only one who'd moved on," Will says.

My chest constricts, and I can't breathe. I want so badly for him to mean that he wants me, though I'm not even sure he could possibly know *what* he wants after all of that.

"I'm angry with Sarah for what she did," Will says. "But I don't exactly feel like I have the moral high ground."

"You weren't cheating on her." It comes out more like a question than I intend it to, and my stomach drops as I imagine all the things he might be about to confess: an affair with June, or one of the women in the writer's room, or maybe even another extra.

Right, Gabby. Because it would *have* to be someone on set. As if Will isn't allowed to have a life outside of the people I know.

Will shakes his head, and now he's looking up somewhere near the crown molding by the ceiling. "Sarah blamed you, you know."

My mouth falls open. "Me? But we didn't—"

"Before I found out about her and—well, before. She said she and I weren't working as well anymore. That we didn't talk like we used to. And she blamed it on how I feel about you."

I freeze. I know where I want this to go, but my heart is too timid to hope for it.

"She wasn't totally right," he said, and his green eyes lock on mine. "But she wasn't totally wrong, either."

I'm pretty sure my heartbeat can be heard over the infomercial now. "What do you mean?" I manage to ask.

"I like you, Gabby. I always have. I liked you back at the bookstore, and when I saw you again, I . . . I really like you. Way more than a man engaged to someone else should. It didn't cause the problems between Sarah and I, those were definitely already there, but it—well, it did make me start to question things."

I gape. New Gabby who saves lives of geriatric soap stars should probably be able to take a little confession of Will's feelings for her in stride, but apparently she's decided to take a backseat with some popcorn and watch this like she would a scene on *Passion Medical*.

I can't make words form around my shock and relief and, well, trepidation. Which is probably good, because I have no idea what to say.

I'm in love with Will. I know I am. And of all the things I don't want to mess up, a possible relationship with him is at the top.

"I feel like I should tell you I feel the same about you," I say finally. "But I guess I already yelled that at you."

Will winces. "I deserved that. All of it and more." He digs his spoon back into the ice cream, and I try to find my footing after that emotional whiplash. He says he has feelings for me, and my heart is definitely doing a little jig to celebrate that. But he's back to not meeting my eyes, and our hands are still inches apart on the table, even though I said it back. So if he likes me and I like him, then—

"I just keep thinking about what a mess I've made of things," Will says. "I wasn't happy with Sarah, haven't been for a long time. We stopped talking a long time ago, way before I met you again. If I was so miserable, I should have ended it. Instead, I decided to be a coward and have an emotional affair. That doesn't make me much better than she is, does it?"

My heart freezes. Is that what the problem is? Yes, he has feelings for me, but now I'm the girl he cheated with? This is another version of *that girl* that I never wanted to be. "It wasn't an emotional affair," I say. "Just having feelings isn't the same thing."

Will looks dubious. "Yeah," he said. "You're right. All I did was hang around the entrance and the craft services table when I knew you'd be arriving or leaving or finishing a scene. Asked you out to coffee, went out of my way to be around you even though I knew my feelings were wrong, and then lied to Sarah about it all."

I take a deep breath. When he puts it that way, it does sound worse. But not as bad as he's making it out to be. "You also set me up with your brother."

Will scoffs. "Yeah, that was a great plan. I decide to find you a boyfriend so that I can get over you, and pick my own brother, just so you'll still be close. I've clearly been writing too many soaps."

My voice catches. "That's why you did that?"

Will nods miserably. "I'm sorry I made that comment about you needing direction. Really, I was talking about myself. Everything I've been for the last two years has been what Sarah wanted me to be. I'm honestly not sure who I am at this point, besides someone who might have leapt into an affair if things hadn't blown up in my face first."

I shake my head. "That would never have happened."

Will meets my eyes again. "I know," he says. "Because you wouldn't have let it. But I'm the one who was engaged."

I'm not sure what to say to that. I mean, I want to think I wouldn't have welcomed advances from Will, knowing full well he was engaged. And I'm pretty sure that my hyperactive sense of guilt would have kept me from actually sleeping with him. But I probably would have let him kiss me. At least once, before I realized I was making a huge mistake.

Will must not know what to say either, because he's quiet long enough that I pretend to be incredibly intrigued by the remnants of the Breakup Tub. We've actually managed to plow through it with remarkable speed. He pulls his hand back down from the table, and I do the same with my own.

Our knees, though, are still touching that tiny bit. I should move mine, I should. But I can't bring myself to do so. Even though I'm clearly not helping things. I want to be the friend who lets him talk, the one who is there for him without ulterior motives. Not the girl who reminds him of his own personal failings. "So, um, I bet it's been tough being at work after all

240

that." I decide not to mention that I know about Sarah having been fired.

He shrugs. "It would be. I quit. I haven't been back since I left that day."

I grimace. "So now you have to find a new job on top of everything else?"

Will rolls his eyes. "Please. I do not get sympathy from you for being unemployed after what I did to you. How are *you* doing? Do you know what you're going to do now?"

Despite the emotional roller coaster of the last few moments, or most likely because of it, this makes me smile. He looks back at me, startled, which is probably fair, because with the way my whole body is buzzing from emotional overload, my smile probably looks a little crazed.

"I'm sorry," I say, fighting the giggle that threatens to burst out of me. "I'm—no, it's not funny, not really. It's just . . . Well, I don't know if you remember this, but that first day we saw each other on the set, you asked what I wanted to do with my life. And I—it made me think. I mean, it made me embarrassed that I was a twenty-three-year-old with absolutely no idea what I wanted."

He cringes. "That was a truly ridiculous question for me to ask, given how little I've ever had figured out."

Maybe. But I'm glad you did. Because . . . I think I'm just now starting to figure some things out for myself. That I might want to take my old people saving powers and go professional, for one. Nursing school," I clarify at his confused expression. "And maybe my life will end up somewhere different entirely, but I'm really excited about it. And that's enough for now."

Will actually looks impressed. "Good for you," he says. "I bet you'll be great at that."

"I'm afraid to hope for that much. I'm just aiming not to quit instantly the moment I find out that I suck."

Will shakes his head. "You're too hard—"

"—on myself," I say. "I know. You're one to talk."

Will rolls his eyes again, but he does smile faintly, which is an improvement. "What about your brother?" he asks. "How is he doing?"

I smile, happy he remembered. Again. Now that I think about it, Will has always remembered the things I tell him, even when I told him years ago. "Better," I say. "Still in rehab. Doing well, according to my mother. Though now my older sister is maybe getting divorced, so who the hell knows about my family."

Will looks pained. "God, the last thing you need is me dragging you through my shit."

"No," I say. "No, I'm glad to be here."

He looks like he very much doubts this, and to avoid wading through the tangled conversation in which he inevitably tells me he'll never see me as anything but a mistake, I turn the subject back to him. "What about you?" I ask. "What are you going to do?" And then it hits me. "Your novel! You're going to finish it, aren't you?"

A slow, shy smile spreads across his face, but he shakes his head, and the smile slips. "I don't know. I mean, yeah, I've spent the last few days making some notes and . . ." he gestures with his spoon towards the piles of papers in the living room. "It's dumb, right? It'll never sell. I know I need to get another real job, but it's been taking my mind off of things."

"I don't think it's dumb at all! Will, it's fantastic!"

He raises an eyebrow at me, though he looks bemused. "My impending poverty?"

I make a face at him. "*Now* you're being dumb. No, I mean . . ." I twirl my own spoon around in my fingers before setting it down on the nearly empty foam container. "Look, I've spent my whole life looking for something that would make me as happy as you are when you talk about your book. It doesn't matter if it sells, not really, or if you have to get another job until it does. You have something you care about, something you love to do, something that excites you—"

I flush, realizing how much I'm probably overreaching. I have no right to tell him what he needs to be doing with his life, with his dreams. But he's leaning in towards me and his knee is isn't just brushing mine anymore, it's pressed up against mine, and as my breath catches, I can smell the pine-scented cologne (deodorant, maybe?) mixed with the slight funk of a shirt that's been worn for a day too many. And chocolate.

It should be a repulsive mix, but on him, with his face mere inches away and those green eyes locked on me, it is intoxicating. My heart is doing cartwheels, or maybe it's my stomach. All I can see is his eyes and then his lips.

Maybe that's all he can see on me too, because he leans in even closer and I follow, and before I can determine whether kissing under the influence of despair and Breakup Tub is really a good idea, his lips are pressed against mine, and his hand is in the hair at the back of my neck, and I taste chocolate and caramel and sunlight and oh my god Will is kissing me and—

And then he pulls away, sitting back against his chair. "I'm so sorry," he says, looking slightly dazed, his eyes trailing back to the Breakup Tub. His hands no longer in my hair, or on me at all. Even his knee isn't touching mine anymore. "I shouldn't have—"

"No, no, it's all . . ." My mind doesn't seem to be able to form coherent thoughts. I am still lost in that incredible, perfect kiss and now his regret, all tangling together into a pit in my stomach. "Good," I finish weakly. I sit further back into my chair, too. We're still not terribly far apart, but it feels like miles now.

He didn't want to kiss me. But *why not?* He's already admitted he has feelings for me. He's known for an embarrassingly long amount of time that I have feelings for him.

"I just keep thinking," Will says, in a tone that says he hates himself for this, his shoulders slumped, "that if I'm the kind of person who would rather be miserable in a relationship, who'd rather cheat and self-destruct than just take the risk and get out and figure out how to put my life back together on my own, well. . . I'm about ten seconds out of that relationship and if that's who I am, then what's going to keep me from turning around and doing that exact same damn thing?"

My blood rushes in my ears. Of course. I'm like Ryan was for Sarah. He doesn't want me; he just didn't want her. And now even worse, I'll always remind him of these doubts about himself. I'll always be the girl he might have cheated with.

This is far, far worse than being friendzoned.

"I should be going," I say, even though part of my brain is screaming at me to stay and see if another bout of making out will make it all better. Screaming that I'd much rather be a rebound than leave it like *this*.

But the other part, the part that is embarrassed and heart-broken and not sure I can take any more rejection—that part's louder. And probably way more rational.

He clears his throat. "Yeah, no, that's fine." His chair scrapes against the tile as he stands and brings the Styrofoam container and spoons to the counter by the sink—which is really not cleaning up so much as moving things from one cluttered surface to another, but I can respect the effort.

Even as I'm dying inside, because Will kissed me and now I'm leaving because of New Gabby and her desire to not continually muck up my life by making stupid, regrettable decisions. Stupid New Gabby.

I give him what I hope is a normal smile, but feels too tremulous. Then I turn to head to the door. I can say goodbye to him as I'm walking out, and then it won't be really like saying goodbye to him, right? He won't see how much I hate this, how much it hurts me.

I make it to the door, my hand on the doorknob, when Will says "Gabby, wait."

My relieved sigh comes out louder than I'd like. Fortunately, the sound is drowned out by a chipper infomercial hawking a blender than can apparently mash zucchini and golf balls with equal ease.

I wait for him to tell me he's changed his mind. That he's scared, but he wants this, and he's far more scared of watching me walk out the door and then losing me forever. I turn and see Will standing in the living room by the coffee table, not near enough to make me believe he's going to grab me for another kiss. Which is probably a good thing.

Right?

"It wasn't because of the microwave fire," he blurts out.

Of all the things I thought he might say, this wasn't it.

"Back at the bookstore," he says, and I hope he doesn't think I've suffered so many microwave-related job losses I need that clarification. "The wiring in that break room was a lawsuit waiting to happen. I set fire to the coffee machine like a month before you started."

I blink, unsure what to say or feel.

"The district manager told me I had to fire someone, for cost reasons," he continues. He jams his hands into his jeans pockets, and stares down at the floor. "It was either you or Margaret, and, you know, she was a single mom and I just couldn't—"

"It's okay," I say. The last thing he needs right now is to feel guilty about a management decision he made two years ago, and one that was clearly the right call. "I'm sorry I even brought it up. That was petty of me."

It's then I realize what we're doing. We're clearing up all the misunderstandings. He's searching, making sure nothing goes unsaid.

Because barring more unexpected run-ins at the community college, after this I'm never going to see Will again. I'm not going to get to tell him how nursing school goes or how things end up with my family. I'm not going to get to read his book and cheer him on and share jokes over sugary snacks.

He's only been back in my life a few weeks, but already I'm losing so much more than the possibility of a romance. I'm losing a friend. I'm losing *him*.

He gives me a gentle smile, and it's one I could stand to

see for the rest of my life. "I'm glad about the nursing thing, though," he says. "I'm really happy for you, Gabby."

I try to smile back, but it comes out as a pained wince. "What you should be really happy about is that if I can start to figure things out, you definitely should be able to. With way fewer microwave fires and cake decorating classes."

He raises an eyebrow, and I shake my head. "Never mind. Just . . . take care, Will."

"Thank you," he says. "For the ice cream, and for everything."

I say goodbye and leave with tears burning unshed in my eyes. I hate myself—both for letting him see how much this hurts me, and not staying and letting him see the rest of what's going on in my head.

It doesn't matter. It's over before it even really began. My heart feels like it's going to break into a thousand pieces, or maybe already has. It's time to leave Will behind me now.

Or soon, anyway. I realize there's one more thing I need to do, a way I can say goodbye and let him know that I'll always wish the best for him. On the way home I stop by a costume shop and buy a cheap top hat. At the post office I seal it in a box with a note I write on the back of a customs form that the postal employee looks askance at me for repurposing:

Will-

No matter what, you're a real writer, and you always have been. You just need the proper finish. -Gabby

(Sorry there's no monocle. The costume shop was sold out. Which is kind of strange. Is there some Sesame Street convention in town and everyone decided to go as the Count?)

No matter what happened between us, I hope he will take this to heart and believe.

TWENTY-SIX

Four Weeks Later

I carefully balance the stack of papers and books along with my large orange mango smoothie while unlocking the door to my apartment, relieved when I manage to set it all down on the counter without turning my books and notes and self a very bright shade of orange. Normally the sight of all this paperwork and study material would make me want to scurry to the nearest mall to apply for a job cleaning fro-yo dispensers, but after the first day of my five-week training course to be a certified nursing assistant, I am actually . . . excited.

Not that we did a ton today to kick in the fear instinct, but I filled out paperwork like a pro, didn't manage to kill anyone—dummies or otherwise—didn't start any break room fires, and honestly found myself interested in everything the instructor was saying.

Plus, after my stint at *Passion Medical*, I have learned one very important truth about myself: I really like working in scrubs.

The training is just one step in a process to nursing school that turns out is much more difficult than just going back to my college and hoping they'll usher me into the nursing program on the merits of the *Soap Opera Digest* article that mentions me (by name!) as the woman who saved Bridget Messler. But my guidance counselor helped me get enrolled in the right pre-reqs for next fall, and assured me that working as a CNA would be a huge help in getting a much-coveted spot in the school.

No guarantees, but then again, my life has never seemed particularly given to fit with the typical guarantees.

Like, for instance . . . how my traitorous brain keeps checking and rechecking my phone with a regularity reserved for day traders and *Candy Crush* addicts, just to see if somehow my ringer got turned off and a text or call made it through without me noticing. Hoping to hear something—*anything*—from Will, even though everything about that last conversation screamed well . . . *last.*

My bright mood darkens with the thought, but I push it aside. New Gabby tries not to focus on all the things that can, and have, gone wrong. After all, focusing on them can't change the past, and it's never stopped these things from happening in the future.

Now, though, my Will thoughts are offset somewhat with the much healthier school plans and figuring out student loans and actually paying attention to Anna-Marie's tales of the new guy she's dating, Max, the cute boom mic operator for *Passion Medical,* who also has connections to another soap on the lot, *Southern Heat.* And now that she just found out she got the role as *Southern Heat's* sexy debutante Maeve LaBlanche, I expect to hear more on set intrigues soon as well.

A knock on the door jerks me out of my study of the mess I've made on the counter and decision of whether I should move these things to my bedroom to leave counter space for tonight's now-weekly Girls Night In (sponsored by Doritos and Wine, naturally). I open it, with the usual hopeful twinge that maybe I'll find Will standing there.

Instead, I find my mom.

"Mom," I say, trying to sound slightly more pleased than just plain shocked. It doesn't work. "What are you doing here? Is Felix okay?"

My mother raises an eyebrow, especially as she looks me up and down, taking in my scrubs (which may not be covered in smoothie, but do already have a mustard stain over my left boob from lunch). "Are you back on the show?"

"No, mom, it's for the CNA training I . . . Is everything okay?"

"Of course. I can't come visit my daughter?"

A normal mother could, I want to say. A normal mother probably would have at some point in the last several years. My mother, as far as I'm aware, has never actually been to my apartment before.

"Um, yeah, I guess." I shift uncomfortably. "Do you want to come in?"

"I'd prefer that to standing out on the stoop like some religious zealot." This is said with a little more wry amusement and a little less biting tone than usual.

"Okay, yeah. Come on in." I wonder what she'll think of my small apartment, with its cluttered counter and sink full of dishes, with the well-worn and wine-stained couch and the tangle of cords from Anna-Marie's various game systems.

And then I realize I don't care. It's my life, and I'm at a point where I actually like it this way, cluttered and stained and all.

Though the presence of a certain adorable writer I can't stop thinking about would certainly improve things.

Surprisingly, she doesn't say anything about the state of my apartment, or even give so much as a pointed sniff. She does, however, look at the strewn paperwork and books on my counter. "So you're really doing this nursing school thing?"

"Yeah," I say, a small flush of pride welling in me. "I am. I mean, it'll take time to get into the school and there's some classes I need to do first. But I'm going to do it."

She meets my eyes, and her lips twitch into the smallest smile. "I showed all my friends that article about you in the soap opera magazine. It certainly beats Marcy Schulman's daughter starting that charity for kids with malaise."

"Isn't it for orphaned kids in Malaysia?"

She rolls her eyes. "Either way. Saving Bridget Messler's life makes for much better lunch conversation."

I laugh, shaking my head. I shouldn't want any part of being compared to her friends' daughters, but I will admit I'm ridiculously happy I finally did something that merits being mentioned at one of her ladies' lunches.

I don't expect mom to actually say she's proud of me, not in those words. But this, for my mom, is the equivalent of her hiring a sky-writer to spell it out for me.

I smile down at the books on the counter, because I'm not sure I'm ready to show her how much that means to me.

"Felix is doing well, though, yeah?" I ask after an awkward moment. "He texted me the other day. He thinks one of the nurses there is pretty cute."

"Yes, and the week before, it was one of the receptionists. I'm starting to think he considers rehab to be nothing more than a really expensive place to pick up women." But she is smiling while she says this. Felix is doing well. I'm sure it won't be the end of his troubles, but I'm so happy he's making progress and texting me again.

"That was one thing I wanted to talk to you about," she says, and suddenly she looks nervous. My stomach squeezes at the sight. Are there any more major family problems that can possibly still be unloaded after the last few months?

"I sold the Lladros," she says quickly. I blink, confused. I mean, I'm surprised she did that, given her attachment to them, but I can see how there might not be much room for them in her small (but impeccably furnished) townhouse.

"Um, good?" I'm not sure how to respond. "Is that what you wanted to do?"

She makes a dismissive gesture. "I decided I didn't need them anymore. They were memories of a life I no longer really need."

I'm not sure if she means that she no longer needs the memories or the life, but I decide not to make her elaborate.

"The point is," she continues, "I used the money to buy Felix's cello back." She purses her lips, as if steeling herself for a bad reaction from me.

"That's fantastic!" I grin. Felix having his cello back is like being given back part of his very soul.

She narrows her eyes. "Felix said that you refused to help him get it. That you said you'd just be supporting him in using the drugs by doing that."

"Well, yeah. Because it was different then. He was a mess. Now he's actually getting help and working at it." It is different, isn't it? It feels like it is. Not that Felix will never slip again or make mistakes, but I can't help but feel that he'll never sink so low again as I saw him on the street that day.

Or at least I really, truly hope so.

Her expression relaxes. "Good. I hoped you'd agree."

Then it occurs to me: Mom wants my approval.

She values my opinion.

I can't remember the exact words I said when I yelled at her and Dana that day, but apparently I'm better at righteous speechifying than I thought.

Or maybe she, too, realized that my life isn't any more messed up than the rest of theirs. And maybe that sort of thing isn't actually a competition.

She clears her throat and reaches into her large Louis Vuitton handbag (which somehow survived the eBay purge, though I distinctly remember Dana tossing it on the "to sell" pile) and pulls out something wrapped in a silk scarf. "I saved one for you, though."

I unwind the scarf and find the Lladro statue I always loved the most, the graceful ballerina, reaching towards the sky with her long, elegant arms. Confident. Luminous.

Tears fill my eyes as I take it from her hands. "This was always my favorite," I say. And what's more, I don't remember ever telling her that.

"I know," she said. "You used to sit in front of the case and draw that ballerina over and over again."

I blink back the tears and throw my arms around her, hugging her tight. She stiffens a bit, then relaxes into me, squeezing me equally tightly against her.

"Of course," she says, speaking over my shoulder, "it was hard to be sure that's what you were drawing. You were a terrible artist."

I laugh. "Thanks, Mom," I say. And I mean it.

The apartment feels emptier after my mom leaves, off to go out to dinner with Dana and Paul (who are back to living in the same house now, though I imagine they've put off any Greek Isle cruises for awhile). She's invited me, but I don't want the moment we had tainted by the inevitable misery of another family dinner.

I know my limits.

I set my Lladro Ballerina on the nightstand by my bed and stare at her for a few minutes, until I hear my phone ding with a text.

My heart twists, still stupidly hoping it's Will.

Again, I am wrong. It's Anna-Marie. I remind myself that it's better this way. No need to put us both through months of trying to be together before ultimately realizing we can't outrun the past. I have a shiny new career to look forward to and, like I once said to Will, I don't need a man to fix me.

Still, I can't help but wonder, if I hadn't spent so much time with him on set, then when things inevitably fell apart with Sarah, he would be the one calling me right now.

I shake myself, turning my thoughts to the message that I do have, even if it's not the one I wish it was.

Hey, come meet me at Fong's! I have some news we need to celebrate!

I'm surprised by Anna-Marie's choice of celebration location, but maybe that last Breakup Tub she ate with me made her come around. I'm eager to hear how work went today, not to mention her lunch with Bridget, who has started taking Anna-Marie under her wing since we visited her in the hospital and explained the whole statue situation.

Bridget didn't seem nearly so upset that her statue was broken in a sex-related incident as she was that June Blair had nothing to do with it. I left the hospital with the distinct feeling that the old dame was already thinking of something else to create a feud with June over.

Now?

Yes. I'm already there.

I agree to meet her and head out. I personally have no problem kicking off Doritos and Wine Night with ice cream, but I have a feeling I'm going to hear about it tomorrow when Anna-Marie spends the day doing cardio beatboxing, or whatever the latest fad workout DVD is.

Fortunately, it only takes me a few minutes to get to Fong's. I walk in and am immediately surprised to see someone other than Su-Lin at the hostess station. Instead, a bored-looking red-haired kid in his late teens slumps over the table.

"Table for one?" he asks as soon as he sees me in the scrubs I have yet to change out of.

I ignore the insinuation. "Where's Su-Lin?" Not that she has to live here or anything, but it feels strange to see anyone else in her place.

He shrugs lazily. "She quit. Her YouTube videos got big. You know, the ones where she does the sock puppet reality show? *The Real Sockwives of Los Angeles?*"

"Her *what?*" I can't believe I've never heard this from her. Then again, I was always so focused on myself when coming in here, I never got to really know Su-Lin.

"Yeah, they're pretty cool. She was on that *Ellen* show last week and everything."

"Wow," I say. Good for her. I wasn't a particularly great friend, apparently, but I am really happy for her.

"So," the kid drawls. "Table for—"

My heart stops, because I have just looked past the new kid at a booth facing the door, and in it sits—

Will. It's Will, and he's watching me with a mixture of surprise and nervousness. He looks like he's about to throw up, actually, and I have a sudden panic that he's meeting someone else here—a tall, willowy blonde with a silhouette identical to Sarah's who will sweep in any moment to meet her new boyfriend for dinner.

Will recovers first, forcing a smile. "Hey, Gabby!"

I stare, trying to think of a way to spare us both the awkwardness and gracefully make an exit without appearing like I'm running away.

I come up with nothing. Running away is starting to seem like a good option.

Will swallows. "Want to join me?" he asks, indicating to the other side of his booth.

"Um," I say. "Are you not expecting anyone? I mean, not that I can judge, I come here alone all the time, but . . ." My face flushes. Yes, running away would have been a far better idea than admitting that. Now I'm pathetic *and* easily startled.

No. That's Old Gabby. New Gabby was just asked to join the guy she's still madly in love with for dinner.

"I mean," I say, "yeah, I'd love to."

I sit down, though Will looks more nervous than I've ever seen him, possibly even more than when he was helping us break in to *Passion Medical*.

"I'll get that Breakup Tub," New Kid says.

Oh, god.

Will and I aren't even dating. Is he about to tell me once and for all that he's realized I was just a distraction from his bad relationship, that our connection wasn't any more real than Sarah's with Ryan?

Or . . . "Did I get you hooked on the Breakup Tub?" I ask.

"Because it's good to know I'm not the only one who comes here and orders it alone."

"I was expecting someone, actually," Will says, and despite my determination to be New Gabby, I have another image of Willowy Blonde, who is now wearing high heels and a cocktail dress, even though I doubt anyone in the history of ever has worn that attire to Fong's.

"You, I mean," Will says. "I was expecting you."

It takes me a minute to fully understand. "Anna-Marie," I say.

He nods. "Yeah, I asked her to get you here. Seemed like a good idea at the time." His eyebrows draw together, and I am suddenly struck by a realization: Will is worried that *I* might not be happy to see *him*.

This should actually make me feel more confident, but my mind is boggled by it. My palms sweat against the cracked vinyl of the booth. Though now that I'm no longer under the impression he's horrified to see me here, that fluttery feeling in my stomach I've come to associate with him returns in full force.

New Kid brings us a Breakup Tub with two spoons jutting out and ice cream already sliding over the edges.

"I don't know if you already ate," Will says, "but hopefully you still have some room for dessert?"

"Always," I say. "Especially here."

And with you, I want to add, but I still really have no idea why he's here and I don't want to embarrass myself further than I already have. Neither of us touch our spoons. There's this awkward silence wherein I know that whatever it is, he's dreading telling me. Is he going to want me to just be his friend? Invite me to meet the Willowy Blonde? Ask me to be in their wedding party, or the godmother to their children?

"It's okay if you're seeing someone," I blurt out, with so much force that Will leans backward. "I mean, unless it's Sarah. Although it's also okay if you got back together with Sarah. I mean—if you guys really worked it out. If you're really happy! That's what I mean. I just want you to be happy."

255

Will looks even more stunned than he did when I walked in. He puts his face in his palm and shakes his head.

I actually look behind me to see if Sarah is somehow standing there listening to all of this.

She is not.

"God," Will says. "I am *so* bad at this."

I press my lips together. "Bad at what?"

"At telling you why I lured you here," Will says. He winces. "*Lured*. Like some kind of creepy stalker. It really did sound a lot better in my head." He rests his elbow on the table and looks up at me like he has no idea what he's doing here.

That makes two of us.

"So why did you?" I ask. "Decide to stalk me, I mean," I add with a tentative smile to try to soften the nervousness that's more palpable in the air than the smell of today's lunch special: Sweet and Sour-kraut.

Will takes a deep breath and folds his hands in front of him on the table, in exactly the same pose my dad assumed right before he told us my grandma's cat Simon had been run over by a school bus. "I've been doing a lot of thinking since I saw you last," he says. "About myself, and about my relationship with Sarah, and about how everything went wrong."

Uh-oh. I am definitely that thing that went wrong. I want to stop him. I want to tell him that he doesn't owe me an explanation and, really, it's just fine if we never see each other again—even if in reality I know that wouldn't ever be fine for me at all.

But I am New Gabby, so I just lean back against the seat of the bench, look into Will's deep green eyes, and wait.

"I realized," Will says, "that it's been a long time since I knew who I was, without Sarah to tell me who I'm supposed to be, you know? It wasn't that way in the beginning, but somewhere along the line I stopped trying to work things out with her and started just letting her choose everything. She stopped giving me direction, and instead she was just pointing me and giving me a push."

"Like taking the job writing for a soap opera," I say.

256

Will nods. "Exactly like that. I mean, she had a point that managing a bookstore was neither lucrative nor the best use of my skills. But instead of being inspired by that, I just let her shove me into the first opportunity that came along, rather than take the risk of trying to figure out what I really wanted."

I identify with that. "I think that's what I was doing with my long string of very short jobs," I say. "I just grabbed at the first opportunity, so I wouldn't have to do the scary thing and admit I had no idea what the hell I was doing."

Will nods. "Exactly."

Despite the freakout currently in my head about how the safer option was definitely to have run away the moment I saw him, I find myself smiling. Even if we don't see each other again after this, it's nice to have this moment.

For the first time, I feel like I'm actually being a good friend to Will instead of just wanting to be, and it's a peaceful feeling. Ten points for New Gabby.

"So I thought," he continues, "that I needed to figure out what I really wanted, you know? I mean beyond finishing the novel, because that is really not a life plan, at least not in the short term. And I thought after I figured that out, maybe I'd be ready to have a relationship again. Maybe that would mean I could do that without making the same mistakes."

Despite New Gabby's newfound zen, my voice comes out strangled when I ask, "Did you figure it out?"

Will shakes his head. "No," he says. "And I think I know why."

My heart stops. I'm pretty sure literally. I at once must know the answer to this question and am terrified to hear it.

"I think it's because of my feelings for you," he says.

Our eyes meet, and an electric current travels down my body. I'm not sure what he means by this—is this an exorcism of those feelings, or does he—

"The way I feel about you is so strong," Will says, "that it's hard to think about anything else. I'm trying to figure out who I am without Sarah to tell me who to be, but I think the truth is that who I am is a person who's in love with you. I'm trying to stand on my own and be true to myself, but I can't, because if I'm going to be true to myself, I have to admit that what I most deeply want is to be with you."

My brain is still stuttering somewhere back around the word *love*, chugging through each of these proclamations like a computer that has run out of processing power. And before I catch up, Will reaches under the table and pulls out a top hat.

The top hat.

The one that I sent him a month ago, with that note.

"Will," I say, because I'm suddenly at a loss for any words that aren't his name.

And then he reaches under the table again and pulls out a huge stack of paper, setting it on the table. I'm a little afraid that my first words to Will after he's said that he loves me are going to be to ask if he's decided that his new life plan is to be a magician, what with the top hat and all the things that are appearing from under the table.

Instead, I reach across and take his hand in mine. His breath catches, and then he smiles. Warmth spreads through my body, warmth and a shy, burgeoning feeling of pure happiness, and I lace my fingers through his.

He pushes the stack of paper toward me. "So this is me," he says. "Taking the risk. Doing the scary thing. Laying my heart out on the table for a chance at what I want."

I look down at the pages. "Is that . . . ?" I slide the note off the top and see the words typed in that old-fashioned type-writer font that the *Passion Medical* scripts were written in:

The Lost Starship

By: Will Bowen

My eyes wide, I look up to see him watching expectantly—hopefully, even. And while I want to tell him all the things—that I love him, that he's what I want, too—this is too big of a thing to go unremarked on. "You did it! You finished your book!"

His grin stretches wider than I've ever seen it. "Yeah, I did.

Thanks to you."

"Thanks to Mr. Peanut, you mean."

He laughs, but shakes his head. "No, really, Gabby. I kept wanting to give up. Just like I've done over and over and over again for years. But I kept reading your note and thinking about how much you believe in me. How much you always have. And I didn't want to let you down."

My heart pounds, and my throat feels strangely dry. He's squeezing my hand and I'm squeezing back, like our fingers are working out their own version of Morse code to say all the things we have not yet said. "I'm glad. But don't give me too much credit. You did all the actual work. You're an easy person to believe in."

"You are too," he says. He lets out a little breath that sounds like relief. His thumb brushes gently over my knuckle in a way that sends tingles up my arm. Then he raises an eyebrow at me, his expression mischievous. "So are you ever going to answer my question, Gabby Mays? What *do* you really want to do with your life?"

I take a deep breath and let go of Will's hand. His smile falters as I stand up, those green eyes widening. But I smile back at him—maybe even managing to do so flirtatiously!—and I slide in next to him. He's still wearing that stupid top hat, and though I've never found Abraham Lincoln's dressing choices particularly hot, Will makes it look like the must-have accessory for gorgeous guys, especially with that look in his eyes, like he wants this every bit as much as I do. My insides are shaky and my legs feel numb, but I no longer need New Gabby to tell me to go for it anyway.

Because I *am* New Gabby, and I'm willing to take risks for what I really want. I know what I really want.

"This, for one." I lean forward, closing my eyes, and suddenly his lips are on mine, and his hand pressed just under my ear, and this time, I know for sure it's me he's kissing, me, with no one else in his mind, no regrets, no rebounds. My whole body feels warm and happy and whole, and I wonder how I've ever settled for any lesser kiss in my life. I lift myself onto my knees on the booth, and Will's arms wrap around my waist, and all my brain cells are firing at once like it's the Fourth of July.

I am Gabby Mays, and I know exactly what I want to do with my life, and nothing is going to stop me from doing it, even the sound of the waiter slamming the check down on the table. We stay there, brazenly making out in Fong's, until the Breakup Tub we have somehow not yet touched is a puddle of melted ice cream and floating cookie dough chunks, and Will's top hat has long since fallen off to roll somewhere under the table, and the glaring owner comes out to tell us it's time to close.

I realize, as we walk out with his arm around my shoulders and mine around his waist, laughing like we're drunk about the look on that waiter kid's face, that I may never be welcome back to Fong's again.

But it's okay. Will's worth it.

Plus, they deliver.

ACKNOWLEDGMENTS

There are so many people we'd like to thank for helping make this book a reality. First, our families, especially our incredibly supportive husbands Glen and Drew, and our amazing kids. Thanks also to our writing group, Accidental Erotica, for all the feedback, and particularly to Heather, our first genuine superfan.

Thanks to Michelle of Melissa Williams Design for the fabulous cover, and to our agent extraordinaire, Hannah Ekren, for her love and enthusiasm for these books. Thanks to Dantzel Cherry for her help with brainstorming and outlining, and thanks to everyone who read and gave us notes throughout the many drafts of this project—your feedback was invaluable and greatly appreciated.

And a special thanks to you, our readers. We hope you love these characters as much as we do.

Janci Patterson got her start writing contemporary and science fiction young adult novels, and couldn't be happier to now be writing adult romance. She has an MA in creative writing, and lives in Utah with her husband and two adorable kids. When she's not writing she can be found surrounded by dolls, games, and her border collie. She has written collaborative novels with several partners, and is honored to be working on this series with Megan.

Megan Walker lives in Utah with her husband, two kids, and two dogs—all of whom are incredibly supportive of the time she spends writing about romance and crazy Hollywood hijinks. She loves making Barbie dioramas and reading trashy gossip magazines (and, okay, lots of other books and magazines, as well.) She's so excited to be collaborating on this series with Janci. Megan has also written several published fantasy and science-fiction stories under the name Megan Grey.

Find Megan and Janci at www.extraseriesbooks.com

The Extra Series

The Extra
The Girlfriend Stage
Everything We Are
The Jenna Rollins Real Love Tour
Starving with the Stars
My Faire Lady
You are the Story
How Not to Date a Rock Star
Beauty and the Bassist
Su-Lin's Super-Awesome Casual Dating Plan
Ex on the Beach
The Real Not-Wives of Red Rock Canyon
Chasing Prince Charming
Ready to Rumba
Save Me (For Later)

Other Books in The Extra Series

When We Fell
Everything We Might Have Been